All Our Yesterdays

A novel by

Forest Bowman

SPECIAL THANKS

I am deeply appreciative to three folks for their help,
their criticism, and their enthusiastic support:
My wife, Myla, who, as with my earlier novel,
has read it so often she must have it memorized
and who brought her English Literature background
into play again and again during the process of writing;
My High School English teacher, Mary Lee Ruddle,
who, while in her late 80's, reviewed the manuscript
with a heavy red pen in hand and provided invaluable
advice and encouragement;
And **my neighbor and avid supporter, Christa Elder Kupac,**
who gave fearless criticism and valuable suggestions
that fleshed out the characters and brought vital scenes to life.
The novel simply would not have made it
without these three.

Tomorrow and tomorrow, and tomorrow,

Creeps in this petty pace from day to day,

To the last syllable of recorded time;

And all our yesterdays have lighted fools

The way to dusty death.

Macbeth (Act 5, Scene 5, lines 19-23)

All Our Yesterdays

CHAPTER 1

"As you are dying, your whole life rolls in front of your eyes, like a magic lantern show, 'cept it goes backwards. Everthing you ever did, you watch again." At least that's what old man Charlie McIntyre had told him. But Adam didn't want to believe it. If that were true, it would mean he would have to re-live that horrible scene when his whole life had been ruined, and at fourteen he was turned into a freak. It was the most terrible moment in his life, or – as he imagined – in anyone's life. And that it happened merely because of the incredible cruelty of two brutish boys only made it worse.

It was that cruelty Adam dwelt on as he lay awake waiting for dawn, waiting for daylight to arrive so that he could run away. He spent a restless night, waking every half hour or so. At least it seemed that way. He couldn't really tell, not having a watch or being near a clock, and the Jepsons were too poor to own a clock that chimed. But when Jehu Jepson called up to the boys to "git yore asses down here!," Adam knew he had tossed and turned most of the night. Every time he woke up his first thought was about running away, how he would explain it to the County Court, and how he would try to get some kind of control over where they would send him next. Then, invariably, he would be overwhelmed with the fear that the justices would send him back to the Jepsons. No, he would say to himself — he even shouted "*NO*" out loud once sometime in the middle of the night. *No. I am not coming back here! After I've told them what the Jepson boys done to me, the justices won't dare send me back here.* Then he would toss and turn some more, as much as anyone could toss and turn on a straw tick stuffed between the floor joists of the grim little attic where Adam and the Jepson boys, Luke and Paulie, slept.

It had been a disaster for Adam, coming to live with the Jepsons, a disaster that the "gentlemen justices" of the Polk County Court had sort of backed into. Pap had died in the damndest, dumbest way. Actually, Pap always did *everything* in the damndest, dumbest way. So it was probably fitting he had died the way he had lived. Pap loved to pull a cork and got drunk, which he did with regularity, and fell into the mill race beside the Bloody Bucket. (The sign over the tavern door read, "The Bluebell Tavern," but the decent people of Stendahl, who avoided the tavern at all costs, knew it as the "Bloody Bucket," after the vicious fights that marked the place.) Anyway, Pap had passed out by the side of the mill race, which was only about two feet deep at its deepest, but he was so drunk that his head had simply dropped beneath the water and he had drowned. From the chest down he was completely dry, so that his watch, which he kept in a pocket of his shabby vest, never even got wet.

A week later the justices of the Polk County Court had met briefly, under pressure from the womenfolk of Stendahl, to find a home for the orphaned, under-sized fourteen-year-old Adam. They sat in the dusty little room off the courtroom and hemmed and hawed about the problem until someone said maybe Jehu Jepson would take Adam in. "Ain't the Jepsons been lookin' for another hand since their oldest boy died?" one of the onlookers had said.

Samuel Oldaker, the skinny, pock-faced President of the Polk County Court leaped on that idea. "Yes, and they're as poor as Job's turkey. I 'spect they could use another hand on that miserable little place of theirs." So the Justices agreed to send someone to talk with the Jepsons. After no discussion at all the court adjourned with the understanding that if the Jepsons would take Adam in, it would be "so ordered" by the court.

So it was that a week later, in August of 1897, Adam Richter was formally consigned to the Jepson's hardscrabble farm seven miles out in the country from Stendahl. It was nobody's fault, unless you want to say that Jehu Jepson's greed for a "free" hand on his farm was a fault. But, fault or not, the result was the same. Adam was sent to live with the Jepsons and the nightmare began.

-o-

Jehu Jepson was a runty little red-haired man who looked like he had been hacked from a diseased pine tree, then let dry and turn pale gray and start to rot. He had only two or three teeth and his sunken-cheeked face that was always two or three days overdue for a shave. He walked with a pronounced limp. Adam never knew why and never really cared enough to ask about it. Besides, at the Jepsons, asking questions only got you in trouble.

While Jehu Jepson was pretty much a nobody in Polk County, for old Wilbur Botts he had been a godsend. Wilbur was a red-haired, freckled, hot-headed man, built along the lines of President Theodore Roosevelt. He was a descendant of one of the oldest families in Polk County, his earliest ancestors having staked out land claims on over five thousand acres in the Oremander Valley in the mid-1700's. Down through the years, as generation after generation of Botts patriarchs had divided their estates among their sons, the farms grew smaller and smaller. By the time Carson Botts – four generations removed from the founder of the clan – died in 1870, his son Wilbur had inherited a farm of just under six hundred acres. But, within two years of his father's death, when he was thirty-seven, Wilbur married a widowed distant cousin, Lucinda

Morgan, an incredibly homely woman thirty-two years his elder, whose eight hundred acres adjoined Wilbur's farm. With fourteen hundred acres in hand, only Armistead Watson was a larger landholder in Polk County than Wilbur Botts. In a county where the average farm was somewhere around two hundred acres, fourteen hundred acres made Wilbur a major player.

Wilbur's marriage was a marriage in name only and he fully expected his bride, who was, after all, sixty-nine at the time of their marriage, to pass on within a few years. But, incredibly, she lived for another quarter century, dying in 1897 at the age of ninety-four. Since he found no comfort in the marital bed, Wilbur had turned to a succession of hired girls to meet his sexual needs and one of them, Emma Stark, had become pregnant. Eager to avoid his wife's wrath and the condemnation of the community, Wilbur had paid red-headed Jehu Jepson two hundred dollars to marry Emma and claim paternity of her child. Their agreement also provided that Wilbur would pay Jehu fifty dollars a year to support the child, who turned out to be a boy, until he reached twenty-one.

Emma continued to work for Wilbur and bore him two more sons, each son bringing the same terms to Jehu Jepson – two hundred dollars up front and fifty dollars a year support until the boy reached twenty-one. The oldest boy, Abel Jepson, died in January 1895, at the age of twenty, from some mysterious fever.

In addition to farming and romancing the hired girls, Wilbur had turned his attention to politics with considerable success. By the time he reached the age of forty-five, he was the major political figure in Polk County. While he never personally stood for public office, it was virtually impossible to win an election without the support of the machine Wilbur had cobbled together over the years. Want to teach school in Polk County? See Wilbur Botts. He would assure that the members of the district school board he had maneuvered into office assigned a teacher to a one-room school at a salary of one hundred eighty dollars for an eight-month term. Concerned over the real estate assessment of your farm? Call on Wilbur Botts. He would make sure that the Polk County Assessor, who owed his job to Wilbur, would keep the assessment as low as possible. In these and numerous other examples, the voters of Polk County had come to depend on – and fear – Wilbur Botts.

The sheriff, too, was a minion of Wilbur Botts. So when Wilbur's sons by Emma Stark Jepson turned out to be regular hellions, Wilbur, out of a distorted sense of paternal pride, intervened to get them out of trouble. If a neighbor's calf came up missing on a farm near the Jepson's, Wilbur would call on the sheriff and the prosecuting attorney, and no arrests would be made and no charges would be preferred. The farmer was quietly paid for the calf and peace would reign in Polk County. Mysterious fires, minor vandalism, drunken fist fights, and threats of serious physical harm, all were pushed aside and the Jepson boys continued on their bullying ways. Of course, this protection only emboldened the boys, who knew nothing of their paternity but, dull as they were, understood that Wilbur Botts was, for some unknown reason, shielding them from the consequences of their acts.

-o-

Life had never been easy for Adam. His family lived from hand to mouth, with seldom even enough to eat, mostly because on those rare occasions when Pap did manage to find some work, he spent all his earnings on alcohol of some sort. What kind of alcohol didn't really matter: beer, wine, whiskey – it was all the same. Whatever it took to get drunk was what Pap drank.

At fourteen Adam was already the man of the house although his small size belied the role he had undertaken. He stood barely five feet tall and weighed no more than eighty-five pounds, about the size of a normal eleven-year-old. Actually, eighty-five pounds was probably a bit high since he had weighed himself on the feed scales at Havel's Mercantile Emporium on Main Street when he was fully clothed.

He had a dark mole high on his right cheek, about three-eighths of an inch in diameter, that merely emphasized the pasty hue of his skin. When he was younger some of the boys called him "Mole," but by the time he had reached his teens the nickname that finally stuck was "Runt." Runt Richter. What a sight he was, smaller than boys two or three years younger than him, his face marked with a mole and his jet black hair, always in need of a haircut, flying in all directions. But he was tough in the way that a five-foot tall, eighty-five pound boy had to be to survive. You had to fight, he had learned – even the bigger boys – or they would torment you to death. So, while he accepted the nickname "Runt," and even ignored the snide comments about the mole on his cheek, he was always ready to fight when anyone made fun of his pap, or the miserable hovel in which they lived, or the tattered clothing he was forced to wear.

His hands, small and delicate in keeping with the rest of his physique, were heavily callused and his arms, while small, were packed with muscle earned by hard physical labor.

Despite his poverty and the rags he wore, he would not tolerate pity. When you pitied someone, he had come to understand, you couldn't respect them. And Adam Richter wanted respect. But respect was the one thing he had never known.

He was obsessed with being clean. Probably, he recognized that was from the experience of cleaning the small animals he trapped for food and for their hides. Once he had ripped the guts out of a rabbit or squirrel, it seemed to take forever to get the smell off his hands.

He was especially proud of his teeth, which were gleaming white, most likely because he ate almost no sweets. He brushed his teeth every day with a twig, the way old man McIntyre showed him one time when they were scraping hides.

"You take a twig from a sweet gum tree," the old man had said, "and you chew on it for a while. It will become soft and bristly. Then you can brush it around over your teeth and all the things that cause your teeth to rot can be brushed away." The old man smiled. "Lookee here. I am sixty-seven and I still have all my teeth. That's 'cause I never eat anything sweet and I brush my teeth ever day."

By the time Adam was eight he started doing odd jobs for folks in Stendahl, picking up barely enough to eat by doing work that others avoided at all costs. For a two-week period the summer after Ma died, he had cleaned out four outhouses for families in Stendahl, the nastiest job imaginable, but it paid him a total of three dollars, enough to keep him and Pap in salt, potatoes, flour, eggs and milk for over two months.

It was around the same time that he had learned to construct deadfalls to catch rabbits that roamed the fields around Stendahl. He cured the hides of the rabbits by rubbing the flesh side of a freshly killed rabbit with its own brains and then holding it up to a fire to warm it. "A animal's brain is just big enough to tan its own hide," old man McIntyre had told him as he described the process of tanning a hide. "A mouse's brain is big enough to tan a mouse's hide, and a deer's brain is big enough to tan a deer's hide. Yes sir," the old man McIntyre laughed, "God was pretty smart when he figgered this out."

This process worked, Adam learned. It would not only make the hair turn loose but would also tan the hide at the same time. A tanned rabbit skin could be sold for eight cents to ten cents at Havel's Mercantile Emporium on South Main Street. In a good week, Adam could make twenty cents to thirty cents this way.

After he moved in with the Jepsons, however, Adam never let on that he possessed any such skill. With the Jepsons, he learned early on, anything out of the ordinary led to a whipping.

The troubles began the day he moved in. Paulie Jepson, a tall, skinny red-haired brute with watery eyes and a pocked face, picked a fight with Adam. Being over a foot taller and a good thirty pounds heavier, Paulie gave Adam a challenge. He didn't whip him but he let Adam know that life with the Jepsons would be no easy ride. Afterward, looking at Adam's bloody nose and swollen face, Jehu Jepson had merely said, "I reckon you best learn to take care o' yourself, boy." When Emma Jepson saw Paulie's battered face and noticed that he was limping slightly, she stared at Adam with a look of absolute disgust — a condition that never changed during the time Adam lived with the Jepsons — and said not a word.

That same day Jehu confiscated Pap's boots and watch, the only items of value Adam had brought with him to the farm. Adam kept his spare pair of pants and shirt only because they wouldn't fit any of the Jepsons.

CHAPTER 2

Calling the Jepson place a farm was to suggest a grandeur it did not deserve. The place was a dump, was what it was – a filthy, run-down, blotch on the soil of Polk County. It was located in a part of the county called The Bleaks, because the countryside was simply bleak and barren. A man would need at least a hundred acres of land, a good team of horses, and an abundance of drive to make a farm go in The Bleaks. Since the Jepsons had only thirty acres, two horses (neither of them work horses), and nothing approaching a spirit of enterprise, they eked out what passed for a living by raising a few scrawny chickens, a milk cow, and a few pigs, all of which could pretty much fend for themselves, at least during the summer. In addition to the hundred dollars a year Jehu received for the support of Luke and Paulie, Jehu and the boys hired out as farm hands for threshing and the like on more profitable farms and, on occasion, as timber workers when a farmer decided to cut and sell some lumber to Brubaker's Mill in Stendahl. They also stole anything that wasn't nailed down in The Bleaks.

But their main source of income was the production and sale of moonshine liquor which they produced from three stills that were ensconced among the scrubby trees and shrubs at the back of their thirty-acre plot.

The tax on liquor had been $1.10 a gallon since 1894 and, by making and selling their own liquor without paying tax, the boys were breaking the law yet again. But, protected as they were by Wilbur Botts, their liquor sales were a safe source of income. And, when word got out that the brothers could safely sell tax-free booze, other moonshiners in the county began selling their products to the Jepsons at a discount and the boys had even more tax-free liquor to dispense for profit.

9

On the evolutionary scale for buildings the Jepson house fell somewhere between a lean-to and a cabin. It had two rooms, a kitchen and a bedroom. There had originally been no ceiling, being open to the ridgepole. But after Abel, the oldest son of Wilbur Botts, was born, Jehu scrounged some planks, laid them across the joists, and put the boy to sleeping up there on a pallet of straw surrounded by rough boards. When Luke came along, Jehu nailed the planks under the joists to give the house a ceiling. Then he put two pallets between the joists and both boys slept there. Paulie's arrival a year later called for only the addition of yet another straw pallet. The boys had access to this attic by a ladder that was fastened to the wall separating the kitchen and the bedroom.

Adam had no quarrel with his bed in the attic. It was, in fact, the first real bed he ever had. At home, while Ma was still living, he had slept wherever he could. Usually, when bedtime came, he would gather up whatever rags and pelts and anything else soft he could find and pile them on the floor before the fireplace, nestle in among them, and go to sleep. After Ma died, Adam slept with Pap for a spell, until he could no longer stand the smell of vomit and stale beer and unwashed body and filthy clothing beside him. So he went back to his makeshift bed on the floor before the fire.

But aside from having a bed of his own, the attic was, like the rest of the Jepson farm, generally a place of misery for Adam. The split shingle roof leaked in heavy rains. The autumn Adam lived there was unusually warm, so hot the boys often slept outside on the ground when it wasn't raining. Then, when the weather turned colder, there being nothing between the boys and the outside but the thin layer of wooden shingles on the roof, it was freezing in the attic. On one or two particularly cold nights Luke and Paulie would steal the thin quilts that were his covers, and Adam would go down into the kitchen and sit before the fire, keeping some heat going all night, secure in the knowledge that Jehu would threaten to thrash him the next morning for "wasting" firewood. Stoking the fire to keep warm at night was, however, one of the few things for which Jehu did not subject Adam to a whipping.

The whippings from Jehu had begun the first week Adam moved in, and like most of the trouble he encountered from the Jepsons, it came about over nothing. He had been asked to move some sacks of corn and oats that sat near the door in the barn. One of the sacks had upset and some of the grain had spilled. Jehu was on Adam in a flash, beating him about the abdomen and beneath the ribs. Two or three hard blows to the kidneys and Adam could barely get his breath. But Jehu continued to beat on the helpless boy. He took care, Adam noticed, not to hit him on the face where the beatings would show. But while he had no scars or bruises on his face, he peed blood for days after one of Jehu's beatings.

If Jehu avoided hitting Adam in the face, Luke and Paulie made up for this oversight. They seemed to delight in watching his face swell after a beating. Only after Luke broke Adam's leg with a piece of firewood because Adam had eaten an apple instead of giving it to him did Jehu insist that the beatings stop. "If'n the County Court finds out you broke his leg, they'll come and take him away. Then you'll have to do his chores, too," Jehu had told the boys. That was an equation they could understand.

Jehu was too cheap to send for a doctor to set Adam's leg, but the leg knitted pretty well on its own, leaving Adam with a small lump on his left shin but, miraculously, no limp.

During the six weeks or so that Adam was allowed to stay off his feet, Jehu put the boy to work in a makeshift carpenter shop in the farm's ramshackle barn. "Can't have you sittin' on your ass doin' nothin'," the old man had said. "Got to earn your keep," as if staying at the Jepson's was some sort of treat or something. But Adam nodded dutifully and hobbled out to the barn on the makeshift crutches Jehu had fashioned for him. He took to working with wood immediately, as if he had always known he wanted to be a carpenter. Put to work making a three-legged milking stool, the boy relished the way the drawknife peeled back the wood from the legs and allowed him to shape a rough stick of tree limb into a sturdy leg. He laboriously hacked a three-inch thick chunk of pine from a fallen log and with a rasp and drawknife, carved out a seat, bored three holes into the seat, and secured the legs with wedges. Jehu gave no sign of approval to Adam, but the boy knew he approved by the fact that he was put to work on other woodworking projects for the farm.

Jehu's tools were quite limited. Adam also assumed they were mostly stolen since, when he wasn't working with them, Jehu made him wrap all of them in gunny sacks and lay them beneath the rickety work bench under two or three layers of lumber. Still, it was pleasing for Adam to learn that he could create things with his hands, even with the limited tools Jehu possessed.

The most immediate benefit of this work—aside from a lessening of contact with Luke and Paulie—was a growing sense of purpose. For the first time in his life he felt that he had the beginnings of a trade. He was a FURNITURE MAKER. He began to look closely at the few pieces of furniture in the Jepson household, figuring how they had been put together, trying to divine the purpose and reason behind their construction.

-o-

As he lay in his pallet thinking over his time with the Jepsons, Adam realized that the hours spent in the carpenter shop constituted the only time approaching a moment of happiness he had ever known in this miserable household.

With the Jepsons he kept his mouth shut and did as he was told. Asking questions or making any kind of comment could only lead to a whipping. Once, when he was lying on his pallet late at night thinking of his miserable condition, he calculated that he had only spoken seventeen words in the Jepson household in the preceding month. In all his time with the Jepsons Adam had never had – with any of them – a moment of idle chatter or conversation. He survived by staying as much in the background as he could.

He had learned, too, that he had to fight Luke and Paulie. They were big, gawky boys, with shocks of red hair that was always in need of a comb and usually a good washing, too. Their light blue, watery eyes were always darting about, as if it would be a sign of weakness to settle a gaze on any one target. They had learned early on in Adam's stay at the farm that, despite his size, he could hold his own with either one of them. So when they jumped him, it was together, when he was over-matched.

Nevertheless he made it a practice to always strike back. Once he broke Paulie's big toe by smashing it with a rock a day or so after Paulie had beaten him up. He had waited by the corner of the house and as Paulie reached the building with an armload of firewood Adam had smashed the rock down on his foot. Paulie was laid up for over two weeks and walked with a limp for months after that. But Paulie stopped picking on Adam from that time on, unless Luke was there to help him.

As for Luke, Adam had smashed him beside the head with a pine stick one morning, just a few minutes after Luke had punched Adam in the face as he lay asleep in the attic. Luke had hit Adam and then scurried down the ladder and out of the house. Still dazed, Adam crawled out of his pallet and went down to the kitchen, where he got a rag to press against his bleeding nose. Holding the rag to his nose, he had walked

13

the half mile down to the creek where the Jepsons got their water so that he could soak the bloody rag in cold water. Luke was there, having just filled two buckets from the stream. As Luke started for the house, Adam picked up a pine stick about two inches in diameter and three feet long that lay by the side of the stream. Dropping his bloody rag he yelled, "Luke!"

When Luke turned, with both hands laden with water buckets, Adam swung the stick into Luke's forehead with all his might. Luke dropped in his tracks, collapsing like a half empty bag of feed sliding off a farm wagon. He was unconscious for over ten minutes, and it was two or three days before he was back to his normal vicious self. Like Paulie, Luke stopped picking on Adam unless his brother was there to help him.

Every time Adam struck back, Emma would horn in. If Luke or Paulie showed any signs of having been in a fight with Adam, whether the boys had won or lost, Emma would deny Adam supper as a punishment. "You ain't gettin' no supper tonight, you nasty little son-of-a-bitch, not since you hurt my boy." Adam would slip away from the primitive table and wander out to the barn while the family ate supper.

One of his chores was to milk Mollie, the Jepson cow. He would trudge out to the barn every morning, plop down beside Mollie on the three-legged milking stool he had made and aim her streams of milk into a wooden bucket. After a few weeks of mistreatment and not enough food, he began to drink his fill of milk from the bucket before taking it to the kitchen where he would cover it with a white cloth and place it beside the stove. Later Emma would use it for the day's cooking or, occasionally, churn it into butter. One morning, after a particularly savage beating the night before and having no supper, he drank his fill from the bucket and then, without even thinking twice about what he was doing, opened his pants and peed into the milk. He carefully stirred his urine into the milk with a sliver of wood he had taken from the workbench.

After a week or so of drinking milk into which Adam had systematically peed every morning, the Jepsons began to complain about the sour taste. "Mollie must be eatin' sumpin sour," Jehu had said. "Got to watch her." For his part, Adam avoided the contaminated milk and took care not to eat anything that contained milk. That was not very difficult, given the meager fare he was offered anyway.

The beatings continued. Once, when the boys had him down and were pummeling him pretty severely, Adam had managed to lock his teeth onto Luke's left ear. He bit hard and hung on for dear life. Luke squalled like a wounded panther and managed to get separated from the other two. With his ear spurting blood, he cursed at Adam. Meanwhile, Paulie alone was no match for Adam and the fight ended with Adam bloodied about the face, Paulie with a swollen cheek, and Luke with a piece of his ear hanging loose and bleeding profusely.

Emma, furious over the damage done to her boys, denied Adam supper that night and breakfast the following morning. She had to pack a dinner for him to take to school out of concern for what the county court might do if he got sent to school without dinner. But his dinners always consisted of the dregs of the Jepson larder.

Jehu ranted and raved about Paulie and Luke being unable to work while they were recuperating from the fights, and he usually gave Adam a beating in revenge. But, deep down, Jehu had to know that the boys had it coming. Luke and Paulie were simply mean. They were pitiless brutes whose fury fed on each other and whose every instinct was purely animalistic. Knowing there would be no consequences for their actions, they were insolent and churlish with their family, and sullen and shifty with strangers. To Adam they were absolute terrors. Luke, being the smarter of the two, was also the more vicious. What Paulie lacked in brains he more than made up for in his willingness to do any devilment Luke set him to.

The only positive trait Adam ever sensed from the brothers was that they loved dogs. The family had three dogs but their favorite was Lizzie, a female hound that was, unlike the family's other two dogs, allowed to sleep in the kitchen. The boys made over Lizzie, fed her scraps from the table and graced her with affection they showed to no other living creatures, including their own parents.

Adam took care when he moved in to show no fear of the boys, despite their difference in size. As far as he was concerned, the only consequence of his striking back at the boys, other than the brothers' increased viciousness when they could corner Adam together and being deprived of a few miserable meals, was that he had to take over their chores while they were abed. Paulie's chore of chopping and hauling firewood didn't bother Adam much, but the long haul from the creek to the house with two heavy wooden buckets of water was a burden Adam hated.

Adam knew they only took their water from the creek because Jehu was too lazy to dig a well. One of their neighbors, Andy Riemann, was a "dowser" who found underground streams for folks by "dowsing" with a forked stick. Adam had heard him tell Jehu more than once that there was a "right smart stream of water, five or six feet down" just a dozen feet or so from the corner of the Jepson house. Jehu talked a good deal about his intentions of digging a well there but, like the chicken house he was "goin' to" build, the well was never dug. So Luke — and for a time, Adam — had to haul water up from the creek. Meanwhile, the chickens still roosted in trees, or in the barn, or anywhere else they could find that was reasonably safe from foxes and weasels.

The place had no outhouse either. The Jepsons relieved themselves wherever they could find a spot of privacy or something remotely comfortable to lean up against. Adam learned on his first day at the farm, that he had to be constantly watching where he was walking unless he wanted to foul his shoes.

CHAPTER 3

That last morning Adam rolled out of his bed the moment Jehu called up to the boys, as he had done every morning since Luke had bloodied his nose that last time.

He scrambled down the steep ladder and made his way through the kitchen. He already had his coat on — he slept in it during the cold weather — and he ducked out the kitchen door, turned round the corner of the house and relieved himself against the corner of the building. Hunching his shoulders against the cold morning air, he headed for the barn to milk Mollie.

On his way across the squalid barnyard he looked at the sky. The clouds were low and threatening and the wind, blowing up from the southwest, was harsh and rough-edged, carrying with it the promise of a cold rain. It would be a wet, raw day, good to stay inside and sidle up to the fire. He had known it was going to rain today because smoke from the chimney had dropped and hugged the ground the day before and the birds had been flying low. No, it would not be a good day to run away. But he couldn't wait any longer. Maybe by nightfall it *would* be a good day. Anyway, he was leaving. That was settled. Still, Adam wished he was going to school. If things had been different, he thought, he would.

Like his new-found interest in carpentry, school had been an escape for Adam. Back in Stendahl he had attended school only sporadically, given his family's dire need and his mother's health. He had been a quick learner, though, and the "three R's" had come easy to him. In fact, as Ma lay dying Adam, though he was only ten, had read to her from the Bible — the one Pap had later traded to Jason Whittaker for a bottle of homemade wine. That same year as his mother suffered through the last phases of tuberculosis, he had dropped out of school to care for her. Adam and Ma were close, driven together by Pap's growing love affair with the bottle and their need to try to find some shred of dignity in their tragic lives. Now, as he thought about it, he realized that the loving memory of Ma, the only true nurturing presence he had ever experienced, had been slowly drained away by the bitter experience of living for six months with the cruel and callous Jepsons.

After Ma's death he had gone back to school but now he was behind boys his age. The teacher, an uppity little shrew named Sarah Teals whose face was perpetually wrinkled in disgust, disapproved of the ragged boy who had shown up at mid-semester and interrupted her carefully-planned lessons. So Adam quit school all together and trapped small game and did odd jobs for folks in Stendahl.

Luke and Paulie didn't go to school — which was one of the reasons school was such a place of refuge for Adam — but one of the rules the Polk County Court had laid down when Adam moved in with the Jepsons was that he was to go to school through the eighth grade. So that September he entered the grandly named "Jeffersonville School," two miles east of the Jepson farm. The dilapidated one-room log structure had been "up-graded" a year or two before by having a puncheon floor laid over the dirt floor that had served students for thirty years. At the age of fourteen, he was placed in the third grade, with two other boys who were each a year or two younger. But it didn't bother Adam, who wasn't any bigger than either of them.

The schoolhouse measured about fifteen by twenty feet. On the right, just inside the school a row of pegs had been pounded into holes drilled into the logs for the students to hang their coats and hats. Beneath this coat rack, sitting on a stool made from a split log, was a water bucket with a dipper. Everyone, including the teacher, used the same dipper.

Toward the front of the room a large, round, cast iron stove sat on flat stones protecting the floor beneath. The stove was surrounded by a metal guard rail to keep the children from bumping into it. On cold rainy days, when the children's mittens were wet, they would hang them on the guard rail to dry. Adam, who had no mittens of his own, grew to love the odor of the drying wet wool.

Along the outside wall of the school facing toward the Jepsons was a covered wood storage bin. Each day a different boy was responsible for bringing armloads of this wood into the school and placing it in the wood box that sat beside the stove. The fathers of the students at the school took turns weekly seeing that the bin was kept full of wood, cut and split for burning in the stove. The Jepsons, although Adam was now a student at the school, did not share in this burden of filling the school's wood bin.

In front of the stove the children sat on benches set before a writing surface raised to a height of about four feet. There were three such arrangements on each side of the room, with the boys sitting on one side and the girls on the other.

The teacher's desk was a large, heavily-scarred kitchen table that sat in the front corner of the room, on the other side of the stove from the students. A picture of George Washington hung on the wall behind the desk. To the left of the picture three wide boards, each about six feet in length, had been nailed together and painted a dull black. This was the school's "blackboard." The only light in the room poured in through three windows set into the wall on the right, or southern, side of the building. A kerosene lantern hung on a peg between the teacher's desk and the windows on the southern wall, but Adam never saw the lamp lit while he was a student at the Jeffersonville School.

The teacher was a short, portly, bald-headed man named Calvin Grimm. He had a pudgy, flabby face, and jaws that flapped when he spoke, but his name fit, for he was a grim observer of all that was wrong with the world. Nonetheless he and Adam hit it off well, probably because Adam set the tone for the rest of the students by being absolutely obedient to Mr. Grimm and by displaying respect bordering on awe for any bits of knowledge he handed out. Adam had learned years ago that pompous little men like Calvin Grimm always took well to submissive behavior. "Pay a little attention to them, give them the impression that you think they are really something, and you can get anything you want out of them," old man McIntyre had once told Adam. Calvin Grimm merely reconfirmed that notion.

Mr. Grimm fancied himself to be something of an artist, and it was at his urging that Adam began to develop an incredible ability at drawing. More specifically, Adam found he could reproduce any drawing he saw. When he was drawing a scene from life, he displayed only slightly more skill than other students, but when a scene had already been reduced to a sketch, he could reproduce it to perfection.

And he could copy a person's handwriting so well they would think it was their own. After school, hiding in the corner of the hay loft where he could look out for Luke and Paulie, Adam delighted in reproducing the drawings from his *McGuffey Reader* and copying the handwriting samples his classmates had shared with him. He hid these papers behind a board in the wall of the barn's workshop.

His schoolmates were a slack-jawed bunch from the farms of The Bleaks, and Adam's two-mile walk to school was about average. One boy, Philo Hooker, walked slightly over four miles each way and Belle Tanner, a pretty little blond girl of thirteen, had only to walk two or three hundred yards across her father's fields to reach school. Most mornings

Adam would walk out of sight of the Jepson farm and then wait under a sycamore tree for two other boys and a girl who walked to school from west of the Jepson farm. The four of them would then walk to school together, laughing and talking. The other kids carried dinner buckets, small bucket-type pails with a wire handle, and kept their books and slates in book bags of muslin-type material. Having neither a dinner bucket nor a book bag, Adam carried his dinner and school materials in a gunny sack he had rummaged from the Jepson barn.

His dinner was generally a chunk of bread and a piece of fatty meat. If the Jepson's had corn cakes for breakfast, his meat would usually be wrapped in a corn cake instead of bread. Occasionally there would be a hard little apple or a pear that was past its prime. But, for the most part, his dinners were pitiful. One of the boys with whom he walked to school, Jesse Little, conscious of the meager meal Adam carried to school, started bringing an extra sandwich. He would always say, "I told Ma not to make me a second sandwich, but she wouldn't listen. Here, Adam, you take it. If'n I carry it home Ma will throw a fit." Adam knew what Jesse was doing and appreciated it immensely. But, being hungry all the time, he always took the sandwich. It was obvious to him, as well, that the other kids were aware of what was going on for they, too, would often bring bits of cake or pie and, claiming they were extra, would give them to Adam. He found their pity embarrassing, but he also appreciated the kindness that lay at the heart of their sharing.

After he had been at school for a week or so, Adam and Belle were drawn together. Belle was already in the eighth grade and stood several rungs above Adam on the social ladder, but there was no other boy near her age with whom she had anything in common. With Adam, however, she could share her love of sketching and, for a while in the fall of 1897,

23

there in the Jeffersonville School, Adam and Belle were what the other kids in school called "sweet on each other."

Adam loved school, not only because it was a refuge but also because he liked the sense of order that Mr. Grimm imposed on his charges. The day always began with what were called opening exercises. They would begin the exercises by reciting the Pledge of Allegiance to the flag, with each child taking turns holding the American flag before the class. Then they would sing *America,* during which Adam tried without much success to stay in tune. He had no understanding of, or appreciation for, music, never having heard singing or whistling around his home and certainly never having heard much instrumental music. But he noticed that some of the kids sang out lustily and enthusiastically. Belle's voice, he found especially sweet and always appeared to be in tune with what Mr. Grimm was trying to make *America* sound like. Then one of the students would recite a Bible verse he had been assigned the day before. After that Mr. Grimm would relate some incident from the past that had occurred on that date, usually something with a military or patriotic theme. Then they would set about their work for the day.

Around mid-morning, and again in mid-afternoon, they would have recess and would play various games in the little field beside the schoolhouse. At first Adam was uncomfortable at recess since he had never really learned to play. As far back as he could remember – and his earliest memory was helping Ma put his drunken Pap to bed shortly before Adam was three – he was either working at some chore to make a little money or trying to trap small animals for food and their pelts. But he soon came to enjoy the gaiety of the playground, racing around in games of tag, or learning to roll a hoop from a broken wagon wheel that one of the boys had brought to school.

The girls mostly played hopscotch, which involved scratching a series of squares on the ground, sometimes single squares and sometimes two squares side by side, which were numbered one through ten. A pebble would be tossed onto square one and the girl would jump into that square on one leg. Then the pebble would be tossed onto square two and the girl would start at the beginning and hop onto square one and two. This was repeated through all the squares with the goal being to make the necessary jumps and keep balanced on one leg as the girl progressed through the series of squares. Adam enjoyed watching the girls try to toss the stone into the proper square and then hop on one leg from square to square. He and the other boys would whoop and holler and encourage the younger girls while trying to get the older girls so flustered they would be unable to make their way through the squares.

Among the boys' games, Adam's favorite was "Red Rover." In this game, all the kids in the school formed two opposing lines, facing each other and holding hands. Then one side would start by picking a person on the opposing team and saying "Red Rover, Red Rover, send (calling one by name) right over" Then the chosen child would let go of his teammates and rush headlong for the other line, trying to break through the line by overpowering the kids' hold on each other. If the child broke through, he or she would then choose one person for the opposing team to join his team, and he or she became part of the other team. Each team would alternate calling people over until one team had all the people and was declared the winner. What Adam especially liked about Red Rover was that, since all the players were on the winning team at the end, there were never any losers. The kids would all stream back into the schoolhouse after a game, sweaty and exhausted, but happy "their side" had won. The games fascinated Adam, who had never realized that children could actually spend their time doing something for no other reason than that it was fun.

The last period of the day was usually spent in some relaxing activity such as drawing, at which Adam excelled. Or, sometimes, Mr. Grimm would read a passage from a classic work of literature. Once, for three days in a row, shortly before Halloween, he read Washington Irving's *The Legend of Sleepy Hollow* to the class. The spooky story excited the children immensely and they clung together on the long walks home those three evenings. Adam was especially pleased that the kids with whom he walked home looked to him for comfort, as if he would protect them if the headless horseman were to suddenly come rushing down The Bleaks road.

In the brief time he spent at the Jeffersonville School, Adam had begun to revel in the companionship of his schoolmates, especially his friendship with Belle. And, as one of the older boys, he enjoyed something approaching a special relationship with Mr. Grimm, who encouraged his skill at drawing and always treated him, Adam noticed, with more respect than he had ever received from anyone in his life, except for Ma.

-o-

The day it happened Adam was caught by surprise. But as he thought back on it he realized he should have seen it coming. For days Luke and Paulie had been sneaking around, whispering to one another and laughing and pointing at him. It was a cold, raw February day and when he came home from school the two grabbed him as he opened the door to the woodworking shop in the barn. Paulie held his arms as Luke tied his hands behind his back.

They bound his arms and legs and laid him on the workbench. Paulie placed a block of wood between Adam's head and the wall and Luke jammed his knee against the other side of Adam's head. "Open your mouth," Luke snarled. When Adam clamped his mouth shut tightly, Paulie struck him across the top of his head with a mallet. Stunned, Adam opened his mouth and gasped for air. Luke took a pair of heavy pliers and began pulling on Adam's upper front teeth. Methodically and bloodily, the teeth came out, one after the other. Every time Adam tried to speak, to plead with the boys, one of them would slap him soundly aside the head. After a while, Adam realized that the harder he fought the more gum and cheek flesh the boys would tear from his mouth. So he gave up. An hour later the six upper teeth and the six lower teeth in the front of his mouth were gone. When the boys untied Adam Luke grinned. "Now, you little son-of-a-bitch, you won't be bitin' no one's ear." Then he laughed and headed to the house for supper.

Adam stayed in the barn and sobbed in frustration and despair. His teeth! The bastards! They had pulled his teeth! The teeth he was so proud of! He couldn't believe it. Even these two savages should have had enough feeling to know what losing all of your front teeth at the age of fourteen could do to a boy. But, no, Adam saw immediately, they could wreak a terrible vengeance on him for his having the audacity to fight back when they picked on him. Since everyone knew Wilbur Botts would prevent them from being called to task for the terrible act, there was no consequence attached to the deed from their viewpoint. What was just a random act of cruelty for them had, however, changed Adam's life forever, and for the worse, that much was certain.

Enraged, and in despair beyond belief, Adam waited in the barn until dark. Then, suppressing his rage, he slowly made his way to the house. Jehu took one look at him and said, "Well, you won't be eatin' nothin' tough for a while, will you, boy?" Then he gave a short snort of a laugh and went back to sharpening the scythe he had been working on.

Emma looked at Adam, curled her lips into a snarl, and snorted, "That'll learn you to bite Luke's ear, you little bastard." Then she laughed as though his toothless condition was the funniest thing. Adam glared at her for a moment and then went up to the attic and lay down for a while, conscious of the growing pain in his jaws. When the boys came to bed later, they left him alone, but he arose shortly after midnight and went to the kitchen to sit by the fire.

He avoided school for the next two weeks as his mouth healed. Surprisingly, there was no infection (probably because he put very little in his mouth except an occasional sip of water) and little pain.

When he finally went back to school he realized how terribly his life had been altered. The boys, who had always been so kind to him, laughed the moment they saw him. Reuben Costner, a small freckled boy in the second grade, called him "Gummy," and the name stuck. By dinner time everyone in the school was calling him "Gummy," even the ones who seemed to feel sorry for him. But Belle's reaction had been the worst. The moment she saw his toothless mouth her eyes widened in horror. "Oh," she shrieked, "you look AWFUL! You look just like an old, old man. Get away from me!" At that moment, which he later recalled as the worst since Ma's death, Adam knew he had to find a new life.

-o-

The morning he was leaving, after milking Mollie and drinking his fill of milk, Adam peed in the bucket. Then, after thinking about it for a moment, he dropped his pants and pooped in the bucket. To his delight a small brown turd floated atop the foamy milk. He watched the kitchen window from a crack in the barn wall until he saw Luke and Paulie sit down for breakfast. Then he went to the house, set the milk pail by the stove, carefully covered it with a cloth, and climbed the ladder into the attic. He put on both pairs of his trousers and tied his spare shirt around his waist under his outer shirt. (It wouldn't be noticed there. He was skinnier than he had been when he moved in with the Jepsons.) He waited until he heard Jehu and the boys leave for the Tanner farm where he had heard Jehu say they were going to help clean the chicken house. When he figured they were out of sight of the house he shifted his attention to Emma. Shortly after Jehu and the boys left the kitchen, she went outside to relieve herself.

When he heard the door slam, Adam slipped down the ladder and stepped into Jehu's bedroom. He reached inside the top drawer of the rickety dresser and felt for Pap's watch. His hand clasped around it and he slipped it out and dropped it into his pocket. Then he grabbed Pap's boots from beside the bed and slipped back up the ladder into the attic. He crawled to the end of the attic and waited. When Emma came back into the house Adam silently opened the window at the end of the attic and dropped Pap's boots to the ground. He quietly closed the window and crawled back across the attic. He went down to the kitchen and drank half a cup of coffee. He placed the cup by the stand where Emma was washing dishes and walked outside and picked up Pap's boots. Holding the boots close to his chest, he walked to the workshop in the barn where he reached behind the work bench and pulled a board loose, took out his collection of drawings and handwriting samples, and replaced the board. He uncovered the tools and carefully surveyed them. There was nothing worth taking. Finally, he spied the heavy steel penknife on the bench and shoved it into his pocket. The knife belonged to Jehu and he had loaned it to Adam to do some carving on a drawer he was repairing for the dresser in the Jepson's bedroom. Adam smiled a toothless grin. He had Jehu's treasured penknife. It belonged to Adam now. It was a victory. A small victory, but a victory nonetheless.

He went back into the kitchen. Emma was finishing the breakfast dishes and didn't look up at Adam. He reached into the pie safe and took out about a half of a loaf of bread and shoved it into his jacket. He glanced around at Emma, noticed she wasn't watching him, and took a small jar of blackberry jam off the shelf. Pulling his jacket tightly about him, he left the house and walked back to the barn, picked up Pap's boots, and strode off in the direction of the schoolhouse. He never looked back.

CHAPTER 4

When he was out of sight of the house Adam veered off the road and down into a deep hollow below the schoolhouse. At the bottom of the hollow he began walking toward the southeast, following the small stream from which the Jepson's took their water. After about three hours of walking a cold rain commenced. Adam pulled his jacket collar up, hunched his shoulders, and kept on walking. Everything around him was sodden and gray. In the distance the fog and mist cloaked the landscape and Adam walked on through a formless countryside, head down, plodding one foot after the other. About noon he had reached the place where the stream he had been following flowed under a small wooden bridge on the main road to Stendahl.

About three hundred yards down this road he veered off to the left and walked to the edge of a small outbuilding on the back lot of the Grenville Franklin farm. There, sheltered by the eaves of the building he pulled the bread from his jacket and ate it gingerly. He tossed some of the crust onto the ground but managed to swallow the soft inner core of the bread. The remainder he slid back inside his shirt. He crouched for a while, hunched up out of the rain beneath the sheltering eave of the outbuilding. With his shriveled, red fingers he removed Pap's boots, which he had put on when he was out of sight of the Jepson farm. They were rubbing his bare feet raw, but at least they gave a little more protection from the weather than did his wretched shoes. After a while he slipped his feet back into the boots, stood up, looked out from under the building's eaves, and squinted his eyes into the misting skies. Then, shaking himself like a dog to shed water, he returned to the road and resumed walking toward Stendahl.

It was nearly four o'clock and darkening somewhat under the heavy clouds when Adam walked up the steep hill above Stendahl and began the long stroll down toward the town. Stendahl lay just inside a sharp loop in the Oremander River, a loop that took in about three miles from beginning to end. About forty years ago Isaac Brubaker had hired a group of men to dig a channel from the beginning of the upstream loop of the river to where the loop ended downstream. Viewed from the air it was as if Brubaker was trying to eliminate the loop in the Oremander River and give the river a straight shot through the middle of Stendahl. But Brubaker built a heavy lock out of 12" by 12" timbers and controlled the flow of water out of the Oremander into what was now a mill race. By the side of this mill race Brubaker built a woodworking shop powered by a water wheel.

The wheel was an undershot wheel, turned by the swift flowing water of the millrace. The big wheel turned a huge shaft, which ran the length of the building, from which wide leather belts drove lathes, drills, a plane, saws, and other equipment. Brubaker had made himself wealthy and had given the village of Stendahl a pretty little stream that flowed through the center of the village. It was in this mill race that Pap had drowned.

The road Adam was following, which had by now become the town's main street, was a mud hole after the morning's rain. Here and there stones had been placed in the street, spaced so that folks could walk across without getting totally muddy and wagons could navigate the gaps between the stones. But there was nothing Adam could do to keep out of the mud as he walked down the hill into the center of town.

Adam had always liked Stendahl, in the way that he imagined most folks favored the town where they had been born and raised. As he passed the Methodist Episcopal Church he looked with what he recognized was something approaching a sense of civic pride at the church's spire with its cross on top. Then he gazed across the street at the schoolhouse and considered how, even if it wasn't as fancy as the church, it was still solid brick and had a suggestion of community prosperity to it. It was a darned site more impressive than the Jeffersonville School, that was for sure.

At the foot of the long hill Adam turned right up Mill Street and walked alongside the mill race for a couple of hundred yards until he came to Brubaker's Furniture Mill. The mill was a three-story red brick building, with dirty windows around three sides on the second floor, through which Adam could make out two men working at different machines. The bottom floor of the building was open on one side, and lumber was stacked down there, drying. The enormous water wheel, set into the windowless side of the building, groaned slightly as it turned, flipping water forward as the mossy green paddles were pushed by the current. Above the front door a wooden sign measuring about four feet by six feet announced "Brubaker's Furniture Mill" in peeling letters. The yard in front of the building was stacked with logs waiting to be cut into lumber. At the far end of the yard sat a huge pile of sawdust. All in all, the place gave the appearance of having fallen on difficult times.

Adam walked across the mill race on a sturdy wooden bridge and climbed a set of steps to the main floor of the mill.

Just inside the doorway to the left was a thick oak workbench about thirty inches deep, running from the doorway to the front wall of the mill, a distance of twelve feet. A woodworking vise was attached to the end of the bench nearest the front wall, and an iron box vise at the other. Another shorter bench stood along the wall on the right side of the door.

Short scraps of lumber were stored under both benches, along with usable scraps of iron. Shallow flat shelves for small tools ranged along the walls of the mill at random. Saws and large tools were hanging from pegs in the wall over the bench. Rows of other pegs held patterns, chains, and forms for bending wood in various locations around the walls. Running down the middle of the room were three heavy machines which could be attached to the constantly-moving drive shaft of the waterwheel by wide leather straps. First, about eight feet out from the water wheel wall was a massive lathe, and about six feet or so from the lathe stood an up-and-down saw. Another six feet beyond that was a complicated-looking drill press with a huge spoon bit attached. Adam knew without being told that when these machines were connected to the water wheel's drive shaft, each one of them could perform, in minutes, work that would take hours by manpower alone. Two men were at work, one running the lathe on which he was turning what appeared to be a chair rung, and the other was pushing a heavy board through the huge up-and-down saw.

Beyond the three powered machines stood a treadle saw, stacks of lumber, and a pot-bellied stove. On the south end of the room a partition had been erected, creating a room about eight feet deep at the end of the building. This was the office.

Adam looked about again and then headed toward the office. An old man, thin and shrunken, with white hair hanging in oily, shaggy locks down over his grimy collar, was bending over a table writing in a small, crabbed hand. Adam stood at the door and, when the man didn't notice he was there, he cleared his throat and spoke: "Uh, excuse me, sir."

The man looked up, peering at Adam through a pair of small, thick, steel-rimmed glasses flecked with sawdust. His eyes were hard and watery. He squinted slightly and then said "What do you want?" The emphasis was on the word *you*.

"I'm Adam Richter, sir. My pap was Job Richter. When Pap died the County Court sent me to live with Jehu Jepson. I've left there now — after his boys pulled my teeth — and I'd like to apprentice with you ... sir."

"Don't need an apprentice'," the old man replied as he turned back to his desk.

Adam swallowed hard. "Sir," he said, "I already know somethin' about workin' with wood. I'd be free labor fer you. All you'd have to do is teach me some more, I mean, how to be a real woodworker. I don't drink like Pap did and I am a hard worker. You won't be sorry, sir. Besides ...," he let his voice drop a bit. If the boys had disfigured him, there was no reason Adam shouldn't take advantage of this outrage if it could help him. He calculated it just might now. He continued, "I kain't go back there, not after what they done to me."

The old man turned and looked at Adam again. "I still don't need an apprentice.'" He narrowed his eyes, like he was thinking. Adam took that as a good sign. At least he hadn't been told to get out.

The old man exhaled deeply. He was thinking. Finally he spoke. "You say you know somethin' about workin' with wood. How about I give you a try? You work here for a month – I won't pay you anything, but if you do know somethin' about workin' with wood and if you know how to work hard, mebbe I'll think about takin' you on as an apprentice.' How's that sound to you?"

Adam tried not to show his excitement. "Sir, I kain't ask for nothing more."

Mr. Brubaker nodded. "You'd best go on home now and git outa them wet clothes." Then he jerked his head with a start, like he had just realized something. "Where you livin' now, boy?"

"Since I left the Jepsons I ain't got no place, sir. I could maybe stay under the mill here, back of that lumber that's dryin' down there. It oughta be dry back in there. I kin wrap up and keep warm."

Mr. Brubaker shook his head. "Kain't have that. You'll have to stay here in the mill. I'll feed you, too. You'll take your meals here in the mill— three meals a day." He peered sharply at Adam in the dimly-lit room. "You say them Jepson boys pulled your teeth?"

Adam paused and then said, as clearly as he could, "Yessir. Jehu Jepson's boys pulled my teeth jist fer the fun of it. They're mean boys. Both of them. God knows what they might do to me next. That's why I kain't stay there no longer. Well . . . that and the fact that they broke my leg one time because I ate a apple." Might as well get some good out of the broke leg, too, if that was possible.

"Well," the old man said, "I'll show you where we can fix up a bed. Don't suppose you've had supper."

"No, sir," Adam answered, "I ain't et yet. But I kin wait."

"I don't eat 'til around seven or so. Let's go see about your bed."

Adam followed the old man out onto the main floor of the mill. Lumber was stacked everywhere and the pungent smell of curing wood — an odor Adam found pleasant — permeated the building. Set into the side of the mill, about midway along the wall facing what passed for "downtown" Stendahl was a huge pot-bellied stove which was set on flat stones, insulating it from the wooden floor of the mill. The stovepipe ran out through the wall behind and above the stove.

Mr. Brubaker gestured toward the floor beside the stove. "You'll make your bed here." You kin keep a fire going 'til nine o'clock. Then, you'll have to go to bed to keep warm. We'll get some shavin's from below and you can make a frame with some scrap wood over there." He pointed to a pile of lumber at the end of the room. "I'll bring you some quilts from the house. Now, get busy and make your bed frame." With that, Mr. Brubaker turned and walked back toward the office.

Adam walked back to the pile of lumber. A man who looked to be about thirty years old came over to him. "You're Job Richter's boy, ain't you?" he said.

Adam nodded.

"Gonna 'prentice here?" he asked.

"I hope so. Right now Mr. Brubaker is just gonna try me out for a while – to see if I am worth takin' on as an apprentice."

The man smiled. "I 'spect you'll make out just fine. I heered him talkin' 'bout makin' a bed frame. Kin I help you? My name's Will Perse. That there's my brother, Davy." He pointed at the man running the lathe and whispered softly, "Davy ain't all here."

"Oh," Adam said, "That's too bad. But, yes sir, I'd appreciate your help with the bed."

Will Perse was a man of medium height with thick dark brown hair that hung out from under a soft cap. He had dark, kind eyes that twinkled when he smiled. His hands were delicate, but also callused from years of handling rough lumber. His nails, Adam noticed, were carefully trimmed and clean. He was clearly a member of the working class but there was, nonetheless, an air of gentility that hung about him. Most likely, Adam decided, it was just a reflection of the fact that he was an exceedingly decent man, kind and considerate of others.

Together the two men selected three pieces of lumber, about two inches thick by twelve inches wide and six feet long. With Adam watching carefully how Will engaged the saw's mechanism with the turning shaft above, they cut one piece in half on the up-and-down saw, creating two three-foot pieces. Then they drilled holes in the ends of the six-foot long pieces and pegged them to the two three-foot pieces making a rectangle three feet wide by six feet long. That done, they set the frame on the floor and went downstairs and filled two feed sacks with wood shavings and brought them back up and placed them inside the frame. Will and Adam massaged the sacks until they were fairly flat and even.

"There," Will said, "that'll make you a pretty nice bed. You get that stove good and hot by nine o'clock and you'll have heat until midnight. If Mr. Brubaker gives you enough quilts, you'll be right cozy there, I'll fancy." He smiled at Adam and Adam knew he was going to like Will Perse.

After making the bed Will introduced Adam to Davy, who smiled softly and offered Adam a limp hand. Then Adam followed Will back to the saw and the older man showed him how to run the saw, cautioning him to keep his hands away from the spinning leather straps that engaged the spinning shaft above. A few minutes before six, Mr. Brubaker came out of the office holding his pocket watch in his left hand and said, "Quittin' time." Then he turned and went back into the office. Will nodded at Adam and turned to his brother. "Come on, Davy, let's go home." He turned to Adam and smiled. "I hope you're comfortable here tonight. See you tomorrow."

After Will and Davy left Adam opened the stove. He took a few pieces of scrap wood and tossed them into the stove. Then he stirred the fire and closed the door. He looked around. Mr. Brubaker was still in the office so Adam took Jehu Jepson's penknife from his pocket and walked to the front of the mill and slid the knife into a pile of walnut lumber, taking care not to disturb the accumulation of dust on the lumber. Just as he had walked back to his bed, Mr. Brubaker emerged from the office. He closed the door and locked it with a long, thin key. "Come on," he said to Adam, and walked toward the mill door.

They walked down the stairs and out a narrow, muddy path to Mr. Brubaker's house. Adam followed Mr. Brubaker into the kitchen. The old man turned to Adam and said, "Wait here." Then he disappeared up a narrow set of stairs. When he returned he was carrying four quilts, all in good shape and quite thick. As he lay beneath them later that night, Adam realized he had never before had so many covers to keep warm. Brubaker's supper, prepared by his sister Fannie, had consisted of two fried eggs and a dollup of potatoes, all cold by the time he had delivered them to Adam, but they were soft and easy to chew. Dried out from his day's walk and with the remains of the bread and jam he had taken from Emma Jepson's kitchen, he went to bed very contented.

Jehu Jepson appeared the following day, as Adam had expected he would. He was furious over the loss of his knife and accused Adam of stealing it. "And you shit in our milk, too, you little bastard! Ruined a whole bucket of perfectly good milk."

Adam drew himself up to his full size and faced Jehu squarely in the face. "I left your miserable place because of the crimes your boys committed against me," he said. His words were somewhat indistinct and lost some of their sense of outrage because of the absence of any front teeth. "You kin search me or my bed or the whole place, if you want, but I didn't take your miserable knife." As he spoke he waived one arm about the mill as a signal that the whole place was Jehu's to search.

Mr. Brubaker had come up from the lower floor where he had been sorting lumber with Davy. When Jehu explained what he wanted, Brubaker asked Adam straight out: "Did you take his knife?"

"No, sir, I did not," Adam said, as distinctly as he could.

Mr. Brubaker looked back at Jehu. "I guess you can search him and his bed over there, but I'm damned if I'll let you search this mill."

Jehu stared at Adam for a few seconds, his eyes flaming with anger, and then he turned and limped out of the mill, slamming the door. As Jehu was crossing the bridge over the mill race, Adam opened the door and shouted after him. "I been pissin' in your milk for over two months, too, you miserable old fool. Hope you enjoyed the taste of it."

Mr. Brubaker laughed. "Good for you," he said, and then he looked at Adam very seriously and said, "Wouldn't blame you if you had stole his knife, neither. Just don't tell me 'bout it. And don't let me ever catch you stealin' from me."

Adam looked squarely at Mr. Brubaker and said calmly, "Sir, I would never repay your kindness by stealing from you."

Mr. Brubaker said, "Humph!" and went back downstairs shaking his head and laughing. Adam heard him say, "He pissed in their milk. Ain't that sumpthin'! That boy, he's got grit. "

CHAPTER 5

The next morning Isaac Brubaker left the mill around ten o'clock. When he returned he said to Adam: "I've been to the County Court. There's a hearing set for next Wednesday. You'll have to be there. They'll ask the Jepsons, too, but I doubt if them no-accounts will show their ugly faces. Anyhow, we'll git you away from under the Jepsons. In a month or so, if you work out, we'll make this apprentice thing all legal." He turned abruptly and walked into the office.

Adam went back to work. He was using a table treadle saw, pumping the saw up and down with his feet and cutting salvageable pieces of lumber from defective slabs of walnut that a larger mill would have discarded as culls.

He had begun this work on the simple order of Mr. Brubaker to "see if you can save anything out of this bad wood. Put the scraps in the wood box for the stove." He had worked for about an hour when Mr. Brubaker came out of the office and saw that Adam had created a sizable stack of usable lumber. Mr. Brubaker studied the stack of lumber. "Only problem with small stuff like this is that it's hard to stack so you know what you have. You have a nice lookin' piece on the bottom of the stack that's just the width you need but when you pull it out it's only seven inches long and the piece you need has to be eight inches long."

"Yessir," Adam said "Been thinkin' 'bout that. Seems to me if we measure each piece and write its length on the end in pencil or chalk we could stack it with the ends showing and know without diggin' in the stack whether a piece'll do. If we took some scrap pine we could build a set of racks along this here wall and we wouldn't have to worry about upsettin' the whole pile ever time we wanted a piece off'n the bottom. We could put different kinds of wood in separate racks, too."

Mr. Brubaker studied the wall where Adam had pointed and pondered for a moment. "Richter," he said softly, "You're gonna do all right here. For right now you just keep on cuttin' good wood outa them culls. In a day or two, if we have time, you and Davy can build some racks."

Adam went back to the treadle saw and continued cutting up the disfigured walnut. Anybody watching him would have thought he was just a boy doing his job. But, deep inside, Adam was ecstatic. Mr. Brubaker had clearly approved of what he had done and had paid him a compliment! As Adam maneuvered the wood through the saw, he carefully studied the matter. It was, he decided, the first time in his life anyone had ever paid him a compliment — except for when Ma was dyin' and she would tell him how good he had been to her and how much she 'preciated it. But that was to be expected – Ma was kin. But this was the first time he had ever received anything other than a cuffing or a cussing or, at best, profound lack of interest for anything he had done. "Yes", Adam thought, "Mr. Brubaker was right. Adam Richter was going to do "all right" at Brubaker's Furniture Mill!"

The only question was would the Polk County Court send him back to the Jepsons?

-o-

The hearing before the county court turned out to be a mere routine. The justices were aghast at what the Jepson boys had done to Adam — and he had described in great detail the pulling of his teeth and Luke breaking his leg, and how he had received no medical attention either time. As he testified he made no effort to make himself more distinctly understood, letting the words slither out as best they would, and reasoning that if he was hard to understand because he had no teeth that would just make the nature of the outrage committed against him even more abhorrent. In the end, the justices announced that an order would

42

be entered approving of his staying with Mr. Brubaker. If Mr. Brubaker decided later to take Adam on as an apprentice, there would have to be formal apprenticeship papers drawn up. But Adam was through with the Jepsons . . . in the legal sense, at least. Deep down, though, he knew this would never be quite enough.

Adam worked his heart out at the mill for the next three weeks. In addition to his regular duties as an assistant to Will and Davy, who taught him how to operate the various machines, he had the room heated by six o'clock every morning, kept the stove stoked all day long, and swept the main floor at least four times a day. He slopped Mr. Brubaker's hogs and kept the wood box stocked at Mr. Brubaker's house and Miss Fannie's cottage. If anything needed lifting, he was "Johnnie on the spot" to help lift. If something needed to be fetched, he was there to fetch. He had decided to make himself indispensable to Mr. Brubaker and the Perse brothers. That it was working out that way became apparent when he overheard Will tell Mr. Brubaker, "That boy is a powerful worker. He's a little bit of a thing, but he's been worth two men twice his size." Mr. Brubaker had replied, "Yes, he's a good worker, eager and quick to learn. Not at all like his pap, thank the good Lord."

About a week after Adam overheard this conversation, Mr. Brubaker returned from a visit with Valentine Burner, one of the town's three lawyers. Mr. Burner had drawn up what he termed an "indenture contract." Mr. Brubaker called Adam into his office and showed him the document. "Read this," he had said. "I thought we might as well make your position here legal."

Adam took the document in his hands and read very slowly. It provided that Adam had "voluntarily put himself an apprentice to Isaac Brubaker, furniture maker of Stendahl, to learn his art, trade, and mystery and after the manner of an apprentice to serve him until March

8, 1904, at which time the said Adam Richter will attain the legal age of twenty-one."

The contract required Adam to faithfully serve Mr. Brubaker, keep his secrets, and "obey his lawful commands." He could not waste Brubaker's goods, play cards, dice or "any unlawful game" and he was forbidden to absent himself from work without Brubaker's consent or to "haunt ale houses, taverns, or play houses." (This last provision suggested to Adam, who knew nothing about how lawyers worked, that the contract must be a form contract, for Stendahl had no "play house" and never had.)

For his part, Mr. Brubaker was required to pay Adam one dollar and fifty cents a month and provide him with "sufficient meat, drink, apparel, washing and lodging, doctoring and nursing if needed, fitting for an apprentice during the said term." He was also to cause Adam to "read, write, & cipher if capable of learning" and at the end of the term Adam was to be dismissed with "two good suits of apparel suitable for an apprentice, the one for the Lord's days and the other for common days," and a "set of tools suitable for a beginning furniture maker." All in all, Adam decided, it was a good deal for a runty, toothless fourteen-year-old with no other prospects.

-o-

Luke and Paulie showed up at the mill a week or so later, strutting in as if they owned the place, followed by their dog Lizzie. "Hey there Gummy. We kinda miss you at the farm. You shit in any milk buckets lately?" Luke picked up a plane, turned it over in his hands and then dropped it noisily onto the workbench just as Mr. Brubaker came out of the office.

The old man reacted with shock. "What do you think you're doing there with that plane? That's a finely tuned instrument. We don't treat our tools like that."

44

Luke turned to Mr. Brubaker. "Listen, old man, me and my brother go where we want and do what we want. Nobody tells us what to do." He shoved Mr. Brubaker in the chest with both hands, pushing him against the wall.

In one swift move Adam grabbed a bark spud, a three-foot-long steel-tipped device for peeling bark from logs, off the bench behind him and swung it violently against the side of Luke's head, dropping him to the floor instantly.

In shock, Paulie snorted, "Jeezus Christ, you coulda killed him!"

"Well, if I did, it's long overdue."

Paulie dropped to his knees and lifted Luke's head. "Luke! Luke! Can you hear me? Are you dead? If you are, say so."

Mr. Brubaker looked down at Luke and shook his head in amazement. Then he turned to Adam, his eyes wide with surprise. 'You sure made quick use of that bark spud, Richter."

"Well, sir, I fought with these bullies plenty of times when I had to live with them. I learned early on you have to move fast, before they know what's happening, or they'll beat you up real good."

Mr. Brubaker looked down at Luke again and at Paulie hovering over his brother. "I don't think either one of these boys is going to beat you up today." As he turned to go back into the office he shook his head and murmured to himself, "I never saw anyone move that quick."

Will and Davy, who had been sorting lumber in the lower level of the mill, came charging up from below, both of them breathless. Will, armed with a club about three feet long and two inches thick, was obviously armed for battle. "What's all the commotion about?" he gasped.

Adam replied quietly. "The Jepson boys needed to understand something."

Will looked down at Luke, sprawled prostrate on the floor. "Well, you sure took care of him. He looks like he never knew what hit him."

"He may not remember what hit him," Adam replied softly, but I'm sure he will remember that something did, 'cause he's going to have a bad headache for a while, I imagine."

Finally Luke moved slightly and groaned. "Jeezus, Gummy. What did you hit me with?"

"A bark spud, Luke. Just be glad I didn't happen to pick up a hatchet or you would be missing the top of your head right now. Now you and Paulie get out of here and don't come back. I'm not afraid of you boys . . . you should know that from when I lived on the farm. So get out of here, NOW! And don't you ever come back!"

Paulie helped Luke to his feet and, with Lizzie trotting behind, Paulie helped a moaning Luke across the millrace bridge and onto his horse. Then, with Lizzie settled into her saddlebag travel compartment alongside Luke's saddle, where Luke usually carried moonshine jugs for sale, they went slowly down Mill Street toward town.

Adam stood silently at the door to the mill for a few seconds, looking out over the lumber yard. He felt a curious sense of peace and satisfaction. He had struck again at his tormentors and, more to the point; he had acted in defense of Mr. Brubaker.

Then he spoke softly. "I don't like violence but sometimes with people like Luke and Paulie, violence is the only way to make your point."

"Well," Will said, "You made your point with those two today."

CHAPTER 6

After this "settling of affairs" with Luke and Paulie, life at Brubaker's Mill settled into a rhythm that Adam found comforting, even though the food was awful and Miss Fannie Brubaker was nothing short of a terror. A short, dried-up woman with two crooked teeth that jutted out from between her tightly pursed lips, her face was set in a perpetual scowl. She wore her gray hair in a bun that always appeared ready to unravel into a million oily strands and showed no signs of ever having been washed. She wore only black, except for mealtime when she donned a dirty white apron that only served to emphasize her slovenly nature.

Since the end of Adam's first summer as an apprentice, he had been taking his meals at Mr. Brubaker's table, the old man having decided it was silly for the boy to carry his meals back to the mill. Miss Fannie disapproved, but Adam now sat at the table with the two of them and ate. They just ate in silence, but eating at this table in this house was a real "step up" for Adam Richter, and he appreciated that fact immensely.

While hot meals were never a high priority with Miss Fannie, even after Adam was invited to eat in Mr. Brubaker's kitchen, he noticed that, while Mr. Brubaker's meals sometimes had steam rising off them, his were always cold. Many times, when Miss Fannie had served Mr. Brubaker and was standing behind him dishing out Adam's meal, she would look at him with a sneer and spit on his meal. She took special delight in serving foods which Adam could eat only with difficulty, such as a particularly tough piece of meat or corn on the cob. Once, when he was having difficulty eating a tough pork chop she had screamed at him, calling him a "toothless, white trash nobody." But Adam never let on, never complained, and never treated Miss Fannie as anything but an elderly lady who was entitled to his respect. "Don't rock the boat," he thought. "Don't do anything to interfere with the good thing I have going here."

She yelled and cussed at her brother, too, and would slap or kick him when she was in a particular rage. For his part Mr. Brubaker never seemed to get aroused by his sister's behavior. Once, after Fannie had thrown a particularly nasty scene in which she had screamed at Adam, Mr. Brubaker had said to Adam the next day, "She don't mean nothing by it. She's jist high strung." But Adam, who had experienced plenty of nasty behavior in his lifetime, recognized Fannie Brubaker as pure meanness personified. Still, he kept his silence on the matter.

All the while, Adam was learning how to be a real furniture maker. He knew now that, when he was of legal age, he would have a trade of his own. Then, when he had put aside enough money, the first thing he would buy would be a set of false teeth. Meanwhile, he decided he would watch, keep his mouth shut and learn everything he could about furniture making — and about life itself.

When he had figured out Mr. Brubaker's routine, he began to explore the mill. After supper he would lock the door, and then take off to peer into some corner of the building. Only the office, which Mr. Brubaker locked every time he left the building, remained a secret.

One night, after he had lived at the mill for about a month, Adam pried loose a board in the floor along the wall just beyond the stove. The board was about a foot long and was held in place by two ten penny nails. He pounded on the point of one nail so that it protruded about an eighth of an inch from the wall, just enough to get a grip on the nail head. Then he filed a groove in the nail about two inches from the point and broke it off with a pair of pliers so that only a half inch or so remained to fit in the nail hole behind the board. He did the same to the nail at the other end of the board. Then he took Jehu's Jepson's penknife from the pile of walnut and placed it a small cloth bag he had found on the top floor of the mill. He placed the bag in the hole where the board had been removed. When he tapped the board back in place, with the shortened nails holding it there and the eighth of an inch of a nail head protruding, it looked perfectly natural, as if the nail had worked itself loose from the expanding and contracting of the wood. This became his "strongbox" which could hold a great deal more. Many a night Adam went to sleep dreaming of what he would someday place in the strongbox.

-o-

It was perhaps inevitable that most folks came to call Adam "Gummy." He hated the nickname, but he never complained. There would come a time, however, he vowed quietly to himself, when no one would dare call him that.

But not everyone called him Gummy. To Mr. Brubaker he was always "Richter." And Will and Davy Perse always called him Adam. Once, shortly after he came to the mill, Adam overheard Davy and Will talking. Davy said, "Know what, Will? Know what they call Adam? They call him 'Gummy,' on account he ain't got no teeth. Reckon we oughta call him Gummy?" Will had stopped turning a bedpost on the lathe and said to Davy: "Davy, he don't have no teeth 'cause them no-account Jepson boys pulled his teeth just for the fun of it. Adam don't let on, but don't you figger it hurts him to be called 'Gummy.' Don't you 'spect that sometimes he forgets he don't have no teeth and when someone calls him 'Gummy' it just reminds him again that he's fourteen years old and don't have any front teeth? If'n you was Adam, Davy, would you want to be called 'Gummy' or 'Adam?'"

After a long pause Davy replied very seriously, "I'd wanna be called 'Adam,' and that's what we oughta call him."

"Yes, Davy," Will said, "you're right. We oughta call him 'Adam.'"

Will Perse was kind in other ways, too. Once or twice a month he and his wife, Cora, would have Adam over for Sunday dinner at the home they rented just up the mill race beyond Mr. Brubaker's lumber yard. Adam noticed that the food was always soft and tender, easy to eat.

In August when corn on the cob was available, Cora would always have creamed corn or baked corn, corn fixed in some way that took it off the cob. The meat she served was usually a soft meatloaf or chicken and dumplings, or some other easy-to-eat dish. Nothing was ever said about it, even by Davy, who lived with Will and Cora. And, God knows, Davy was prone to saying the wrong thing at the wrong time. But Will and Cora had obviously lectured him in advance. And Davy was such a kind-hearted soul that he would never have deliberately hurt anyone, especially Adam, of whom he was obviously quite fond.

Adam came to realize that those Sunday dinners at the Perses were the only occasions in his life when he had experienced anything approaching normal family life. The Perses had no children. Cora had given birth to a little girl who had died at birth and she was never able to have children after that. Adam sensed that, after a fashion, Will and Cora were treating him much like they would have treated a son of their own. The thing he liked most about the relationship was that there was no pity attached to it. They accepted Adam as a friend whose company they obviously enjoyed, not as a toothless orphan who needed their pity.

Another sign of the couple's kindness was how they always had substantial leftovers they insisted Adam take back to the mill with him. It was always food that would not spoil immediately but which would permit him to extend his Sunday dinner over several days. Often, the leftovers would be a cake or sweet rolls or a pie, pleasures he had never known in his earlier life. The Perses always offered the leftover food in such a way that Adam almost believed it was an accident that they had so much left over and that they would be offended if he didn't take it.

Every time he had dinner at the Perses and took food home with him, he vowed that someday he would find a way to repay them. In all his young life he had never encountered anyone who had treated him with such kindness and generosity. They expected nothing and there was clearly nothing he could do for them or give them. Yet they treated him with such gentleness and respect, with such a sense of humanity, that they made him feel like he had blessed their day by just accepting their invitations. That, he decided, was a sign of "class," too. Will and Cora were clearly working-class people. Will never looked entirely comfortable in his Sunday suit and the family grammar often left something to be desired. But they had a sense of – Adam didn't know the word for it – but it was a sense of how to treat others that Adam had usually seen only in the upper classes. The Perses, he decided, had a lesson to teach him about how to treat others.

Will was, in fact, a study in himself. In addition to being talented, he was a steady worker. When they were unloading timber from a farmer's wagon, or setting timber on the roller carriage to drive it through the gang saw, or working with a tool operating off the mill's drive shaft, Will worked steadily and with a quiet rhythm that Adam sought to duplicate. Will never seemed in a hurry, never seemed to tire, but just went steadily about his work. Adam watched him carefully, trying to copy the easy, graceful way Will worked.

Cora had also shown her kind heart in another way after Adam had arrived at the mill. He was ragged, the only items of clothing he possessed were the same ones he had worn when he was sent to the Jepsons. Over the months since then he had grown a bit, his clothing had deteriorated further, and his appearance had become increasingly pathetic. Then one evening Cora appeared at the mill with trousers and shirts and a pair of shoes. She explained that this clothing had been donated to the church for distribution to those who need it. She had guessed at his size — guessed well as it developed — and his appearance was improved dramatically.

-o-

Since Mr. Brubaker was the only furniture maker in Stendahl just about anyone who needed furniture built or repaired showed up at the mill sooner or later. A lifetime of being on the bottom of the Stendahl social ladder had taught Adam to stay in the background, out of the way. But he had discovered that he could learn a great deal about a person just by watching and listening. Perhaps, he reasoned, he could even learn more because he was in the background and almost invisible to other folks. So he became a serious student of human behavior, always watching and listening to the way other folks spoke and dressed and acted.

He noticed that some of the folks who came to the mill displayed an aura that suggested they were members of the "upper class," while others simply did not. This was not a new discovery but something he had instinctively known from as far back as he could remember. But now he concentrated his attention on the matter. As he lay in his bed at night he pondered over what it was that separated the upper class from the lower classes. No doubt, he realized, some of his impression of who was upper class was affected by the fact that he knew who had money in Stendahl and who did not. But, on reflection, he knew it wasn't just that. There were some folks in town who had accumulated some money but who still didn't have that indefinable something that identified them as upper class. But the folks who ran the town, who led the churches and who sat on the County Court and who made all the big decisions for the community, truly were different from the others in ways that were difficult to quantify. It clearly wasn't just their money.

For one thing, they dealt with other people with such ease, treating everyone with dignity. They might be above other folks in social standing but they always treated them with respect, calling them "ma'am" and "sir" and being very dignified and all with everyone. Then, too, they spoke a different language. For example, they never said "ain't," or "et." How they knew to say "eaten" for "et," or "isn't" for "ain't" was a puzzle to Adam.

They dressed differently, too. It wasn't just that the men who worked in the bank wore suits and ties to work while folks like Adam and Mr. Brubaker wore work clothes. On Sundays, when all the men who went to church wore suits, Adam could still tell who was upper class and who wasn't. Some folks just had an "air" about them that told him they were the people who counted in the community. And others didn't. It was that simple. But, then, as Adam thought about it some more, he knew it wasn't really simple at all. He studied on this question a great deal and decided he would learn just what it was that marked some folks as being upper class. Then, he intended to join them. He, Adam Richter, would join the upper class. After he got his teeth, of course. In the meantime, just for starters, he would stop saying "ain't" and "et."

CHAPTER 7

It was Randall Armentrout , the president of the Stendahl State Bank, who gave him the idea. Randall was a short, doughy, prissy, man with watery eyes set in deep sockets. His hair was gray and hung in clumps over his ears and neck, framing his face. Aside from his eyes, which darted about as he constantly scanned his surroundings, the only thing memorable about him were the tiny veins in his cheeks and nose, which gave his face him an almost infantile, pink-cheeked appearance. He was always chomping on a cigar, "Probably," Will once said, "because he thought it made him look more masculine." In truth it didn't. It only made him seem like a fat little schoolboy who was trying to impress the older boys.

Randall had inherited several thousand shares in the Stendahl State Bank from his grandfather who, with two business partners, had started the bank in the wake of the Panic of 1873. Randall now owned over 45% of the shares in the bank, by far the largest chunk of shares controlled by any one person. As a result, he pretty much ran the bank as though he owned it outright. With his money and the power it brought him in the small, rural community of Stendahl, he was an insufferable little man; made even more difficult to endure by the strange conviction – held by him but by no one else – that he was witty. All in all, he was a very hard man to like.

Adam had always avoided Randall. Even in his darkest days with Pap when he needed any kind of work just to stay alive, he had never approached the president of the Stendahl State Bank. Still, Adam watched him and listened to what he had to say, in the strong belief that the folks he considered his betters had something to teach him, even if the lesson was not to try too hard to be clever.

On this particular day Randall was at the mill checking on the progress of an oak roll-top desk he had ordered for the bank. As he was leaving the mill, Will said to him, "Mr. Armentrout, I can have it done a week or so earlier if we skimp on the scraping and finishing of the wood. But I don't think we ought to do that."

"I think not," Randall had said, and he walked out the door and down the steps.

"I think not." That struck Adam as a strange thing to say. Why didn't he say, "I agree with you," or "all right by me," or "no, let's not skimp on the scraping and finishing." Why did he say "I think not"? It was a perfectly fine thing to say, even if it was a bit "lofty." The point was it was something only a man of Randall Armentrout's station in life would have said. And when he said it, it marked Randall Armentrout as a member of the upper class, as surely as if he had said to Will, "You know, I have a great deal of money and I belong to the upper class." Adam wasn't sure why that was, but he was certain it was the case and that was enough. Adam also knew at that moment that he would never learn to speak "upper class" English just by listening to people like Mr. Armentrout talk. It was something he was going to have to study.

So that evening, after supper, Adam put on his clean pants and shirt and Pap's boots and walked down Mill Street, across Main Street, and out Jefferson Avenue to the large brick house of Armistead Watson. Watson was a farmer who had inherited the most prosperous piece of land in the county. The farm backed up against the town of Stendahl which gave Watson the advantage of living in town while still running a farm. For his daughter and only child, Ida, this had been an especially fortuitous development for it meant she could go to school in Stendahl's all-brick two-room school, instead of some primitive one-room school in the country. It was no doubt only a matter of degree, but an education at the Stendahl Public School was bound to be superior to that of any of the county's one-room country schools.

After graduation from Stendahl Public School, Miss Ida had spent a year at a finishing school in Baltimore. On her return to Stendahl she learned that Sarah Teals had resigned as one of the two teachers at Stendahl Public School. So Miss Ida applied and was hired immediately by Miss Sallie Beeker, the school's headmistress and other teacher. In a town the size of Stendahl a member of the family of one of the town's most prominent citizens was seldom disappointed when it came to public positions, even if she was extremely large and not at all attractive. (Truth to tell, if Miss Ida had been the least bit attractive she would never have gone to finishing school. There would have been some young man with an eye on the Watson farm offering to marry her. But such was Miss Ida's girth that not even the prospect of the finest farm in the county could attract a suitor.)

Adam took off his battered hat and knocked on the door, noticing that the door knob was of highly polished brass and that the windows in the door were gleaming. "Must remember to wash the windows in the mill," he thought, as he waited for the door to be answered.

An attractive woman in her fifties, whom Adam recognized as Armistead Watson's wife, answered the door. "May I help you?" she asked. Her manner suggested she was not thrilled with the presence of this toothless, slightly ragged boy on her porch.

"Yes'm," Adam said. He had read the signals Mrs. Watson was giving out and was, quite simply, terrified. But his misfortunes of the past few years had taught him that in such circumstances the best course was usually to get right to the gist of the matter.

"I am Adam Richter and I would like to speak with Miss Ida Watson about teaching me English grammar. I kin pay her." Another thing Adam had observed about the upper classes was that they greatly approved of the efforts of the lower classes to improve themselves — so long as the lower classes still "kept in their place." So before Mrs. Watson had a chance to interject a word, Adam went on: "I am from poor circumstances, but I want to improve my lot and I believe proper understanding of English grammar is necessary. It will make me more valuable at Brubaker's Mill where I am apprenticed to Mr. Brubaker to learn the furniture-making trade."

Just how better grammar would make him a better furniture builder escaped Adam, but he knew the sentiment of the thing, the idea of improving himself while staying in "his place" would be well received. He paused for a second and then decided to butter the bread a little thicker. "I am told Miss Ida is a wonderful teacher and I have sought her out before going to anyone else."

Mrs. Watson softened visibly. When she was satisfied that Adam was finished, she said, "Please come in and have a seat in our parlor, Mr. Richter. I'll fetch Ida." She glided effortlessly out of the room. Adam noted that Mrs. Watson had displayed another sign of "class," by calling him "Mr. Richter," even though she knew, from his appearance and from what he had told her that he was from the lower classes.

Adam looked about him. The room was the very picture of Victorian elegance. There was a cut velvet settee at one end of the room, flanked by an enormous fern on a tall cherry stand on one side and by an elaborately carved platform rocker on the other. The double windows behind the settee were curtained in frilly lace, through which Adam could see the barnyard. To his right was a walnut pump organ, with velvet upholstered pedals. Above the organ was a huge lithograph of a little girl, not more than two years old, sleeping peacefully against an enormous sheep dog.

Adam looked at the other end of the room. There was an ornate quarter-sawed oak table with a kerosene lamp sitting on one end. The lamp had a leaded-glass shade with an ornate scene of flowers and greenery. Around the table were four chairs of a design which Adam had never seen before. They were oak and the backs had designs which appeared to have been burned or pressed into them. Adam wanted to look at them more carefully, but the sound of approaching footsteps caught his attention and he stood and turned toward the door.

Miss Ida Watson came into the room, smiling. "Mama says you want me to teach you English grammar," she said.

"Yes'm," Adam said as he turned his hat nervously in his hands. "I want to git ahead in the world and I believe I oughta learn proper English." He stopped with that. He could see this speech wasn't affecting Miss Ida as it had her mother.

Miss Ida smiled and looked off into the distance. "Before school begins this fall I plan to travel some. I am taking the stage to Whitney on Tuesday and catching the train to Baltimore on Wednesday afternoon. From there I am going to Washington, D.C., to view the sights. After Washington, I am taking the train to Richmond to see my Aunt Grace and tour the sights of Richmond. From there I just might go somewhere else. I just don't know yet. So, you see, I wouldn't be able to tutor you until my return just before school begins."

As she talked Adam watched her intently. She was batting her eyelids and rolling her eyes and twisting her head back and forth and acting, oh so important. Like this trip of hers was the most momentous journey ever undertaken, which to her it probably was.

Lord, but she was fat! That fact overwhelmed everything else about Miss Ida. It was impossible to know whether she could conceivably be pretty under all that fat. Adam thought she was so fat, and had been so all her life most likely, that this dominated her life. At a time when most young women would have been thinking about men or starting a family or at least looking forward to some social arrangements, Miss Ida Watson had to manufacture a trip to have something to look forward to — to give her life some meaning. "We all need something," Adam thought, just like he had now decided to learn English grammar. For Miss Ida that "something," for the time being at least, was her trip.

"I'm pleased for your trip, Miss Ida," Adam said. "It sounds like it will be real educational — and fun. I suppose I could see if Miss Sallie Beeker can teach me this summer."

"Oh, you've not been to her yet?"

"No, mam. I come to you first. I was told you was the best, even though Miss Sallie's the headmistress." No need to mention that he knew Sallie Beeker didn't like him, that she had encouraged Sarah Teals not to "waste any time on this little piece of dirt" when he had returned to school after Ma's death. No need to mention that he wouldn't seek Sallie Beeker's help if she were the last source on earth. "You was the best, they said, the vury best," Adam repeated.

Miss Ida gestured toward the oak table. "Please have a seat. I'll be right back." She glided out of the room as gracefully as a woman of her size could possibly glide.

She was back in a few minutes, carrying a stack of small cloth-bound books. "These are *Hart's English Grammar, McGuffey's First, Second, Third, Fourth and Fifth Readers,* and *Sanders' School Reader,* books I teach from at the public school." She handed the books to Adam as she plopped down in one of the oak chairs. The chair groaned audibly. "I have a proposal, Mr. . . . ah . . . Richter, is it?"

"Yes'm. Richter. Adam Richter."

"Well, Mr. Richter, I propose that you take these books ... I am assuming you *can* read ...."

Adam nodded vigorously. "Yes'm. I can read. I attended Jeffersonville School when I lived with the Jepsons." No need to mention the Stendahl school and his unfortunate dealings with Miss Sallie Beeker and Miss Sarah Teals. "I've already read the first through the third of *McGuffey's Readers.*"

"I will take those three Readers back and you take the rest of these books and study the lessons in them. You learn what you can from these books and when I return we will see whether it is worth our time to continue with your studies. You take real good care of these books. Do not let them get wet or dirty. And study the lessons they contain." She was smiling at Adam in a superior, but not entirely unpleasant, way.

Adam smiled back, keeping his lips firmly together. She could no doubt tell he had no teeth, but out of habit he always smiled with his lips pressed firmly together. "Yes'm. I'll take real good care of them. And when you git back I jist know you'll want to teach me. What do I owe you for the use of these books? I have some money with me now." Adam reached toward his pants pocket.

Miss Ida flipped her hands in front of her ample bosom as though she was brushing away a fly. "Oh, my goodness, there is no charge for using these books. After all, you cannot exactly read the print off them, can you?" She gestured toward the books. "You take these books and study them. When I get back from my trip, I will send word to Brubaker's Mill where Mama says you work and you can come by. We will have a little examination and decide whether to proceed. All right?" She stood up.

Adam stood as well. "Yes'm, that's fine with me. I sure do appreciate what you are doin' for me."

As she led Adam through the hallway and out the front door she said, "That's fine, Mr. Richter. I am happy to help."

Adam turned before walking off the front porch. "You have a real nice trip. I'll see you when you get back." But Miss Ida had already shut the door and was waddling down the hallway.

-o-

After supper that night Adam lit the kerosene lamp beside his bed, unwrapped *Hart's English Grammar* from the flour sack in which he had placed it for protection, and began to read. It was, he could see immediately, not going to be easy. The first lesson was about articulation, and began with a discussion of vocals, which the book described as "sounds which consist of pure tone only." Adam shook his head and read further. There were tables of "long vocals," such as ä, as in "hare", or ē, as in "eve," and "short vocals, such as ă, as in "mat," and ĕ, as in "met." There were diphthongs (oi, as in "oil" – which Adam had always pronounced as "orl" but now understood his error) and subvocals (b, as in "bad") and aspirates (p as in "rap.")

By the fourth page of the text, however, he began to understand the purpose in all this discussion. Under "Faults to be Remedied," was a discussion of the necessity of pronouncing correctly unaccented vowels. The book cautioned not to pronounce the word "sep-*a*-rate" as "sep'rate" or "sep-*er*-ate," or the word *"a*p-pear" as "'pear" or "*u*p-pear." Adam read the words carefully, repeating the correct pronunciation. He read them over and over, slowly practicing the correct pronunciation. But it was hard going. There was so much to learn.

After a while he put the book down and gazed off into the distance, contemplating what little he had just learned. He thought of the various customers who came into the mill and how they talked. People like Valentine Burner, Mrs. Hester Siple, whose husband, Conrad, owned

62

half of downtown Stendahl, and old Doc Glanzer pronounced their words very carefully. With them, "*a*p-pear" was always "*a*p-pear," never "'pear" or "*u*p-pear." "*O*-pin-ion" was always just that, never "'pin-ion" or "*u*p-pin-ion." Will and David Perse, and most of the folks who came to the mill regularly, and Mr. Brubaker himself, might slur or mispronounce their words, but not the "quality" folks of Stendahl. Correct articulation, Adam realized, was one of the ways quality folks could be distinguished from the rest.

It was only 9:00 p.m. but Adam carefully rolled the book up in its protective sack, placed it under his tick of shavings, blew out the lamp, and crawled into bed. There was much to think about. Or, as Adam told himself with a smile, much to "con'-tem-plate."

In the next few weeks, Adam read *Hart's English Grammar* every evening. His practice was to read for a while and then consider what he had just read. If it wasn't completely clear, as was most often the case, he read it again. And again. And again. He did not move on to the next section of the book until he had a complete understanding of what he had just read. "Great God, it was hard work!"

Still it was an amazing journey. Since he had come to work for Mr. Brubaker and had begun studying people, he had come to realize that certain combinations of words were never used by the upper classes. No one from the upper classes ever said "we *was*" or "them *is*." It was always, "we *were*" and "those *are*." He had wondered what made some combinations of words *right* and others *wrong* and how folks knew just what was right and what wasn't.

He discovered the answer to his question on page 59 of *Hart's Grammar*. Verbs – he had long since understood what the parts of speech were – had singular and plural forms! If you were talking about more than one person or thing, it should always be "they" or "we" *WERE*, not "we WAS" or "they IS." "He," being a singular noun, should always be paired with a singular verb, such as "is." "They," being a plural noun, should always be paired with a plural verb, such as "are." It was an amazing revelation to Adam, that there are patterns to grammar, just like there are patterns to numbers. Then Adam remembered the introductory words to the preface to *Hart's Grammar*, which he now turned to and read again.

> Grammar is like arithmetic. It is based on scientific
> principles, and for advanced students it deals mainly with
> theoretical and abstract discussions. But for beginners,
> it requires positive rules and definitions, and above all
> things, clear and copious examples.

Adam wasn't sure what "copious" meant, but the rest of that passage was very clear. Just as six and eight *always* added up to fourteen, so "I" is *always* paired with "am" and "you" is *always* paired with "are." It is not that the upper classes speak differently; it is that they understand the *rules* that govern grammar and follow them precisely. That is the key! Adam knew then that he had just crossed over a divide of considerable magnitude in his life. He may live in a lumber mill and own precious little, but he had unlocked the key to moving from his station in life to ever higher levels.

After he had mastered *Hart's Grammar,* he tackled Sanders' *School Reader* and then *McGuffey's Fourth* and *Fifth Readers. Hart's Grammar*, he realized later, had been the hardest book of all, but it had also laid the foundation for the other books which were, after all only readers, books containing passages from literature. *Hart*, on the other hand, had laid down the rules and set forth the reasons for the rules that made the language consistent, and even eloquent.

Some nights Adam stayed up until one or two o'clock in the morning. On the mornings following a late night, instead of being weary from a lack of rest, he was exhilarated with the new knowledge he had gained. He learned to conjugate verbs, never being quite certain why it was called "conjugating," but fully aware of how it determined the proper structure of an English sentence. He learned about adjectives and adverbs, about prepositions and conjunctions, about the origins of words. He was fascinated to learn that the English language contained thousands of words from Greek and Latin, and Saxon, whatever that was. He made a mental note: "must ask Miss Ida."

After a month of steady review of these texts, Adam realized that he had an understanding of the English language that would serve him the rest of his life. He would, he realized, be learning the proper use of the language for the rest of his life. English, he said to himself, is not something you acquire in a fortnight. (He smiled as he said "fortnight," a new word meaning two weeks. It was fun learning new words.) From now on he was going to make a conscious effort not to slip into the old, lazy ways of speaking, he would take care not to mix up plural verbs with singular nouns, and would never again treat language as anything but a precise undertaking, to be performed in one, and only one way: the proper way.

He also determined that he would take great care not to "show off" his new-found knowledge. If he were an educated man, it would show, without his having to point it out to others. After all, that's the way it was with the upper class folks in Stendahl.

CHAPTER 8

In cold weather, one of Adam's tasks was to have the stove heated before the mill opened at six o'clock. Since he had no clock and couldn't see Pap's watch in the dark, Adam relied on Mr. Brubaker's rooster to wake him in the summer as dawn began to break. In the winter, when the rooster waited for a later dawn, Adam learned that the Teters, who lived about two hundred yards down the mill race, rose around five o'clock. So, in cold weather, when Adam began to suspect it might be getting toward five o'clock, he would go to the window on the Stendahl side of the mill and look toward Teters. If their lamp was lit, he knew it was five o'clock. Otherwise, he went back to bed, rising to check again every few minutes. It became a matter of pride to Adam that, in all his time as an apprentice to Mr. Brubaker, he never once failed to have the main floor of the mill heated by the time Mr. Brubaker came to work. It also interested him that the old man never commented on this fact, as though it never occurred to him to wonder how Adam was always up and had the place heated on time.

Mr. Brubaker was good to Adam in a distant sort of way. A true artist with wood, he showed Adam how to select the various kinds of wood that went into a sturdy piece of furniture. He taught him the correct angle to "approach" the turning stock on the lathe, how to cut and fit perfect dovetails, and how to know which way to run the grain of the various pieces of wood in a piece of furniture to minimize cracking and splitting as the wood swelled and shrank during the year. "Wood breathes just like a man," he told Adam time after time.

Brubaker's Furniture Mill built all sorts of furniture. But what Mr. Brubaker was proudest of were his chairs, which constituted the most common item of furniture the mill turned out. "Any fool can make a decent chest," he told Adam. "But it takes a right smart talent to make a chair that people scoot all over the room and drop their rear ends into and tilt back on and lean into and squirm around on year after year and not have the chair arms or legs break off or work loose."

"A well-made chair," Mr. Brubaker explained, "takes advantage of the different kinds of wood. White oak, ash, and hickory are best for the back spindles of a chair 'cause these woods tend to 'whip' less when you turn 'em on the lathe. Maple, which is hard and stiff and resists shock and bruisin' probably better than any other wood, is ideal for chair arms and the back that holds the spindles. Maple and oak, both hard, are what you want for chair rungs and legs. As for the seat, butternut, chestnut, or pine will do fine."

"The secret," Mr. Brubaker explained, "is to use these different woods, use some of 'em dried and some green. A seat of green chestnut," he explained, "fitted with well-dried legs of maple or oak, could be counted on to shrink tight around the socket ends of the legs, making the final joinery absolutely rigid and durable." There was no doubt about it, the old man knew his wood and was masterful at working with it. Adam loved to watch the way his gnarled, arthritic hands could take a wood plane and shape a nothing piece of wood into a elegant piece of molding or the way he tilted the chisel on the side rest of the plane just so and caused the shavings to peel away from the turning stock and a beautiful piece of chair spindle to emerge.

When a log was delivered to the mill, Mr. Brubaker would have the farmer pull the log across the little bridge over the mill race and into the yard in front of the mill where it would be placed to dry. When the log had cured it would be rolled to the front of the mill and placed in front of the gang saw, a huge apparatus in which six to eight saw blades were locked onto a wooden frame side by side. Then the whole assembly would oscillate up and down – driven by the power of the mill's water wheel – and rip the log into flat boards. By adjusting the distance between the gang saw blades, and adding or removing blades if necessary, the thickness of the boards could be varied. Once the logs were cut into boards, the boards were stacked onto racks on the bottom floor of the mill and allowed to cure further.

Adam was entranced by the operation of the gang saw and its supporting apparatus. Mr. Brubaker's machinery was so well designed that even a scrawny teenager could control logs that weighed over a thousand pounds. The power displayed by the blades as they sliced their way through the massive logs and the reducing of mammoth logs into boards of manageable size, created a sense of strength and mastery over his surroundings that Adam had never experienced before.

He also noticed that when Mr. Brubaker was talking with a customer about a piece of furniture the customer wanted built, he often led the customer to the wood of his choice, which was usually influenced by what species of lumber was sitting downstairs, cured and ready for working. If a man wanted a cherry chest and Brubaker had a surfeit of cured walnut but very little cherry ready to work, he would talk about the beauty and durability of walnut, how well it aged and what fine properties it had. If the reverse were true, he would sing the praises of cherry over walnut. The interesting thing was, Mr. Brubaker usually had his way in the choice of lumber, but the customer always went away thinking he had chosen the wood. That, Adam decided, was a valuable talent, being able to talk people into wanting to do what you wanted them to do, all the while having them think it had been their idea.

Adam had been working at the mill for about six months when, one Saturday at noontime, he rushed through his dinner, stood up abruptly and announced, "I have to run to town for a few minutes. I'll be back before we start back to work."

He went straight to Havel's Mercantile Emporium on South Main Street. It was a bright day and it took a few minutes for his eyes to adjust to the dark interior of the store. He hadn't been in the store since he had sold tanned rabbit furs to old Mr. Havel before Pap had died. But the smell of fresh leather harness and dyed cloth and oiled floors brought him back instantly to his earlier days. A dim figure stood behind the counter. Adam approached the counter and recognized the figure as a long-time clerk for Mr. Havel, a man he knew only as Arley.

"Kin I help you, Gummy?" Arley asked, peering out over his glasses, which had slid halfway down his nose.

"Want to buy some wool stockings," Adam said.

"What size?"

Adam blushed. "Don't rightly know," he said.

"Hold your foot up here," Arley said. "Let me take a look."

Adam lifted his left leg and held his foot up for Arley to see. Arley turned, reached up, and pulled a box off the top shelf. "Here," he said, "I believe these will do fine." He held out a pair of stockings to Adam.

"Yes," Adam said as he felt the warm feel of the wool between his fingers.

"How many pairs you want, Gummy?" Arley asked.

Adam paused for a moment and then said, "Three. I'll take three pair." Then he realized he had never asked the price. "How much are they?" he asked, holding his breath.

"Eight cents a pair. That'll be twenty-four cents total."

70

Adam dug into his pocket and pulled out a quarter, which he handed to Arley who reached in a drawer beneath the counter and dropped a penny into Adam's hand.

"Thank you very much, Gummy," he said, as he handed Adam the stockings, which he had wrapped in a piece of newspaper.

Adam nodded his thanks as he walked out of the store.

On his way back to the mill he thought about what he had just done. He, Adam Richter, had just purchased store-bought wool stockings! Imagine. He had never before even worn stockings, ever. Now he owned three pairs. *Wouldn't Ma be proud!*

The afternoon seemed to drag on forever as Adam thought about the stockings, wondered how they would feel, and half wondered if he hadn't been entirely too extravagant. Finally, at precisely six o'clock, the mill closed. When everyone was gone Adam went down to the lower level of the mill and opened the small door that led directly to the mill race. He sat down on a large rock which he always used when washing up and removed his shoes. He immersed his feet in the cool water of the mill race and washed them thoroughly with the lye soap Mr. Brubaker had given him. When he was finished he took the pair of stockings he had brought with him and pulled them on. Then he pulled his shoes on and laced them.

They felt wonderful! The rough edges of the worn leather insides of his shoes were softened by the heavy wool stockings. "This," Adam thought, "is how it must feel to be rich."

-o-

Miss Ida Watson had been home for nearly a month when she sent one of her father's farm hands to the mill to ask Adam to meet with her at her home that night. Adam sent word back that he would be "de-light-ed" to meet with her, taking great pride that he had not said "du-light-ed."

In Armistead Watson's parlor that night Miss Ida was very matter-of-fact. Adam began by politely inquiring about her trip, but she dismissed him brusquely, "Oh, it was a fine trip, very educational and all, but those folks in Richmond are so taken up with their 'society' ideas, that it became such a bore."

"The boys in Richmond don't pay much attention to fat girls either," Adam thought. But he followed Miss Ida's lead, turning to *Hart's Grammar.*

"I found this book particularly helpful, Miss Ida." He took great care to enunciate the "u" in "par-tic-*u*-larly." "The lessons were very de-mand-ing," he added. "If anything, this book has increased my o-pin-ion of the need for an ed-*u*-cat-ion." He could barely keep from smiling. He had not pronounced "particularly" as "par-tic-*er*-ly" "demanding" as "d*u*m-mand-ing," "opinion" as "'pin-ion," or "education" as "edj-*a*-cat-ion," as he would have in the past. His pronunciations had been as polished as if he had graduated from at the top of his class at Stendahl's public school. Even his elocution had been flawless, surprisingly so given that his voice had to glide out over toothless gums. More to the point, it all sounded quite natural to him. It obviously did to Miss Ida, too, as she smiled softly at him.

She opened the book and questioned him briefly about articulation, pronunciation, emphasis, and modulation. Then she had him open *McGuffey's Fifth Reader*, and read William Allingham's poem, *Robin Redbreast,* Goldsmith's *An Elegy on Madam Blaize,* and a page from James Fenimore Cooper's *A Chase in the English Channel.* When Adam had finished, Miss Ida said quietly, "Very good, Mr. Richter, very good. Cooper's *A Chase in the English Channel* in particular is very difficult reading. You have obviously taken the study of this book seriously. I am going to be happy to help you with your studies." Then she handed him a pile of books. "Here is the last of *McGuffey's Readers*, the *Sixth Reader* and this is *Ray's New Practical Arithmetic*. I presume you wish to study arithmetic, too."

"Yes ma'am," Adam replied, wondering if she noticed he was no longer saying "yes'm." "A knowledge of arithmetic will be essential to my work with Mr. Brubaker." Adam was feeling pretty good, now, talking like a regular "quality" man-about-town. His comment had a nice "ring" to it, too. His learning arithmetic would help him be of more assistance to Mr. Brubaker. Here it was again, the lower class boy knowing his place and seeking only to improve the quality of his service from that place. People like Miss Ida would like that.

Miss Ida then laid out a schedule for Adam's studies. He would read the *McGuffey's Sixth Reader*, and then he would read the arithmetic book. He could keep *Hart's Grammar* as a reference should he need it to understand anything not fully clear to him in the *McGuffey's Reader*. After he felt he had mastered the materials in a book, or if he felt he needed some help with some of the material, he would drop by the Watson farmhouse and Miss Ida would either meet with him or set a time for a meeting. "There will be no charge for this, Mr. Richter," she added. "I greatly approve of folks in your circumstance seeking to better yourselves."

"Yes," Adam thought, "I'm sure you do."

"In fact, Mr. Richter, I am going to give you *Hart's Grammar* to keep as your own. I have another copy and I, like you, find it an invaluable resource."

He left the Watson home feeling elated. *I, Adam Richter, am going to get an education! I even own a book, my very own book. The first I have ever owned. I am going to be an educated man!* Then he furrowed his brow, remembering a passage from a story by John Greenleaf Whittier that he had read in *McGuffey's Fifth Reader*: "Never brag of catching a fish until he is on dry ground." Adam nodded his head, as if talking to himself. He would keep quiet about his learning. There would yet be time enough for others to know what was being stuffed into his head. In the meantime he would learn and keep his own counsel. He would watch and listen and learn.

-o-

One of Adam's chores as Mr. Brubaker's apprentice was to feed his pigs. The pig pen was set behind the house next to what had been a stable at one time, but Mr. Brubaker no longer kept horses.

Next to the pig pen was a large black walnut tree. The fall Adam came to work at the mill Mr. Brubaker had told him he could have the walnuts if he wanted them. Adam leaped at the opportunity. He gathered the nuts and took them to the mill where he peeled off the wrinkled green husks, cracked the nuts open with a small sledge hammer on a rock, and extracted the meat. The husks dyed his hands a dark brown that would not wash off and took over two months to wear away completely. Adam, who had always cared about cleanliness, was ashamed of his stained hands but realized that folks in the community would understand that they were not dirty, merely stained by walnut husks. He had plenty of company with stained hands as other folks in the community sought to earn a little money by harvesting walnut meat as well.

The first year he cracked walnuts he sold over seven pounds of walnut meat at eight cents a pound and had a pound or so left over which he wrapped in a sack to give to Cora and Will Perse at Christmas.

It was, he realized, the first time he had ever given anyone a Christmas present. Even when Ma lay dying, he had never had anything to give her. And the family never had a Christmas tree to put a present under anyway. Every penny Adam could come up with went toward survival, while every bit of money Pap scrabbled together went to liquor of one sort or another.

By the following spring he had over sixteen dollars stashed in his strongbox, saved up from the one dollar fifty cents a month Mr. Brubaker paid him and the fifty-six cents he had made selling the walnut meat. It helped that he never spent a penny on anything. He washed himself and his clothes in the mill race, using lye soap Miss Fannie Brubaker had made. Will Perse cut his hair every two or three months and he ate what Miss Fannie fed him. At this rate he calculated he would have saved up nearly seventy dollars when his apprenticeship was over. With the set of tools Mr. Brubaker was obligated to give him and his knowledge of woodworking, he would have the beginnings of a trade. He could buy set of store teeth and start life anew, probably some place out West where folks wouldn't know about him and his background.

CHAPTER 9

By the spring of 1899 Adam had pretty well explored the mill from top to bottom. It was time, he decided, to inspect Mr. Brubaker's office. He had never outwardly shown the slightest interest in the office, but he always watched carefully — when he knew Mr. Brubaker was unaware he was watching — as he locked and unlocked the door. One evening, when the days had grown longer and the sun didn't set until around eight o'clock, Adam took a piece of soft pine and whittled it until it was just a tad thinner than the keyhole and inserted it. He twisted the pine softly, hoping the lock would make an impression. But there was nothing.

Then he took the piece of pine to the stove, opened the door and rubbed the end of the pine against the soot that was caked on the door. He went back to the door and re-inserted the piece into the lock and twisted it softly, hoping to make an impression on the soot-covered piece of pine. Again, nothing.

Adam played with this piece of wood for several nights and then began a different approach. He had been given a key to the mill. It didn't open the office door but perhaps, Adam reasoned, he could use some variation on that key to make a key for the office. He had seen the key hanging from Mr. Brubaker's suspender button and was familiar with its general shape. So he carved out a key with the same dimensions as the mill door key, leaving the end blank. Then, carving from memory, he tried to reproduce Mr. Brubaker's key. After three weeks of carving and re-carving every night after Mr. Brubaker had left for the house, Adam finally succeeded in getting a key that wouldn't jam in the lock. But the lock was so difficult to operate that the homemade pine key was certain to break off in the lock. That, Adam knew, would be a disaster.

He took an oil can that was used to lubricate the machinery and squirted a little oil into the lock, hoping that as Mr. Brubaker locked and unlocked the door day after day, the lock would become easier to operate — not easy enough that Mr. Brubaker would notice, but easy enough that a homemade wooden key would work.

As he waited for the lock to become easier to operate, Adam carved another key out of maple, the hardest wood in the mill. When it didn't work he shaped another unworkable key and yet another. Finally, one evening in the early summer of 1899, when Adam had been living at the mill for just over a year and had come to believe he would never fashion a key that would work, the lock opened with a quick "snap." Adam's heart stood still. He was in! But what if Mr. Brubaker came back to the mill for some reason or other? He never had during all the time Adam had been living there, but what if he suddenly changed his pattern? Adam locked the office door and sat down on his bed to think. After a while he got up and placed a heavy board across the mill door. If Mr. Brubaker tried to get into the mill, Adam would explain that he always barred the door out of fear of the Jepson boys. He might suspect Adam was lying, but he wouldn't know for sure, and Adam would have time to get out of the office and get the door locked.

With the board in place, Adam unlocked the door to the office and began snooping around. There was no money, and if there had been Adam wouldn't have bothered it. Mr. Brubaker had been too good to him, and things were going too well to steal from the man. Adam just wanted to know what was in the office.

Mostly it was a disappointment. Brubaker's accounts were a mess, and they took up most of the space in the office. There were two or three books about carpentry and furniture making and an old Bible in German.

The high, sloping desk was covered with papers, mostly drawings of chests and the like and bits of paper crammed with calculations. Everything had a layer of dust, including the stool Mr. Brubaker was supposed to sit on when he used the desk but which, since the old man usually just leaned over the desk, had gathered its share of dust.

It was the safe that stood opposite the desk against the back wall that interested him most. On those occasions when Adam had been in the office when the safe was being opened, he had conspicuously paid little attention to Mr. Brubaker's fiddling with the dial, knowing that any interest shown in this exercise would only make the old man suspicious. He had, however, taken note of things: Mr. Brubaker began turning the dial clockwise; he turned the dial to four different numbers; and the last number was 64. He knew that because the old man always left the dial set on that number when he turned the handle to open the safe. When he closed and locked the safe, he always spun the dial at random. But Adam knew from observation that the last number Mr. Brubaker dialed to open the safe was 64.

He fiddled with the dial to the safe for nearly an hour, holding it delicately in his fingertips and trying to sense if any tumblers were falling. It was no use. He could not open the safe without the combination.

Finally Adam set the dial at 47, the number to which he had noticed Mr. Brubaker had randomly spun the dial when locking the safe for that night. He did a bit more snooping around the office, carefully picking up papers and looking at various documents. But there was nothing of great interest. In the growing twilight he quickly glanced around the room and, satisfied that he had left no sign that he had been there, carefully closed and locked the door.

Over the next couple of weeks he went into the office nearly every night. Mostly he fiddled with the dial on the safe, hoping that by chance he might stumble onto the combination. That never happened though it did start him to thinking.

He had noted that Mr. Brubaker's desk was littered with papers containing minute calculations in the old man's crabbed hand. He was always calculating one thing or another – how much to pay a farmer who had brought a load of wood to the mill, how much to charge for a piece of furniture, how many board feet were in a load of timber – numbers, numbers, numbers. It stood to reason that once in a while, after having been immersed in calculations, Mr. Brubaker would simply have a lapse of memory and forget the combination to the safe for a brief time. When that happened, he had to have it written down somewhere handy. It could always be kept in the house, of course, but that would be too inconvenient. He could carry it in his pocket, but that meant he might lose it sometime and someone who found it would recognize it for what it was and break into the safe. No, he had to have written the combination down somewhere in the office.

Then, too, Adam remembered the time he had come into the office when Mr. Brubaker was trying to open the safe. He was very frustrated, moving the dial carefully in a clockwise and counterclockwise manner. He had turned to Adam and said, "You git out of here. I have something I need to do." Adam had left the office and Mr. Brubaker had closed the door. After a few minutes he re-opened the door and said to Adam, "You can come in now." Adam noticed the safe was open. Obviously Mr. Brubaker had hidden the combination somewhere in the office. He had told Adam to leave because he didn't want him to see where the combination was hidden.

For the next few nights Adam carefully sifted through all the papers in the office, looking for a list of four numbers, the last of which would be 64. Nothing. There were occasionally columns of numbers, but never just four and never containing the number 64. Then, late in June, about three weeks after he had gained access to the office, he saw something he had never noticed before. As he moved some papers in the drawer of Mr. Brubaker's desk he caught a glimpse of pencil markings on the wooden bottom of the drawer. There were four numbers: 11, 72, 9, and 54. That can't be it, Adam thought. The last number has to be *64* not *54*.

Then it suddenly came to him. Mr. Brubaker had written down the four numbers of the combination *after deducting ten from each one!* If that was true, the combination would be *21, 82, 19,* and *64*. With his hands shaking, Adam turned to the safe dial. He turned clockwise to 21, then counter-clockwise to 82, then clockwise to 19, and finally counter-clockwise to 64. The handle wouldn't budge.

Then he thought about it some more. When he opened the safe Mr. Brubaker spent a little more time than would be necessary just to go to four numbers. He went clockwise several times, then counter-clockwise several times, and so on. He seemed to get to the last numbers faster than the earlier ones. Adam spun the dial clockwise four times to 21, then counter-clockwise three times to 82, then clockwise twice to 19, and finally counter-clockwise once toward 64. As he approached the number 64 the dial tightened. The tumblers were falling into place. Adam grabbed the handle of the safe. It opened effortlessly. He pulled the safe door toward him and peeked inside.

His heart beating rapidly, he closed the safe and went back outside to make certain the door to the mill was properly barred. He came back and opened the safe again. It was, like Mr. Brubaker's desk, a mess.

There was a sack of what Adam took to be coins from the weight and the way the sack jingled. He didn't bother to open the sack. He wouldn't have taken them if they were gold doubloons. He would not steal from Mr. Brubaker. There were account books and plans and piles of papers.

It was in a wooden cigar box on the middle shelf of the safe that Adam found the most intriguing item in the safe: Mr. Brubaker's will. Adam read the will in the growing twilight. It was a purely homemade will, written on a piece of light blue lined paper like the ones on which he kept his accounts and done entirely in Mr. Brubaker's hand. The will had been written six years before. It left $100 each to Will and David Perse and the rest of his estate was to go to his sister, Fannie. Adam read the will two or three times, studying the old man's peculiar handwriting carefully. Then he placed the document back in the cigar box, put the box back on the middle shelf, and slipped out of the office, carefully locking both the safe and the office door behind him. He had a lot to think about.

-o-

It was about this time that he overheard Miss Fannie arguing with Mr. Brubaker about keeping an apprentice. "That boy's just another mouth to feed," Fannie complained. "One of these days he'll start drinkin' just like his daddy did and set the mill on fire. Then where'll you be?"

"He's a good boy," Mr. Brubaker replied. "I think he's so happy to have a place to stay and a chance to learn a trade under someone who treats him right that he'll not do anything to jeopardize all that. Besides, the boy is a good worker."

"Hmmph," Miss Fannie snorted. "He's just a worthless, toothless little shit. He's probably stealing you blind, and you're too stupid to see it."

Miss Fannie had made it clear to Adam as well that she did not like him. All her dealings with him, which were abrupt to the point of rudeness, reinforced this impression. Spitting in his food, feeding him hard to chew food, and looking at him with a look of sheer hatred, all left no doubt how she felt about the homeless boy her brother had taken on as an apprentice. Nonetheless, Adam went out of his way to be kind to the old lady, something most of the folks in Stendahl had long since given up trying to do with the short, skinny woman whose face was set in a constant snarl. But Adam refused to let her behavior determine how he would treat her. He called her "Miss Fannie," although he had noticed that others simply called her "Fannie." (Actually, Adam had noticed that the folks he considered to have "class" always addressed her as "Miss Fannie." To these folks an unmarried woman was always "Miss So-and-so." It was the others who called them by their first names. This was, he reasoned, yet another reason to call her "Miss Fannie.")

Her cooking was unbelievably bad, but at least he was getting more of it than he had ever received when living with the Jepson's. She did nothing else for him. He washed his own shirts and pants and took care of his own belongings at the mill. Miss Fannie just "harrumphed" along saying very little and scowling constantly. She lived in a three-room cottage about a hundred yards away from Mr. Brubaker's house. Adam had never been inside the cottage, but one of his chores was to chop wood and keep the wood box on the cottage porch full. So he had spent some time around the place. Other than to tend a small garden she kept out behind the cottage and to traipse up to Mr. Brubaker's house to fix three meals a day for her brother and Adam, Miss Fannie tended to stay in the house. It was obvious that the old woman had no friends.

She was physically abusive to Mr. Brubaker. Several times Adam had heard her slap her brother or had heard him shout at her to stop kicking him. A couple of times he had limped about for a day or so and Will had told Adam he believed the old man was limping because Fannie had kicked him. One thing was certain. Adam was going to steer as clear of Miss Fannie Brubaker as he could.

-o-

Adam had also heard Mr. Brubaker sing his praises to Randall Armentrout. "He's a good worker and a good boy," he had said. But the banker as well had not reciprocated Mr. Brubaker's positive impression of his apprentice. "Well, I hope you're not disappointed," he had said. "His old man was a serious drunk who never amounted to a hill of beans. An apple doesn't fall far from the tree, Brubaker. Frankly, I'll be surprised if the boy doesn't turn out just like his old man."

Mr. Brubaker had responded, "I have a little more faith than you do, Randall. I think the boy is going to be all right. He saw what drink did to his daddy and I reckon he has decided not to let it do that to him."

But Randall had laughed. "Just you wait and see. Just you wait and see. When he gets drunk some night and burns your mill down, don't say I didn't warn you!"

CHAPTER 10

With every passing day Adam was becoming more skilled as a furniture maker. He was securely settled in as a "resident apprentice" at the mill. After his first few days at the mill, he and Will had built a lid for his bed. Otherwise, they had noticed, the quilts would be covered with sawdust each evening. He kept his spare pants and shirt folded up beneath this bed lid every day, alongside Pap's boots. At night he carefully swept the sawdust off a pile of walnut lumber near the bed, laid the clothes there, and placed Pap's boots alongside the lumber.

One thing Adam didn't like about living at the mill was that the building had large double-hung windows on three sides. They were necessary to get sufficient light into the mill for the workers to do their jobs, but they gave him very little privacy in the winter when it got dark early and he was inside the building with a kerosene lamp lit. The only saving grace was that the side of the building facing the mill race and the street – the side with the mill wheel – had no windows. That was the north side of the building and offered no chance of sunlight anyway. The south side of the main room had no windows since the wall separating the office from the mill blocked those windows. But, Adam reasoned, all the windows were so dirty it would be difficult for anyone to see in, anyway. Still, just to be safe Adam confined his after-hours roaming into Mr. Brubaker's office to Sundays or evenings when it was light outside after he had eaten supper.

The mill was, as Adam had often considered the scene, an all-together efficient arrangement for building furniture. There could be improvements, of course, such as moving the lumber stored on this floor to a covered area which could be built outside, permitting the east wall to be used for more workbenches. They needed to erect covers over the logs stored in the mill yard. But for now, with the work force Mr. Brubaker had at hand, it was a very efficient arrangement.

Will Perse, Adam had noticed, was a very gifted wood worker, and Adam sought out every opportunity to learn from him. It helped that Will liked him. It was also fortunate that Will was blessed with infinite patience, for some of the tasks were extremely complicated.

Take making crown molding, which required the use of a molding plane that was so large it required two men to push it through the wood. Will had made the task considerably easier by harnessing the power of the mill's drive shaft. He looped a rope around two handles that protruded from the front of the huge plane. Then he turned the rope once around the mill's drive shaft which was turned by the waterwheel and handed that end of the rope to Adam. When Will had the plane in place at the end of the timber, he said, "Okay," and Adam tightened the rope around the drive shaft. The drive shaft pulled the rope taut and then began pulling the plane slowly down the length of the piece of lumber, with Will guiding the course of the plane. When he reached the end, he yelled,"Woah," and Adam loosened the rope. Will pulled the plane back to the beginning of the piece of lumber, fitted it securely into the grooves made by the first pass over the timber, and nodded to Adam to tighten the rope again. The process was repeated over a dozen times until the face of the piece of lumber had been shaped into a piece of crown molding.

The mill always had a good supply of four-inch crown molding on hand. When Adam asked about this, Will explained that it was for caskets. "When someone dies, we might not have time to do all the fancy molding. We have to have it on hand to put the casket together fast. Fortunately, most people use a coffin, which doesn't have all that molding. But nowadays folks with money want caskets. So we have to have plenty of crown molding on hand."

Adam was puzzled. "I thought a coffin and a casket were the same thing."

"No," Will said, "a coffin is narrow at the foot, widens up toward the shoulders, and then narrows again about the head. A casket is just like a small bed. It's the same width throughout all its length. Somehow, caskets don't seem so confining, I guess. Not that it matters much to the corpse. But I suppose the whole funeral and burial thing is for the survivors anyway."

Adam thought about what Will had just said. Both Ma and Pap had been buried in rough coffins. He had never thought about how much room they might have – or need.

-o-

One day Randall Armentrout drove up to the mill in his buggy. He pranced across the bridge wreathed in cigar smoke and bounded into the mill. Will Perse was working at the lathe and Adam was using the treadle saw. Randall looked at Will. "Get your half-wit brother to go up to my buggy and get those two chairs and bring them in here. And tell that simple-minded son-of-a-bitch to be careful."

Adam got up from the treadle saw. "That's all right, I'll get the chairs."

"Fine with me," Randall said. "I don't care whether a toothless wonder or an idiot carries the chairs. Just so they get here in good shape." He laughed, like he had just said the cleverest thing.

Adam was crossing the bridge on his way to the buggy when he heard Will behind him. "That man really gets my goat. He acts like neither you nor Davy has any feelings. Who does he think he is anyway?"

"He's the president of the Stendahl State Bank, that's who he is," Adam said. "People bow and scrape before him and he gets away with that kind of behavior because he's the biggest toad in the puddle. No one wants him to get down on them." As they removed the two chairs from the back of the buggy Adam continued, "but someday, somehow, he'll get his comeuppance."

"Don't see how," Will said. "Those kinds of folks always seem to get their way and walk all over everyone else. You ever hear what he did to the Widow Benson?"

Adam shook his head.

"He bought the lot beside her house, it's about three times the size of the lot her little house sat on. Paid her one hundred dollars. A week later he sold it to Vincent Webster for two hundred fifty dollars. That was bad enough but he had to gall to tell her what he had done. She cried and asked him to at least split the profit with her, seeing as how she had practically nothing to live on. He just laughed and told her, 'Business is business, Rebecca. If you aren't smart enough to look out for yourself, I'm sure not going to do it for you.' She didn't live but about six months after that. Folks say she just grieved herself to death over being taken by Randall Armentrout. That miserable little man."

Adam laughed. "I never heard you talk that way about anyone. You must really hate him."

"I try not to hate anyone. The Bible says you shouldn't. But I sure don't like him."

"You're not alone, Will. You have a lot of company where Randall Armentrout is concerned."

-o-

In January 1900, after Adam had been apprenticed for nearly two years, he had accumulated, from the one dollar and fifty cents a month Mr. Brubaker paid him and from selling walnut kernels, slightly over fifty dollars. So one Saturday, having received permission from Mr.

Brubaker to run to town for few minutes, he left the mill and walked downtown to the office of J. Fletcher Cobb, the only dentist in Stendahl. Cobb's office was over the *Polk County Guardian* on Main Street and as Adam entered the long stairway up to Doc Cobb's little office, he glanced quickly up and down the street, and then darted, self-consciously, into the stairway. The odor of ether and alcohol met him at the bottom of the steps and grew ever more prominent as he climbed higher. Much to Adam's relief Doc Cobb was alone in his office, working on a partial set of dentures. He looked up as Adam entered the office.

"Why, hello, Adam," he said, peering out over his glasses, which were pushed halfway down his nose. "What can I do for you?" J. Fletcher Cobb was a gaunt, cheerful man, who looked as if he never got enough to eat but couldn't have been less concerned about it. His smile was "all teeth" which, considering his profession, was a fine advertisement. His jet black hair betrayed not so much youth as the miracles of chemistry. He was a pleasant man, not given to small talk, thoroughly professional, a real gentleman.

Adam, winded from the long climb up the stairs, replied without waiting to catch his breath, "Doc, I want to buy a set of store-bought teeth."

"Bully for you, Adam, bully for you," Doc Cobb replied. "Of course you want a set of teeth. I was wondering when I would hear from you. You're becoming a solid citizen of this community, Adam, a fine woodworker according to Mr. Brubaker. You have a bright future. There's no reason you shouldn't have a proper set of teeth." He motioned for Adam to take a seat in the dentist's chair.

Adam nodded as he sat down. It was the first time anyone had suggested that he was a solid citizen of Stendahl, but he had to admit that it made sense. *By golly, I AM a solid citizen of this town, even if I am still only an apprentice. And a solid citizen shouldn't go about without his front teeth, especially a solid citizen of my age.*

It was days later before he realized how quickly Doc Cobb had set him at ease about wanting to buy a set of dentures, a venture many in Stendahl would consider a supreme act of vanity. Doc Cobb had made it a matter-of-fact transaction, the sort of thing that would be expected of a solid citizen of the community. And he had called him "Adam," not "Gummy."

Doc Cobb told Adam the dentures would cost thirty-five dollars and would be ready in around six weeks. "When the railroad gets here, I expect we could have teeth made in three weeks or so. Having to send everything in and out of town on the stage practically doubles the time required. It no doubt adds to the cost, too. But six weeks will be gone before you know it. Here, Adam, let me make an impression of your mouth and take the necessary measurements to order the dentures."

Thirty-five dollars! That would take most of the money Adam had saved over the past two-and-a-half years, but he would have proper teeth again. He would no longer be a freakish little man everyone called "Gummy." It would be worth it.

Adam sat in the chair as Doc Cobb made casts of his upper and lower jaws and took a number of measurements of his mouth, carefully recording the findings on a tiny card. The teeth, he reassured Adam, would fit him perfectly and in time he would forget all about ever having lost his natural teeth. That, Adam thought, is extremely unlikely. Doc Cobb talked on, emphasizing how "natural" the teeth would look and how Adam would be able to eat raw apples and corn on the cob and chew tough meat – all activities that Adam had carefully avoided for nearly three years now. The whole process of measuring and making a cast took less than three-quarters of an hour.

As he walked back up Mill Street toward the mill Adam pondered over what he had just done. The idea that he was now a "solid citizen" of Stendahl kept coming back to him.

-o-

It took over two months for Adam's teeth to arrive in Stendahl. Meanwhile, the mill was busy, farmers were bringing in loads of logs every day or so and it was all the boys could do to keep up with the work. There were three orders for dining room chairs, two chests, and a dining room table in various stages of completion. At first all Adam could think of was when the teeth would arrive. But after a week or so he had become so immersed in the mill's workload that he pretty much forgot about the teeth.

Then, on a Tuesday in early March, a boy Adam recognized as Doc Cobb's son appeared at the mill late one afternoon, after the stage had come in, and handed Adam a note. The note read: "*Adam, your dentures are here. Come in when you can. If you like, I can stay late this evening and you can come down after the mill has closed. J. Fletcher Cobb*"

Adam wrote across the bottom of the note: "*I'll be down around 6:30. Thank you. Adam Richter*"

J. Fletcher Cobb was smiling when Adam entered his office. "Adam, your life is about to take a marvelous turn. Let's try out your new dentures."

Adam sat in the chair as J. Fletcher Cobb fiddled with the teeth, washing them off with alcohol and then rinsing them in water. He had Adam gargle a solution and then inserted the teeth into Adam's mouth. They felt strange, almost overwhelming massive, nothing like his original teeth had felt. Adam had a moment of panic. "Doc, these don't feel right. Are you sure you measured me right? I don't think I can wear them."

"Of course they don't feel right now, Adam. Your mouth is not used to having twenty-eight teeth. It's been what, two years, since you lost your teeth?"

"Yes, it was two years last month." He winced as he recalled the experience.

"Then, you can't expect them to feel perfectly normal at first. The important thing is you must wear them all the time. They must be in your mouth except when you are asleep. That way they will become second nature to you." He handed Adam a mirror. "Look at yourself. Smile! Don't they look grand?"

Grand was the word for it, no doubt about that. For the first time since that awful day in February 1898, Adam felt like a complete human being again. He would wear these dentures, even if they never felt comfortable. He was no longer going to be "Gummy" Richter.

No one said anything to him the next morning until Will came up to him around ten o'clock. "Adam, I just wanted to tell you that I like your teeth. They look like they are your real teeth and they make you look years younger." He smiled broadly. "I'm afraid to have you to dinner any more 'cause you look so fine Cora might want to take up with you."

Adam laughed. "Thank you, Will. They don't feel right yet, but Doc Cobb says they will eventually. Meanwhile, I am going to wear them anyway."

"They look just fine, and I'm real happy for you. I suspect the others are, too, but they won't say anything. Me . . . well . . . I just had to tell you."

"Thank you, Will. I appreciate it. And I won't steal Cora from you. Besides, I am sure she knows she has a good man already."

Adam smiled as Will walked away. *Leave it to Will Perse to say the right thing in the right way.*

CHAPTER 11

Adam applied himself wholeheartedly to the art of woodworking. He moved from an awkward hand at the tools attached to the spinning driveshaft of the water wheel to an artist whose consummate skill was evident in everything he made or repaired.

By the time Adam turned twenty-one on March 8, 1904, and his apprenticeship with Mr. Brubaker officially came to an end, he was a master craftsman. That evening the old man gave Adam seven dollars to buy two suits and told him the large tool chest that was stored in the corner of the first floor of the mill was his. Then he asked Adam if he would be willing to stay on as an employee at a dollar-fifty a day. "You can even stay here in the mill and take your meals with Fannie and me, just like you have been doing. The only difference will be that I will be paying you a dollar-fifty a day. I really don't want to lose you, Adam. You've become very valuable to me." That was the nearest Mr. Brubaker ever came to being sentimental in Adam's presence, and it was the only time he ever called him by his first name.

Adam agreed to Mr. Brubaker's offer immediately. Nine dollars a week! Thirty-six dollars a month! One month's pay would cover the cost of his teeth. It was difficult to comprehend. Life was looking up. One of these days he would even be able to move into a place of his own. In the meantime, he would continue just as he had, just putting money away every week.

Indeed, his status at the mill changed very little after he became an employee. He had been treated much better than most apprentices for the past few years and there was little Mr. Brubaker could do to make his situation much better, except pay him, which he was now doing.

Will Perse congratulated him on his new status, and he and Cora and Davy had a celebration at the Perse household on the following Sunday. They gave him a feather tick to place on top of the bags of wood shavings on which he slept. "Can't have you not getting a proper night's sleep now that you're a regular employee of the mill," Cora said. Even Davy was excited at Adam's new status. "Yessir, Mr. Adam," he said, "I'm real happy for you. You're a good man. Good men ought to get ahead."

-o-

On Wednesday, May 18, 1904, Charlie McIntyre was hired to clean the flue of the Mrs. Charlotte Steinmetz, a widow who lived on Main Street. About halfway through the job he collapsed, fell off the ladder and lay on the floor of her kitchen, unable to move. Charlotte screamed in panic and ran outside to get help. By chance, Luke and Paulie Jepson were walking down the street on their way to the Bloody Bucket. Charlotte pleaded with them to come inside and help. The boys entered the house, looked at Charlie lying there in pain and laughed.

Luke leaned down and yelled into Charlie's face, "Remember the time you cussed at us and called us no good sonsabitches? Well you can just lay there 'til the cows come home. Us sons-a-bitches ain't gonna lift a finger to help you." Then the boys walked away, still laughing.

Charlotte ran outside into the street again and screamed for help. Peter Kaufman, who lived two doors up the street, came running out of his house. He told Charlotte to go back in and tend to Charlie while he ran to get Doc. Glanzer.

As it happened, Doc had just left his office a few minutes before Peter arrived and it was over an hour before he could be located and taken to the Steinmetz home. By that time Charlie McIntyre was dead.

Adam was deeply moved by Charlie's death. The old man had been his mentor as far back as he could remember. He had taught him things a boy usually learns from his father, things like how to catch and clean game, how to handle shovels, rakes, grubbing hoes and other tools to make the work easier. He had advised Adam on cleanliness, tooth care and how to keep his clothing from being ruined while performing the filthiest of tasks. He was never down his nose at Adam and treated him very much as he might have treated a son. In fact, if Charlie had not been a bachelor Adam would have run to him when Pa died, but he knew the County Court would never send him to live with an unmarried man.

Nonetheless, Charlie McIntyre was as near to a close relative as Adam had, and his passing was a highly emotional blow that caught Adam totally by surprise. Now, at twenty-two, he was truly alone. He had Will and Cora, of course, but they were newcomers, more like kind neighbors than kin. Charlie, on the other hand, was from the old days, the past, that time when Adam still had Ma and still belonged somewhere. Now, without Charlie there was nothing left.

That Charlie had fallen and was in need of help and that the Jepson brothers wouldn't provide that help convinced Adam the hard-hearted brothers had, in effect, killed the old man. It was an opinion from which he never wavered and it only added to the bitterness he felt toward Luke and Paulie.

Charlie had no family and very little money. Adam asked Will if he thought Mr. Brubaker would permit them to make a casket to put Charlie away in instead of having him buried in a rough coffin. Will's response was, "I wouldn't count on it, but it's worth asking him."

Gathering up his courage Adam approached Mr. Brubaker who was leaning across his desk in the office doing some figuring. "Sir," he began, "Charlie McIntyre has died."

The old man looked up and replied. "Yes I heard he passed away."

"Well, sir," Adam said, "he was a friend of mine from as far back as I can recall. He helped me in many ways when no one else paid me any notice. I would like very much to see him put away properly, in a casket, not just in a rough coffin. You can stop my daily pay until the cost of the casket has been made up. But I would like very much to see a casket made for him."

Mr. Brubaker chewed on his lip for a minute and said, "Richter, if he was a friend of yours then he deserves to be put away properly. Let's make a casket for him and I'm not going to touch your pay.

For the next three hours Adam and the Perse Brothers labored at creating a beautiful casket out of prime walnut. Then the casket was lined with some muslin sheets that Cora donated and Charlie was laid out for viewing.

Word was sent around town that Charlie McIntyre could be viewed at the mill and various town folk who had used his jack-of-all-trades skills at one time or another came by to pay their respects. The following day he was buried in the cemetery beside the Methodist Episcopal Church, his grave lot having been paid for by Mr. Brubaker.

Adam was deeply moved by Mr. Brubaker's kindness and generosity and also bitterly angered that the Jepson brothers had once again shown their lack of any sense of decency to the citizens of Polk County. Someday, somehow, those boys would have to pay.

-o-

One Monday eight months after Charlie McIntyre died, Fannie got into a violent argument with her brother. Adam never learned what the argument was about, but it was apparent the following morning that Fannie had kicked the old man so badly he could hardly walk. In fact his limp was so prominent that Adam, who seldom mentioned anything personal to Mr. Brubaker, asked why he was limping.

"Fannie kicked me last night. Three times. She was mad over somethin' and really laid into me. I can hardly walk this mornin'." He tried to laugh it off, but it was apparent he was in considerable pain. He pulled up his trouser leg to show the wound to Adam. His long underwear was matted with blood on the front of his shin. As he tugged at the underwear the wound started bleeding again. It was a ghastly sight.

"You'd best see Doc Glanzer about that," Adam said.

"No, it will be all right in a few days. It's happened before. I reckon I'm just a good poundin' board for Fannie to take out her fightin' on. I poured a concoction of turpentine and sugar on it. That'll take care of it, I'm sure. It always has in the past."

But it didn't get better. By Friday the leg had become seriously inflamed. He showed it to Adam again. The red streaks that radiated out from the wound, along with the puffiness and the puss that oozed from the wound, were signs that this was a serious infection. Will's concern was obvious, too, and he talked with Adam about his fears that the old man just might die from the infection. "God knows what will happen to the mill then." Will shook his head and looked around the mill, with a worried look on his face.

-o-

Adam, too, was worried. The old man had obviously begun to slow down a good bit in the last year. He had even begun to talk to Adam a bit, complaining about his condition. He had also begun to seek out Adam's advice on some aspects of the running of the mill. It was clear that, although Adam was sixteen years younger than Will Perse, Mr. Brubaker considered Adam the more appropriate person to talk business with.

When the matter involved a detailed problem with a piece of machinery or a complicated aspect of furniture building, he went to Will. As to the operation of the mill in a general sense, how the machinery should be laid out, where things should be situated most efficiently, he turned to Adam. This pleased Adam immensely and didn't seem to bother Will in the least. In fact, Adam sensed that Will wanted little to do with the operation of the mill although, God knows, Will was smart enough to do it, but he wanted only to be an artisan, not a mill operator.

Confronted with the old man's serious injury and his overall deteriorating condition, Adam was deeply worried about what would happen to the mill and Mr. Brubaker's other property if he should die from Fannie's abuse. He knew, from having read the old man's will, that he had left all his property to Fannie who clearly could not run the mill or oversee care of the business. Fannie was a recluse who had no capacity to deal with other people and her pattern of verbal abuse would destroy her as a business owner. In her hands the mill would, almost certainly, end up belonging to Randall Armentrout, who would either close the business or run it haphazardly, while making everyone connected with the concern miserable.

As he pondered the problem Adam realized if the mill failed or working there under Randall Armentrout became impossible, he could always pull up stakes and move west, starting all over. But what about Will? He had Cora and Davy to care for and couldn't just walk away.

No, the mill had to be preserved, and if properly done, the business could even be expanded. Although only four men worked there at present, there was a clear need for another worker just to handle the lumber that came in almost daily. Plus someone in the office who could bring order to the books would be a welcome addition. No doubt the need for other workers would follow.

And there were other factors. The mill was the only business in Stendahl that produced anything exceptional. It brought farmers and lumbermen to town with regularity and provided them with income they otherwise would not see. It marked Stendahl as a place of creation, a place where originality and skill resulted in quality production.

Properly staffed and run, Brubaker's Furniture Mill would continue to provide fine furniture and solid employment for the town in the foreseeable future. But the operation had to be in the hands of someone who knew how to manage it and make the business a smoothly operating, efficient contributor to the life of Stendahl. That person was not Fannie Brubaker.

Adam pondered over this a great deal. That evening after work Adam asked Cora Perse if he could have a quill or two off of the geese that strutted around their back yard. "I've a mind to try my hand at drawing again," Adam said, "and I'll be needing a good quill pen."

"Why, of course," Cora said.

Adam had grown very fond of Cora. A thin, pale-skinned, blonde-haired woman, she was of about medium height but her rail-thin build made her appear much taller. Her folks were Norwegian immigrants, she once told Adam, which explained her blonde hair and extremely fair complexion. She was country to the core, with a long, loping stride that made her appear as if she were walking behind a plow. Her nose was a bit too large and her eyes too deep set to be pretty. But she had a quick smile and an easy way about her, and was so incredibly kind and thoughtful. She had a habit of tossing her head toward her left shoulder when she laughed, which she did often. She loved to tease Will and was always going on about how slow and deliberate he was, which was true, but was also among his strengths.

Cora was an excellent cook and a first-rate housekeeper. Somewhat shy around strangers, she was actually quite talkative within the family circle, of which she obviously included Adam as a member, for she would jabber on at length to him. Adam was always amazed at how she could lay out a wonderful Sunday dinner with only the slightest display of effort, although he knew she had worked hours to make sure everything came out just right. She was such a delight and made Adam feel so much at ease that he had known her for some time before he realized that she was the first woman, other than Ma, with whom he had felt entirely comfortable. It also came as a surprise to him when he realized, after he had known her for a few months, that he no longer saw her as unattractive. With her pleasant, thoughtful ways, and her easy smile, Adam had come to see her as quite pretty. "Beauty is only skin deep," he had read somewhere. Maybe so, but with Cora Perse it went clear to the bone.

That evening he and Cora walked out into the back yard where geese and ducks and chickens roamed about on the slope leading down to the mill race. A few ducks and geese were in the water. The rest were meandering about the yard with the chickens. There was no grass, every blade having long since been plucked up by the birds. Bird droppings were everywhere. Cora pointed at a goose just emerging from the mill race. "We'll try her," she said.

Cora walked up to the goose, which was utterly unafraid of her, and reached down and picked it up. She shoved the bird's head back under her arm, took hold of its two feet in one hand, and began pulling the feathers the wrong way — "against the grain." In less than a minute she had over a dozen long feathers. When she was finished she set the goose down on the ground. It shook itself, ruffling its feathers, and waddled away, unconcerned over the loss of a few feathers.

"We pluck the geese twice a year," Cora said. "You can pick a goose in ten minutes and get a great big pile of feathers. The geese are used to it and don't mind. You can get half a pillow's worth of feathers off a goose. Goose-feathers are nice for pillows or bolsters." Adam smiled. Cora sure did like to talk.

Back at the mill later that afternoon, Adam went to lower level and gathered up a sack of walnut shells from beside the rock where he had shelled the nuts the fall before. He pulverized the shells with the same small sledge hammer he had used to crack the nuts. When he had reduced the shells to a coarsely-ground powder, he carried the powder to the brick-lined fire pit near the mill race corner of the mill's ground floor.

An iron kettle hung over the fire pit and above that was a steam box in which wood was suspended on iron bars as steam generated in the iron kettle circulated around the wood and softened it for bending, to make chair backs and the like. Adam dumped the ground up walnut hulls into the kettle, added a little more than a pint of water, and built a small fire in the fire pit. As the water began to boil he added a touch of vinegar and salt, to "set" the compound. When he was done he had nearly a pint of dark brown ink which he poured into a small jar. He soaked up the remainder of the ink in the kettle with sawdust and dumped the sawdust into the mill race. Then he sealed the jar of ink and set it in his "strongbox" to cool.

He took two of the goose quills Cora Perse had given him and whittled the ends into pen points which he stored in his strongbox with the ink. The following evening, when he tried out his ink, it was a bit darker than he wanted. So he added a bit of water and tried again. After he had diluted the ink for a third time, it was just right.

Satisfied with the ink, he laid a wide cherry board across two small nail kegs, gathered his ink and quill pens and a piece of paper he had taken from Mr. Brubaker's office – the same kind of paper on which the old man had written his will – and began writing. He had Mr. Brubaker's will in front of him and, referring to it constantly, he began to copy the old man's crabbed handwriting.

"In the name of God, Amen," he began. Then followed the litany about "being of sound mind and acknowledging the inevitability of death" (the old man was on the edge of being eloquent here) and finally he came to the disposition of the estate. Mr. Brubaker had left one hundred dollars apiece to Will and Davy Perse. Adam removed the cash gift to Will and raised Davy's gift to two hundred dollars. He had the old man leave Fannie the cottage in which she lived (which Mr. Brubaker owned) and an annual income of one hundred eighty dollars — fifteen dollars a month. Then Adam came to the gist of the matter:

> I leave my house on Mill Street to Will Perse who,
> with his wife Cora, now rents the property. I leave the
> house in which I live, and all the belongings therein
> to my apprentice, Adam Richter. Will Perse and Adam
> Richter have been loyal, hard workers at my mill and I
> wish them to own these homes unencumbered.

> I leave the house in which she lives to my sister
> Fannie for her lifetime and upon her death I leave this
> house to Will Perse and Adam Richter, as joint owners.

> I leave my business, known as Brubaker's Furniture
> Mill, with all the equipment and lumber therein, to Will
> Perse and Adam Richter as joint owners. I do this in the
> fond belief that Will and Adam, in addition to seeing
> that she is paid an income of fifteen dollars per month,

will look after my sister Fannie's needs until her death.
In an earlier will I had left my home and mill to Fannie,
but her increasing age and her lack of knowlege as to
the operation of the mill, together with Will Perse and
Adam Richter's keen interest in and knowlege of how
the mill should be run suggests that Fannie's needs
would be better met if the mill was left to someone who
could run it at a profit, from which Fannie could obtain
an income.

Mr. Brubaker had misspelled "knowledge" in his will, so the word became "knowlege" in this latest version of "his" will. And the old man had the habit of letting his words drop slightly at the end of each line, a trait which Adam dutifully copied.

When he was done, Adam dated the will July 7, 1902, and studied it carefully. He laid the two wills side by side on the cherry board and compared them. They looked as though they had been written by the same person. Indeed, anyone who knew nothing of the forged will would be hard pressed to say it wasn't in Mr. Brubaker's hand.

Satisfied, Adam returned the original will to the safe in Mr. Brubaker's office where the old man could review it if necessary. Then he folded the new will exactly as Mr. Brubaker had folded his will, and placed it in his strongbox.

After he had locked the office and stowed the key in his strongbox with his other belongings, Adam went to bed. It wasn't good dark yet, but he had a lot to think about.

CHAPTER 12

Mr. Brubaker died three days later, in terrible pain and distress. Adam had sat with him for several hours the night before, coming to bed only when he was relieved by Fannie in the middle of the night. That morning, after about three hours sleep, Adam had risen around 5:00 a.m. as usual. He had started a fire in the mill and gone to slop the hogs when he heard Miss Fannie yelling from Mr. Brubaker's house. "Come quick, he's dead! Come quick, he's dead!"

Adam dropped the slop bucket and ran into the house. Miss Fannie was standing in the kitchen, wringing her hands and crying. She motioned toward the steps that led upstairs to Mr. Brubaker's bedroom. "He's dead," she said, sobbing. 'He's dead!"

Adam dashed up the steps, two at a time. At the head of the stairs he turned into Mr. Brubaker's bedroom. The old man was lying in his bed, his form barely visible in the dark. Adam groped around on the table beside the bed, found the matches he knew would be there, and lit the lamp. He held the lamp close to Mr. Brubaker's face. His mouth hung loose and his eyes were half open. He was absolutely still.

Adam felt the old man's face. It was as cold as a wagon wheel. Mr. Brubaker was gone. He set the lamp down on the table and thought for a moment. Then he blew out the lamp and walked back downstairs.

"Yes ma'am," he said to Miss Fannie, "he's gone all right. But I reckon I better get someone to come here and pronounce him dead . . . officially, I mean."

Miss Fannie just stood there, wringing her hands and staring at her feet. "Whatever you think," she said softly. Thinking over it later, Adam would recall those words as the only words Miss Fannie had ever spoken to him that were not tinged with contempt.

As Adam walked onto the porch, he looked back through the window. Miss Fannie was just standing there. Adam raced to the mill, dashed inside, and jammed a board against the door. Then he rushed to his strongbox and took out the key to the office and the copy of Mr. Brubaker's will which he had prepared three days earlier. As he inserted the key into the door to the office his hands shook. With a soft "click" the door unlocked. He stepped inside and hurried to the safe where he twisted the dial to the appropriate numbers of the combination. The handle wouldn't budge. He clasped his hands together and told himself to calm down. Then he repeated the process, more slowly and carefully this time. As he approached "64" the dial tightened and the door opened with a spin of the handle. He reached into the cigar box where Mr. Brubaker kept his will, took out the old man's will, and replaced it with the one he had written. Then he carefully closed and locked the safe.

He left the office, closed and locked the door, and walked over to the stove. He opened the stove door and dropped Mr. Brubaker's will into the fire, watching it burst into flames. Then he looked for a moment at the key he had made that had given him access to the office. He tossed it into the fire, too. Grabbing his coat, he left the mill and headed downtown, to the home of Dr. Solomon Glanzer.

Adam would always recall the rest of the morning as through a thick fog. He and Doc Glanzer had hurried to Brubaker's house where the doctor had formally pronounced Mr. Brubaker dead. He had sent Adam for Isaac Ketterman, the town's harness maker who also doubled as a jackleg undertaker. Isaac had come for the body and, after conferring with Adam and Will and Miss Fannie, had simply washed the old man and dressed him in his best suit of clothes. Adam and Will had gone to the mill where they spent the rest of the day preparing a casket for Brubaker's burial.

It was Will who suggested a casket instead of a coffin. "The old man was good to all of us and we owe it to him to put him away in as fine a style as we can." They picked out some well-seasoned walnut and carefully dove-tailed the sides to the end of the casket. Then, taking some beautifully-planed crown molding and a piece of walnut that measured twenty inches wide by over five feet in length, they fashioned a casket top that Will swore would have been the envy of any casket maker in America. They lined the bottom and the sides – up to a height of one foot – with tin, "to keep the water out," Will said. Cora took two silk petticoats and lined the inside of the casket, fashioning one piece of silk into a small pillow on which to rest Mr. Brubaker's head. When they were done and the old man was placed in the casket, which had been set up on sawhorses in his parlor, Adam and the Perses were proud of what they had done for him. Davy cried when he finished helping place Mr. Brubaker in the casket and the rest of those gathered there remained quiet lest they, too, break down. Only Miss Fannie showed no emotion.

They placed a wreath, fashioned out of walnut shavings and stained black, on the front door of the house. It was the universally-understood sign in Stendahl that a body was inside, prepared for what was called "the viewing." Adam was surprised at the number of town folks who came by to pay their respects. They were from all levels of society. Of course, Randall Armentrout came by puffing at a cigar and darting his eyes in every direction. Even on this occasion he could not forgo the opportunity to try to be funny. But no one laughed at his feeble attempt at humor. Still he gave his typical smile, the sort that men give when they had very little experience at smiling.

Old man Havel, of Havel's Mercantile Emporium, was there along with Arley, who had sold Adam his stockings. Armistead Watson was there, as were Dr. J. Fletcher Cobb and Doc Glanzer. Valentine Burner, the lawyer who had prepared the apprenticeship documents for Adam arrived and met in private in the kitchen with Miss Fannie for nearly a half hour. Old man Reeves, owner/operator of a shoe shop on Mill Street, showed up, uncomfortable in his dress suit, and told Miss Fannie how sorry he was at Mr. Brubaker's death. There were carpenters, farmers who had sold Mr. Brubaker timber over the years, mechanics, clerks, teachers, overall a broad cross section of the town of Stendahl. Many of them, Adam realized, were living with furniture Mr. Brubaker's mill had made for them. All in all, it was a reaffirmation that Mr. Brubaker had been widely appreciated for his work.

Wilbur Botts showed up, too, radiating pomposity and arrogance. "Well, maybe now we can get someone who knows what they're doing to run this miserable little enterprise," he said loudly as he waited in line to express his condolences to Fannie.

Donovan Brumble, a mechanic whose shop on Jefferson Avenue kept all the carts and wagons and buggies in the county running and who was standing in line ahead of Wilbur, turned toward Wilbur and glared. "That's an uncalled-for comment at an inappropriate time, Wilbur. You need to learn when to keep your mouth shut."

Wilbur immediately flared into anger. "Nobody tells me to keep my mouth shut."

"Well, I just did," Donovan replied. "That's one of your problems, Wilbur. Too many people are afraid to speak up to you. Unlike half of Polk County, I don't owe my job to you, and I'm telling you if you have any down-your-nose opinions about the running of this mill, a decent respect for the dead would suggest that this is not the place to broadcast them. Show a little respect, will you."

"I don't need advice from you," Wilbur snorted.

"Well, you just got it," Donovan replied as he turned to speak with Fannie.

Wilbur seethed but said nothing further. When he had spoken with Fannie he stomped out of the house, crossed the millrace, mounted his carriage and drove away in a huff.

Mr. Brubaker was buried the following afternoon. It was late the next morning when Miss Fannie and Valentine Burner, came to the mill. Valentine had Mr. Brubaker's keys and he fumbled around for a few minutes, trying this key and that, and finally opened the office door.

Mr. Burner was a substantial man, tall and tending toward heavy set. His thin black hair was plastered in delicate strands across his head. When he smiled, which was often, a gold tooth peered out from the corner of his mouth. He dressed elegantly, favoring plaid suits with vests that sported lapels. A heavy gold chain hung across his ample stomach and a pair of pince-nez eyeglasses hung from a chain attached to a buttonhole in his lapel.

As they entered the office, Adam heard Fannie say, "He told me he kept it in a cigar box in his safe. He gave me the combination to the safe a couple years ago. Adam heard Valentine Burner spinning the dial of the safe. Then he heard the safe door open. "There's a cigar box," Valentine said, Adam heard the rustle of papers. Valentine Burner said, "Here it is . . . now, let's see . . . ."

After a few minutes he heard Mr. Burner clear his throat nervously. He said, "Well, you aren't going to like this, Fannie, but it appears your brother left this mill to Will Perse and Adam Richter."

Fannie screamed, "WHAT?" It was the loudest Adam had ever heard Fannie speak. Then she said, "Give me that!" From the rustling of papers, it was obvious she was reading the will. After a few minutes, she screamed again, "I don't know what this is, but he didn't tell me nothin' 'bout this and I know he meant to leave everthing to me!"

Valentine Burner said, "Well, is that his handwriting or not?"

Fannie hesitated – a good sign, Adam thought – "It looks like his writin' but . . . but he wouldn't do this."

"Fannie," Valentine Burner said, "it looks like he did. And, you know, his reasoning is perfectly sound. He left you your home and fifteen dollars a month and Will and Adam can see to it that the fifteen dollars a month will always be there. Think about it for a minute. You couldn't run this mill and Will and Adam can. You'll actually be better off the way your brother planned it."

"Shit!" Fannie said. And then again, louder, "SHIT" I don't know how they done it, but somethin' ain't right about all this! I tole my brother a hundred times not to trust them Perses and that Richter trash!"

Fannie stomped out of the office, followed by Valentine Burner. She stomped to the door and down the front steps. After she had slammed the door loudly behind her, Valentine Burner turned to Adam and Will who were standing there, handed them the will and asked, "Do either of you know anything about this?"

Will studied the will briefly and shook his head. "No, this is certainly news to me."Adam, his mind racing frantically, took the will and studied it carefully. He handed the paper back to Mr. Burner. "No, sir, I never saw this before either. Although," Adam peered out the window into the distance, as though he was studying the matter carefully, "last summer Mr. Brubaker told me how worried he was about Miss Fannie and how he'd like to have some way to protect her if he died before she did. He even asked me one time, now that I think about it, if I thought Will Perse and I could run this mill. I told him I was sure we could." Adam looked at Valentine Burner. "I never really give it much thought, you know. It was just like he was thinking out loud."

"Do either of you have a key to the office?" Valentine asked.

Both men shook their heads. Adam spoke, "As you know, I lived in the mill. But Mr. Brubaker always kept the door to the office locked. I just assumed it wasn't any of my business. Never really paid it much mind. Never had any reason to be in there."

"Well," Valentine Burner said, "it looks like the two of you are the new owners of this mill, or at least will be when the County Court settles his estate."

-o-

After Valentine Burner left, Davy Perse, who had been listening to everything, rushed up to Adam and Will. "Mr. Brubaker left the mill to you? That's wonderful! Thank the Good Lord!' We'll keep our jobs after all."

Will looked around the room. "Yes," he said to Davy, "we'll all stay here and run the mill just like Mr. Brubaker is still here . . . if it turns out that we do own it."

Then he turned to Adam with a serious look. "Who would have thought it? Why do you suppose he left the mill to us?"

Adam smiled. "I think the way Mr. Burner explained it to Miss Fannie probably sums it up. Neither he nor Fannie had any children so he left the business to us and we can see to it that his sister is taken care of for life. I don't suppose he really cared what happened to the property after both of them are gone. Or maybe he had a better opinion of us than we knew and thought we deserved it. Anyway, not leaving the property to Fannie does sort of make sense."

Adam stared at the floor and shook his head. He was relieved at the reaction of Valentine Burner and Will. They weren't suspicious, which was a great sign. *The first hurdle had been leapt. Now it was up to the County Court.*

Exactly ten days after Mr. Brubaker's death the County Court of Polk County accepted Mr. Brubaker's will for probate, official recognition of the will as genuine. Fannie Brubaker did not appear to contest the will. She had shut herself up in her cottage and came out only to go to the well and the outhouse.

Since learning they had inherited the mill and the houses Will and Adam had moved very slowly. Adam continued to live in the mill and he and Will worked just as they would have if Mr. Brubaker were still living. After the County Court hearing they met briefly with Valentine Burner at his office on Maple Avenue and were assured there would be no problem regarding their assumption of the properties left to them in the will. "They're yours, officially," Valentine said.

Will and Adam were walking back from Mr. Burner's office, deep in thought, when Will turned to Adam and, speaking in a very serious tone said, "Adam, Cora and I have been talking. We think it's silly for you and me to have to talk over and agree on everything important that comes up in the business, which is what we would have to do as co-owners. So I have this suggestion: You take over the overall operation of the business and I will supervise making the furniture. If either of us comes upon something we think should be discussed with the other, then we'll consult. Does that make sense?"

Adam thought about it for a moment and then replied, "Yes, that seems perfectly rational to me." He then held out his right hand and the two shook hands, smiling.

That night Adam moved into the house. He fixed a light supper of fried ham, black coffee, topped with homemade bread that he had purchased at Mrs. Roscoe's Café on Beacon Avenue downtown. Then he began going through the house, room by room. The Brubaker house was a white two-story frame dwelling that had begun its existence as a two-room cottage, built shortly after Mr. Brubaker had finished the mill. A few years later, as the mill prospered, an additional room was added to the first floor and, still later, a second story. The house was simplicity itself, one room leading into another on each floor, without even the benefit of a hallway for privacy. A small stoop led from the front room to the pasture that rolled out to the south for perhaps a hundred-fifty yards to the Oremander River. At the rear of the building, facing the furniture mill, a small porch was attached to the wall outside the kitchen. On the porch stood a wood box full of oak, cherry, and walnut scraps with which Mr. Brubaker fired the stove in his kitchen, the only room in the house that was heated during the winter.

Inside, the house was sparsely furnished. There were no closets but a plain oak dresser in each of the bedrooms, plus a chest in Mr. Brubaker's bedroom that held the old man's clothing, his linens, and a few threadbare towels and wash clothes. Adam began going through the chest and dresser. There were four pairs of wool stockings – worth eight cents a pair, Adam knew – and three blue flannel shirts, two pairs of heavy brown carpenter's overalls, and a pair of elastic suspenders.

In the bottom drawer of the dresser were three pairs of heavy gray wool button-up, long-sleeved shirts and matching trousers. Both the shirts and trousers appeared to be form-fitting. Adam had never seen anything like them before. He removed a pair of the strange items from the drawer, laid them across the bed, and studied them. Suddenly, it dawned on him – they were men's underwear. He was now the owner of three pair of woolen underwear. He and Mr. Brubaker were about the same size. He would be able to wear everything Mr. Brubaker had left behind.

When he finally went to bed it was past midnight. His mind was reeling with all he had seen and the special knowledge that now it officially belonged to him. As he lay on the feather tick, which itself was atop a thick straw tick, all supported by rope woven between knobs attached to the side rails of the bed, his hands swept over the sheets. Sheets. He – Adam Richter – was sleeping in a real bed between real sheets. Covered with heavy quilts. It was almost too much to take in. *Wouldn't Ma be proud!*

Adam wore the wool stockings the next day and the bottoms of the underwear a day or so later. A week or so after Mr. Brubaker's death, he donned the underwear tops, fully aware that the underwear could be seen underneath his flannel shirt. If Will Perse noticed, he never mentioned it. For Adam it was a feeling of sheer elegance.

In the weeks following Mr. Brubaker's death he and Will began to make changes in the mill's operation. They had Davy wash all the mill's windows, inside and out. One weekend the three of them put a new coat of white paint on the window frames and doors and repainted the sign over the door. After a brief discussion the three of them decided the mill's name should remain "Brubaker's Furniture Mill."

"The old man left it to us," Adam said, "and the least we can do is leave his name on the place." So "Brubaker's Furniture Mill" it remained.

CHAPTER 13

A month or so after Adam and Will had inherited the mill, Valentine Burner stopped by the office to see how things were going. Apparently Fannie Brubaker had seen him enter the mill for, about two minutes after Valentine entered the office, Fannie stomped up the steps to the mill, marched to the door of the office and began screaming: "You sneaky fat-assed son-of-a-bitch! You helped those two bastards steal my mill!"

Valentine pirouetted his two-hundred-fifty pound frame on his heel and toe as gracefully as a ballerina and jabbed his finger in Fannie's face. "Shut up! Right now!"

Fannie opened her eyes wide in surprise, blinked frantically, and backed away from Valentine.

"Let me give you a word of advice, Fannie Brubaker. I happen to know that your brother died from an infection caused by your kicking him . . . not once, but three times. As prosecuting attorney of this county, I would be perfectly within my rights to seek an indictment against you for involuntary manslaughter. You and I both know that you don't have enough friends in this county to hand-pick a jury of twelve men who would vote to acquit you. So my advice to you is to go back to your cottage, close the door behind you, and enjoy the fifteen dollars a month your brother left you – which is fifteen dollars more than I would have left you if you had been my sister. Now go, and don't let me hear another word out of you! Go!"

Fannie gave Valentine a stare of pure hatred, blinked a couple of times, and then wheeled and stomped out of the mill.

"Wow," Adam said. "You sure put her in her place."

"Long overdue," Valentine said, "long overdue."

As the weeks passed they built an outside storage facility for curing lumber, a post and beam, open-sided, roofed structure about forty feet long, by sixteen feet deep, with racks to hold the green lumber. Storing the curing lumber outside in the drying shed permitted the main floor of the mill to be cleared of green lumber. Once the lumber had been removed, Adam had the huge boring machine moved up from the lower floor and spread the remaining machines around a bit, providing more working room. He and the Perse brothers built a cherry four-poster bed, a walnut dining room table, a chest of drawers of oak, three different styles of dining room chairs, and a rocking chair which they placed on the main floor of the mill, just outside the office, where they were certain to be seen by anyone coming into the mill. Will explained to Davy, "We must let folks know what we can do. And there is no better way than to show them our handiwork." He then explained that one of Davy's new duties was to dust these pieces of furniture twice a day with a feather duster.

"This place," Adam announced, "is going to show off our handiwork at its best." Davy and Will nodded. All three of them liked the new direction the mill was taking.

For some time Adam had been thinking about joining a church. He really didn't have much idea about religion. In fact he wasn't sure just what he believed or, indeed, if he believed in anything at all, but joining a church seemed like the right thing to do if he was going to be a solid citizen of Stendahl. With this in mind, he purchased a black round cut cotton year-around sack suit, a boy's muslin shirt which fit him perfectly, a linen collar and cuffs, a black band tie and a soft black fedora at Havel's

Mercantile, for the grand total of four dollars and ninety cents. At old man Reeves' shoe shop on Mill Street, he bought, for thirty-five cents a pair of oxfords Mr. Reeves had rebuilt and polished to a high gleam. One Sunday, shortly thereafter, during dinner at the Perses, Adam said, "Will, I've been thinking about coming to church some Sunday. Do you think folks at your church would welcome me, given how Pap drank and all?"

"Adam, church folks – if they're good Christians – won't care a whit about your background. In fact, they may see it as an opportunity to help someone who has never been involved in a church."

Adam laughed. "Well, that's me, all right. I have never set foot inside a church in my life."

So the following Sunday he accompanied Will and Cora and Davy Perse to the Methodist Episcopal Church on Main Street. To his immense surprise he enjoyed it thoroughly. The preacher, a tall, red-headed man named Walter Rhine, could preach a sermon that would make the hair stand up on the back of the neck. Sometimes, at the end of the service, when the last hymn was being sung, Reverend Rhine would ask folks to come to the altar and give their lives to Jesus. Adam wasn't quite certain what that meant. And he certainly didn't understand what he took to be one of the basic tenets of the Christian church, that Jesus had died for his sins. After all, Jesus had been dead for nearly nineteen hundred years and how he could have died for Adam's sins was a mystery, but one that he pretended to understand.

Sundays began to have a ritual to them. Adam rose around seven o'clock. After breakfast he changed into his "Sunday-go-to-meeting" clothes, and accompanied Will, Cora, and Davy to church. Will and Cora walked in front, arm in arm, and Adam and Davy followed, usually chatting about the weather or some scene along the way. With his fedora cocked on his head at a rakish angle, Adam felt a marvelous sense of family, of belonging to the Perse family.

With his new teeth, his "Sunday-go-to-meeting" clothes, and his increasingly comfortable presence in the Stendahl Methodist Episcopal Church, Adam had the sense that he was truly becoming an upstanding citizen of Stendahl. To assure that status he continued to study grammar or math or to read something of value every evening from one of the books he had borrowed from Miss Ida Watson.

One thing Adam particularly enjoyed about church was the preaching. He marveled how Reverend Rhine could organize his thoughts into a coherent theme based on scripture he had just read to the congregation, and then deliver a sermon with such passion and, most impressive to Adam, such an eloquent manner. He also liked the singing of hymns. He had never been exposed to music at home, certainly not at the Jepsons, and had no real sense of how to sing or even enjoy music. But, here in the Stendahl Methodist Episcopal Church, amid the lusty singing of the congregation, he found that he had a tolerably good voice for singing, especially of those hymns that called for bellowing out of the music. His favorite hymns were Rock of Ages, O Worship the King, Onward Christian Soldiers, Come Thou Almighty King, and, especially, Amazing Grace.

After he had been attending church for about six months, he suddenly felt moved to join the altar call during the last hymn, Onward Christian Soldiers. He still didn't know how Jesus could have died for his sins and wasn't at all certain how he could "take Jesus into his life," as Reverend Rhine kept asking his congregation to do. He felt moved, nonetheless, to go to the altar and affirm himself as a member of the Christian faith.

He was amazed when nearly a dozen members of the congregation, mostly older women but also Will, Cora and Davy Perse, joined him at the altar to pray with him and to assure him that, just as Jesus welcomed him to the church, so did they.

Three weeks later, after four evening sessions with Reverend Rhine, Adam stood before the congregation and officially joined the Stendahl Methodist Episcopal Church. That Sunday, after dinner, Will left the dining room and returned with a package, wrapped like a Christmas present. He handed it to Adam.

"Open it," Will said. "Open it."

Cora was smiling broadly and Davy was grinning from ear to ear. Adam opened the package and found a Bible, bound in what the box said was French Morocco leather. On the inside was an elegantly-printed page titled, "Presented to." Cora had written in a fine hand that the Bible was presented to "Adam Richter, by Will, Cora, and Davy Perse, on the occasion of Adam's joining the Stendahl Episcopal Methodist Church."

Adam was deeply moved. He tried to talk, but tears filled his eyes and he began sobbing. To his immense surprise the entire family approached him, gathered him in their arms and cried with him. After a minute or so he backed away, wiped his eyes, and blew his nose. "I'm sorry," he said. "I don't know what came over me. I don't think I've ever done that before."

Cora spoke first. "There's nothing to be sorry about, Adam. As you could tell the moment was just as emotional for us as it was for you. That's a good sign. It means we all care for each other. It's actually something to be proud of, not ashamed of."

Adam smiled and held up the Bible. "This means a great deal to me, more than you will ever know. Now I will be able to study the Word of the Lord all by myself."

As Adam pondered his breakdown upon receiving his Bible he realized that, for all the pain and mistreatment he had endured, he could only recall crying three times before in his life: when Ma died, when Pap died, and when his teeth were pulled. Why should he have cried now, when something good was being done for him? He concluded that Cora was right, this gift and the tears shed by the Perses were concrete signs that they all cared for one another. They were family. Adam Richter, after all those years alone, belonged to a family! It was a wonderful feeling.

Somewhat to his surprise, he did begin studying the Bible. He marveled at the majestic language of the King James Bible. He especially liked Luke's story of the birth of Jesus. He was entranced with how Luke said Mary was "great with child," instead of just "expecting a baby at any moment," and how he talked about "the days were accomplished that she should be delivered," instead of simply "her time had come." As he read this story in his parlor he recognized that, while the words didn't rhyme, this was not simply prose – this was poetry in its highest form. And he, Adam Richter, poor former apprentice, was being made privy to some of the world's greatest literature.

He smiled proudly and looked around the parlor. This house is nice, he thought, and I own it. But the thing I'm proudest of and which no one can take away from me, is that I am moving up in the world! Someday . . . somehow . . . I am going to BE SOMEBODY!

-o-

One evening, shortly after joining the church, Adam was attending a Wednesday night prayer service when he noticed a very pretty young woman, with her dark hair done in a bun, sitting to his left two pews in front of him. He had never seen her before.

When the service ended and worshipers were leaving the sanctuary Adam very carefully waited and slipped out of his pew immediately behind the young lady. She was short, even smaller than Adam, and carried herself erectly. Just before they reached the door Adam very casually elbowed her in the back. As she turned he reacted as if startled and said immediately, "I'm so sorry! I didn't mean to bump into you." She smiled broadly and replied, "Oh, that's quite all right, no harm done."

Adam immediately held out his hand and said, "I don't believe we've met. I'm Adam Richter."

The young lady took Adam's hand, smiled broadly and said, "I'm Sarah Gifford. I just moved here from South Carolina. I'm living with my sister, Helen Klein." Her eyes were a very dark blue and her smile, framed by voluptuous lips, was striking. She was, Adam decided immediately, a beautiful young woman. He moved very quickly, asking her a few questions about her move and how she liked Stendahl and they found themselves chatting for a couple of minutes. Then Sarah looked toward the door where her sister was standing and said, "Oh, I mustn't keep my sister waiting. It was very nice to meet you Mr. Richter."

"Please call me Adam, Miss Gifford."

Sarah smiled. "Then you must call me Sarah, not Miss Gifford."

"Agreed. I hope to see you again, Sarah."

"I'm sure you will if you attend this church. I'll be worshiping here with my sister."

After they parted, Adam walked up Mill Street smiling to himself and thinking that perhaps it would be nice to get to know Sarah Gifford a lot better. In the days that followed the image of Sarah Gifford reappeared again and again and Adam began to look forward to church on Sunday with increased enthusiasm.

-o-

A few days later a black man in his late fifties, a former slave on one of the plantations in Wiles County east of Stendahl, came into the mill and asked to see the owner. Adam was leaning across the desk recording the price of the load of lumber that had just been delivered that morning from The Bleaks. He stood up when the man entered the office. "Yessir, what can I do for you?"

The man had his hat in his hand and was stooping slightly at the shoulders. The man's head was bent forward slightly, showing the bald spot at the back of his curly gray-haired head. He was a slightly-built man, who looked as if he had seen a good bit of hard work. His clothing was ragged and patched but, Adam noticed, also very clean. The man was clean-shaven, too, and his shoes had been recently blackened. Aside from the mud around the soles of his shoes, mud that everyone in Stendahl would be carrying on this wet July day, he was very presentable. He had obviously "spruced up" for his visit to Brubaker's Mill. Adam offered the man his hand. "I am Adam Richter, co-owner of this mill. How can I help you?"

"Well sir, I'm lookin' for work. 'Scuse me, my name's Tally Monroe I shoulda told you that right out."

"That's all right," Adam said. "Go ahead."

"Well, like I said, I'm lookin' for work. I know lumber right smart. I can't read or write but I can tally up the board feet in a piece of lumber afore you could write it down. That's howcome folks calls me Tally. Tally ain't my real name. But they calls me that 'cause, like I say, I can tally up board feet faster than anyone 'round here.'

Adam knew the mill could use another hand working with the lumber, but he and Will had decided some time ago to wait a while before hiring another worker. Very quietly he said, "I just took over as co-owner of the mill a few months ago. I don't know if we can afford another man right now."

The black man's shoulders sagged slightly. He knew what was coming next.

Adam couldn't do it to the man. He remembered how he felt when Mr. Brubaker had said, "Don't need an apprentice,'" to him. He looked out the window toward the lumber curing shed. He pursed his lips and thought about it for a moment. "But I suppose I could use a man who can tally board feet as fast as you say you can. Why don't you go out there in that shed and tell me how many board feet are in the load that arrived this morning. It's the ten or twelve oak logs that are stacked on the outside of platform. You'll be able to tell which ones, they're the greenest ones out there."

Tally left immediately. Adam watched him from the window of his office. He had brought with him a home-made log rule and a worn cotton measuring tape in a brass-bound case. The logs he was measuring were all fairly straight, measuring about eighteen feet in length and twelve to eighteen inches in diameter, with very few defects such as squirrel holes, fire scars, or forks. Tally slapped his log rule against the narrow end of each log, quickly took the measure of the logs, sighted up and down the logs quickly, did a few calculations in the dirt with a stick, and hustled back into the office.

Adam pretended to be busy when Tally returned. He looked up, acted surprised, and said, "You back already? Well, how many board feet?"

"Seventeen hundred eight board feet. They's eleven logs, all in good shape."

Adam looked down at the papers on his desk. "That's just a few board feet off what we calculated this morning, only it took us a lot longer than it did you."

The man smiled. "I tole you, I can tally board feet real fast, Boss."

"All right, Tally. I'll take you on at the same wage I hired the last man at, a dollar sixty-five a day. We work from six in the morning 'til six at night. You're the bottom man on the totem pole here – 'cause you're the last one hired." He looked the man up and down. "Your color doesn't matter to me. How you work is all that matters – and that you're honest. And get along with the others."

"Yessir, Boss, yessir. You won't be sorry, I promise you that, Boss."

"Two other things. Don't call me Boss. My name's Adam. Everyone calls me that. That's what you'll call me. And your name? You said it wasn't really Tally. What is it?"

"Jacob. Jacob Monroe. I was borned and raised on the Monroe place down the river over in Wiles county. Monroes, they owned me 'til the Lincom folks said nobody could own anybody any more. Anyway, like most slaves my folks just took their family name. My first name, Jacob, that was the name what my mother give me. But everone calls me Tally."

"What would you like to be called here, Jacob or Tally? You pick. Whichever name you want is fine with me. I've had enough experience with nicknames others thrust on me that I don't want to call anyone else by a nickname they don't want. So you decide and that's who you'll be called around here."

The black man studied the floor for a bit. "Well, they's a lot of Jacobs around, but I'm the only Tally I know of. I think I'd like to be called Tally. It says somethin' about what I can do. Makes me feel a little special."

"Then, 'Tally' it is. Here, I'll have Will Perse take you around and introduce you to the others.

Tally wasn't about to go. He obviously had something he needed to say. Adam waited.

"My daddy was just a old slave, but he know'd how to tally lumber board feet. He tole me many a time, 'Boy, the way to survive as a slave is to have somethin' you can do better'n anyone else. Thataway you'll not be just a fiel' hand. You can do somethin' special for the master and he'll even hire you out to others. Makes life a little easier.' Then

124

he teached me how to tally board feet. Kept makin' me do it faster 'n faster, so I got so it was just somethin' I did natural like. Didn't think much about it. I think my daddy was right proud of me. I know I was right proud of him. Weren't easy bein' a slave. Me, at least I lived to see freedom. Daddy never did. But I know he'd be proud of me now, workin' here in this mill and all. Bein' the tally man."

"I am sure he would," Adam said. "Now let's see if Will can show you around the mill." When he had turned Tally over to Will, Adam came back to the office. He sat down in his chair and rubbed his eyes. "Great God," he thought, "I can't be hiring a man just because I feel sorry for him."

He told Will what he had done and Will reassured him. "You're in charge of running the overall operation. If you believe hiring this man now is the thing to do, that's fine with me."

The more Adam thought about it, the more he had a good feeling about Tally Monroe.

CHAPTER 14

The following Sunday after he and the Perse family had arrived at the church Adam stopped at the door, motioning for the Perses to go on in, and began a conversation with Gerald Hoffman, a longtime usher and doorkeeper at the church. He stood there and very carefully made small talk with Gerald while watching to see if Sarah Gifford would be coming to church that morning. After a few minutes he saw Sarah and her sister coming down the street dressed in their finest. He continued to talk with Gerald and when Sarah started up the steps into the church, Adam turned and said, "Good morning Sarah. It's nice to see you again."

Sarah smiled broadly. "Good morning, Adam." Their eyes locked for a moment, and both of them were beaming. Then Sarah followed her sister into the church, found a pew and sat down. Adam quickly ended his conversation with Gerald and slipped into the pew with the Perses. Adam's pew was on the left side of the aisle and Sarah's on the right, one row forward. Adam had a great view of Sarah and spent a good deal of the morning service looking at her.

When the service ended Sarah turned to leave her pew and immediately locked eyes with Adam, again smiling broadly. Adam waited until she was even with this pew and stepped out into the aisle.

"So, are you well settled here in Stendahl?"

"Yes, it's already beginning to feel like home. I'm sure I will like it here. I don't know if you've heard but I'm going to be teaching in the Stendahl Public School. Miss Sallie Beeker is getting married and will be moving. I'm very excited to have the job. I'll be teaching the first through the fourth grades."

Ah, Adam thought. This is a double win for Stendahl! Not only will Sarah Gifford be staying here but that dreadful Sallie Beeker is leaving.

He smiled broadly at Sarah. "Well, that's wonderful. That school is such an important part of the life of this town and I just know you will be a fine addition there."

Sarah showed no interest in catching up with her sister, who had stopped to speak with two other ladies in the church entrance, so Adam quickly continued the conversation.

They talked about how pleasant it was after two days of rain and Sarah said she was looking forward to a summer without the stifling heat that enveloped South Carolina. Adam told Sarah that he had grown up in Stendahl, had worked at the town's furniture mill for seven years and for the last seven months had been the co-owner and operator of the mill. From her he learned that she had taught in a one-room country school in South Carolina and was excited over the opportunity to teach in Stendahl's "elegant brick two-room schoolhouse." She had grown up in South Carolina, just outside the capital city, Columbia, where she had lived after getting her teaching certificate and was delighted to be living here in Stendahl with her sister and brother-in-law.

Sarah paused and shook her head. "My goodness, I didn't mean to talk so much. I'm sure you weren't interested in all my gibberish."

"Actually, Sarah, I find your story very interesting. I would love to learn more about you."

Sarah blushed. "Well, the next time we talk, it's your turn to tell me more about you."

"Mine is not a very pretty story, Sarah. But I would love to talk with you some more." Adam paused briefly and then took what for him was a great leap. "Perhaps I could call on you some evening. W-w-would that be possible?"

Sarah smiled brightly. "Why yes, Adam, that would be very nice."

"Well, uh, would this Tuesday evening be suitable? What time are you finished with supper?"

"This Tuesday will be fine. We're usually finished with the dishes and all by six-thirty. Would seven o'clock be all right with you?"

"Seven will be perfect. I'll see you then."

"I'm looking forward to it, Adam. Thank you." She then walked to the church door where her sister was breaking up her conversation and, as the two of them started for home, Sarah looked back and smiled at Adam.

Adam stood there stunned. *What had he done? How did he ever get the courage to ask that beautiful woman if he could call on her?*

Behind him Cora Perse touched him lightly on the shoulder. "Did I hear you ask about calling on Sarah Gifford? That's wonderful, I'm so pleased for you."

Adam nodded a brief yes and started down the aisle. On the walk home he was very quiet and no one said anything more about Adam's upcoming visit with Sarah Gifford.

-o-

Since he had arranged to call on Sarah Gifford, Adam had thought of little else than the upcoming visit with her. And he was worried. *Would he be able to carry on a conversation or would he be tongue-tied from fear? What would they talk about? Would his grammar be good enough for this schoolteacher?* He was twenty-two years old and had never called on a lady before. Excited as he was about the prospect of visiting Sarah, he was also concerned that he may have made a mistake.

On Tuesday evening he fixed a quick dinner of a softboiled egg and a piece of toast to calm his queasy stomach. Then he carefully washed his face, brushed his teeth, slicked down his hair and, having studied himself in the mirror at length, decided he looked as presentable as he could be. He left the house at a quarter 'til seven, walked out Mill Street, turned up Main Street and started up the hill. As he drew near to

Sarah's sister's house he took out his watch. It was still eight minutes before seven. Too early! So he turned, walked back down the street a bit and paced back and forth until, about two minutes before seven, he walked up the street, turned into the sidewalk leading up to the house, and knocked on the door.

Sarah answered the door, smiling broadly and said, "Please come in. It's so nice to see you." She led Adam into the parlor where she motioned for him to sit on the sofa while she took a seat in an overstuffed chair beside the sofa. Sarah's sister Helen and her husband Charles came into the room and greeted Adam warmly. They all sat and chatted briefly, after which Helen and Charles excused themselves and left the room.

Sarah turned to Adam and said, "Now, tell me about yourself. I yammered on quite a bit about my past when we chatted on Sunday, so now it's your turn."

"Well there's not much to tell you," Adam began. He told her he had been orphaned at fourteen and sent to live on a farm out in The Bleaks, which he described as "a godforsaken part of the county west of here." He told how the two boys who lived there mistreated him, how he escaped, came back to town and apprenticed with Mr. Brubaker, who had willed him and his co-worker Will Perse the mill when he died. He ended by mentioning that the boys on the farm had pulled his front teeth and he had bought a set of false teeth after he had moved.

"Oh, they pulled your teeth? That's terrible! Were they punished for what they did?"

"No. They are two - pardon my expression - hellions and seem to be able to get away with everything, no matter how awful it is. But I survived and I've put them behind me and life is going pretty well for me." He paused and grinned. "I've even been able to call on a very pretty girl, so I consider myself very fortunate."

Sarah smiled softly. "And I have had a very handsome man call on me. So we are both VERY fortunate."

They both laughed and chatted on for a few more minutes when Helen came into the room carrying a tray of coffee and cookies. As they sat there with their coffee and cookies and chatted away, Adam was delighted to find himself feeling very much at ease. And it was clear that Sarah felt the same way. Then the clock in the hallway struck eight and Adam stood. "Well, hasn't this hour flown by? I must be going, It's been a real pleasure to chat with you."

"I have enjoyed it thoroughly," Sarah said, with emphasis on the word *thoroughly*. "I do hope you'll call again."

"I will be delighted to call on you again, Sarah. This has been a very, very pleasant evening. I don't know when I've enjoyed myself more."

"Well then, why don't we pick a time for you to visit again?" Sarah said boldly.

Adam, surprised and thrilled, replied quickly, "What about next Tuesday evening?"

"Perfect," Sarah said as she followed Adam to the door.

Just as Adam was stepping off the porch onto the sidewalk Sarah said very softly, "Thank you again for calling. I do so look forward to seeing you again."

Adam remembered very little about the walk back to his home. But he recalled every word Sarah had said and every expression she had displayed. Life was *really* looking up for Adam Richter.

CHAPTER 15

That Sunday Adam once again motioned for the Perses to go ahead into church while he waited for Sarah. She was beaming as she and her sister walked up the walk toward the church. "Good morning, Adam. Are you the doorman today?"

"No, I was just waiting out here to see if any beautiful women would appear. And here you are!"

Sarah laughed. "Well, on my part it's always nice to see a handsome man waiting at the door." She smiled and walked on into the church with Helen.

His second call on Sarah was even more delightful than the first. They chatted like long-time friends. Sarah taught Adam how to play Old Maid. When Adam ended up with the Old Maid after two games, Sarah laughed loudly and said, "I really shouldn't have defeated a gentleman caller like this. Will you forgive me?

"Sarah, you are forgiven. I have never lost a game with more pleasure than these two games to you. Unlike you, I've had a pretty hard life, so losing a card game means nothing to me, and especially losing to a beautiful young lady."

The smile left Sarah's face and she sat quietly for a few seconds, looking down at her hands which were clasped in her lap. Then she spoke softly. "I guess I need to tell you the dark side of my past. I haven't had my teeth pulled and I was full-grown before I lost my parents, but I've suffered some aspects of what one could call a hard life, too."

She then told Adam how, after her mother had passed away the year before, her father had married again and how very difficult this new stepmother had been. Roseanna Quick was her name and she had, as Sarah put it, been "- true to her name - quick to isolate Sarah and her sister, Helen, from their father." Helen, who was seriously involved with a young man at the time, very quickly married and moved out, leaving Sarah utterly unwelcome at what she had previously thought of as "home." The school where she taught was barely a mile away but such was the icy atmosphere that Sarah had fled her stepmother and her mostly silent father and moved in with a family that lived near the school and had two children enrolled there.

To add to the misery and confusion, shortly after Sarah moved out, her father passed away suddenly, leaving a freshly-drafted will that left everything to Rosanna and nothing to his daughters. Sarah and Helen were told they could drop by and take anything that clearly belonged to them, but they were forbidden to take anything that had belonged to their father. Moreover, Rosanna announced, she would have the final word on whether any item *really* belonged to the girls or should stay in their late father's home. Faced with this intolerable situation, as the school term neared its end Sarah was invited to move in with Helen and her husband in Stendahl.

"So, you see, my life has been no bed of roses as well," Sarah said quietly. "But I'm looking forward to life here in Stendahl bringing me a return to happiness and contentment." She smiled brightly. "And, right now, I'm as happy and contented as I can be."

Adam quickly replied. "If I can do anything to add to your happiness and contentment, I would be thrilled to do so."

"You already are," Sarah said, "just by calling on me."

The atmosphere in the room had heated up considerably and both of them were aware of it. They chatted cheerfully, but a bit more intensely, until the clock in the hallway struck eight and Adam rose to leave.

"Oh, darn that clock," Sarah said. "It takes you away so soon." She accompanied him to the door and put her hand on his coat sleeve. "Thank you again for calling. I do enjoy your visits so much. Next Tuesday evening again?"

"Yes," Adam said, grinning. "Wild bears, or even the Jepson brothers, couldn't keep me away."

Sarah reached up, pulled Adam forward, and kissed him on the cheek. Once again Adam left Sarah's presence walking on air and arrived home with no memory of the trip itself.

-o-

In early June 1905 Oliver Finch, a 55-year-old Scotsman who worked as assistant cashier at the Stendahl State Bank suffered a slight stroke. He stayed at home recuperating for a month during which time Randall Armentrout reduced him to half pay. "I don't have to pay you anything, you understand," he told Oliver. "But I'm paying you half your salary for a reasonable time out of the goodness of my heart."

Oliver came back to work during the second week of July. He now walked with a limp and dragged his left foot slightly. At the end of the week Randall called him into his office. "Oliver, a bank has to look efficient as well as be efficient. It just doesn't look right to have an assistant cashier dragging around the bank like he's half drunk. It looks disgraceful. I'm going to have to let you go."

Oliver was distraught. Adam learned of his plight at church the following morning when he overheard a neighbor of the Finch's talking about their dilemma. "Nell Finch came to our house last night, all upset. She said Randall Armentrout had fired Oliver at the bank because he walks with a limp after his stroke. Nell was crying and carrying on, said she doesn't know how they're going to be able to make it with Oliver out of work."

The sermon that morning was on the Golden Rule. Reverend Rhine worked himself into a frenzy on verse 12 of the Seventh Chapter of

Matthew's Gospel: "Therefore all things whatsoever you would that men should do to you, do ye even so to them: for this is the law and the prophets."

Adam pondered over this scripture and Oliver Finch's dilemma. After dinner with the Perses he and Will, accompanied by Davy, walked along the millrace and agreed that the job of bookkeeper at the mill should be offered to Mr. Finch. So, shortly before nine o'clock the following morning Adam knocked on the door at the Finch's home on Maple Street. Oliver greeted him and ushered him into the parlor, limping slightly, despite every effort not to limp. Out of the corner of his eye Adam caught sight of Nell Finch standing in the doorway.

A short, bald-headed man with a substantial stomach and a pallid complexion, Oliver was direct in his speech and actions, almost to the point of rudeness. Yet he was a decent man and had been a popular employee at the Stendahl State Bank. If you dealt with Oliver Finch, you knew you would get the absolute truth and fair treatment. What he lacked in small talk he made up for in politeness and integrity.

He came straight out. "Mr. Finch, I understand Randall Armentrout let you go at the bank on Saturday."

"No, Randall Armentrout didn't 'let me go,' he fired me . . . because I had a stroke and can't walk fine enough to suit him. He said I was disgraceful."

"Well, Mr. Finch, Will and I need a bookkeeper at the mill. We just can't keep up with all the paperwork, paying farmers for their lumber, calculating of the cost of furniture we're building, buying all the supplies we need – the day-to-day book work that has to be done. I am looking for a bookkeeper. You're just the sort of person I need."

"I don't walk very pretty anymore."

"You won't be walking much at the mill. You'll be sitting on a stool in the office keeping track of the business. What do you say? We'll pay you the same as all the other workers at the mill, a dollar sixty-five a day. I'm sure that's less than you made at the bank, but it's the best we can do."

Oliver thought for a moment. "That's nine ninety a week. Actually, that's more than I made at the bank." He turned to his wife. "Nell, can you believe it? I am going to get a raise and I won't have to work for that dreadful little man anymore."

Nell Finch broke into tears. When she was finally able to speak, she told Adam, "You will never know just how much this means to us. I've been downright sick since Oliver came home Saturday and told me what Randall Armentrout did. Now, I just can't believe our good fortune." She extended her hand. "Thank you Adam, thank you from the bottom of my heart. And send our thanks to Will as well."

Adam smiled. He turned to Oliver Finch. "I assume that means you'll take the job."

Oliver smiled weakly and nodded his head. His eyes, too, were filled with tears. It was the first time Adam had ever seen Oliver Finch show any emotion.

"When can you start, Mr. Finch?"

Oliver cleared his throat and fought to take control of his emotions. "Whenever you want Adam. And it's 'Oliver,' not 'Mr. Finch.'"

"No, it's 'Mr. Finch.' You're my senior. I didn't have a lot of training in proper manners when I was growing up, but one thing my folks always insisted on was that I mustn't call my seniors by their first names. You can call me 'Adam' and I'll be one of the bosses. But we will call you 'Mr. Finch.' Actually, it will add a bit of 'class' to our operation, having a distinguished former banker doing our bookkeeping. Why don't you come to work tomorrow? We open at six."

Oliver Finch stood up. "I'll be there at six sharp, probably a little before six." He extended his hand. "Thank you, Adam. You've restored my faith in mankind."

"The way I see it, Mr. Finch, we both come out ahead. You get a job, we get a first-rate bookkeeper at the mill, and Randall Armentrout will have to scramble around to find someone half as talented as you, even if he can walk prettier."

Walking back up Mill Street, Adam smiled over what had just happened. The odd thing was he and Will hadn't performed an act of charity. They hadn't even simply performed according to the dictates of the Golden Rule. They had just managed to hire the best bookkeeper in town. Sometimes things really do work out for the best.

-o-

In mid-July, 1905, Luke and Paulie Jepson visited yet another peril on Stendahl when they bought an automobile, a 1902 American, nicknamed the American Gas. This, the first automobile on the streets of Stendahl, was a small gasoline-powered buggy manufactured by the American Motor Carriage Company in Cleveland. The two-passenger runabout right-hand-drive vehicle had a steering wheel instead of a tiller. Its water-cooled, seven-horsepower single-cylinder engine fitted under the seat and its seven-gallon fuel tank gave it a driving range of about one hundred fifty miles. The boys had the car shipped from Baltimore where its former owner had wrecked it, restored it somewhat, and offered it for sale. Despite its scars and dents the vehicle was a flashy one, painted "French Carmine," a rich red with a shade of purple. Its seat bench was trimmed in black leather and its minimalistic coachwork included a small compartment in front which the boys kept loaded with jugs of moonshine.

To nobody's surprise the boys were reckless maniacs with the vehicle and, as usual, nothing could be done to calm them down.

-o-

As their relationship blossomed Adam and Sarah began taking long walks together about town and out the trail to "Lovers Leap," a precipice that overlooked the Oremander River two miles east of Stendahl. As they walked they shared their interests and talked of their concerns. Adam confessed to Sarah that he had read very little and asked her to recommend books with which he should become familiar. Sarah told him she had read several books recently but they were mostly 'girly' ones that wouldn't interest him. Then, after thinking about it for a few minutes she suggested he read some of the novels of Sir Arthur Conan Doyle about the fictional detective Sherlock Holmes.

"As a teacher I should probably suggest you read Shakespeare or some of the great works of the ancient Greek philosophers. But I believe it would be much easier, and more fun, to become well read by delving into books that are simply a delight to read. My father loved the Sherlock Holmes character and the mysteries that brilliant private detective gets involved in. I'll do some looking and see if I can come up with a list of some of those mysteries you might want to read. According to Daddy you will get pulled right into those stories and will have a true literary experience that you can share with others."

Adam laughed. "Well, I sure could use what you call a 'true literary experience to share with others.' I don't think anyone would want to talk with me about McGuffey's Readers or Hart's Grammar."

Sarah smiled and took Adam's hand. "Stick with me, Honey, and you'll be the best read man in town."

Adam nodded and muttered, "Okay." But all the way back to town he was really thinking about Sarah calling him "Honey."

-o-

In early October Adam attended a meeting at the Presbyterian Church where Charles Warren, an executive of the Baltimore and Western Railroad (already being called the B&W) addressed the audience on what to expect when the railroad reached Stendahl sometime in 1907. A short, squat, bald-headed man in a sharply-pressed suit with a Masonic pin in his lapel, Mr. Warren described the rapid growth that had accompanied every town and village through which the railroad had passed. His curly eyebrows wiggled up and down as he excitedly told the audience, "You can expect to have a population growth of no fewer than a hundred souls, perhaps as great as three hundred."

Stendahl's population was now about three hundred eighty-five, so that was quite a prediction and the crowd in the little church was appropriately impressed. Mr. Warren emphasized how the railroad would improve life in Stendahl, actually changing it beyond the imagination of anyone in the audience. Working himself into a high-pitched frenzy with his arms flailing and his cheeks turning bright red and beads of sweat appearing on his brow, he concluded his presentation by declaring, "Baltimore is a center of commerce, and we have factories that produce materials more quickly and cheaply than you can ever do it in a town the size of Stendahl. Even accounting for the cost of shipping goods by rail to Stendahl, they will be readily available at a lower price than you can ever create them here. Your standard of living is going to be improved beyond all expectation when the Baltimore and Western Railroad comes puffing and chugging into your fair town." At this vision of an exciting, prosperous future for Stendahl, the audience rose in thunderous applause.

Adam, too, was impressed and pondered over Charles Warren's remarks for the next few days. The following Sunday, after dinner with the Perses, as he and Will and Davy walked along the mill race enjoying the warmth of Indian summer, he shared his concerns with Will.

"Charles Warren gave me a lot to think about the other night. I suspect, since he was with the railroad, he was presenting a rather one-sided picture of what the railroad will do for Stendahl. Nonetheless, if you agree that it might be helpful to our business, I would like to take a trip to Baltimore and see for myself if what he was saying is true. If it is, we may need to do some serious planning for the future. What do you think?"

Will nodded. "I think it's a great idea. We have to keep up with the changing times." The two of them continued walking along the mill race in silence for quite a while, each man deep in his own thoughts. Davy followed along, oblivious to the conversation taking place around him but happy just to be invited to walk with his brother and his friend.

When he walked Sarah and Helen home after church the next Sunday morning Adam described to them the grandiose future Charles Warren had laid out for Stendahl. He talked of how the presence of the railroad would shorten the time for travel and delivery of goods to towns to the east and how that could reduce prices of all sort of goods that could be shipped in from Baltimore and other cities. The ladies listened intently and Sarah then described the trains she had taken on her move to Stendahl five months earlier. Then she laughed as she described what she referred to as 'by far the worst part of my trip,' the two-day stagecoach ride to Stendahl after she had left the B&O in Whitney.

"Well," Adam said, "I guess I'm going to find out for myself how difficult that trip is because I'm planning to go to Baltimore this Thursday to see how the railroad coming here might affect our work at the mill."

Sarah laughed. "I knew you would have to go to Baltimore sooner or later to judge for yourself what Mr. Warren told you. You are too good a businessman to let a big change like the railroad coming to town happen without being fully prepared. "

Adam smiled and as he was bidding Sarah and Helen goodbye at the Klein home he asked Sarah to tell him, when he called on her Tuesday evening, as much as she could recall about the stagecoach trip from Whitney to Stendahl, so she could help him get ready, at least mentally.

She laughed and agreed, and when he called on Tuesday evening she described all the rigors and inconveniences of the two-day trip, including the miserable night in the inn at Watkins Cove. Adam asked about train travel she had experienced, which she described in elegant terms.

"The future is here, Adam, and it has arrived by train. I doubt if we will ever again be traveling individually from town to town like we used to do by horseback and on foot. We will go everywhere by train, faster and in greater comfort. Just you watch. When the B&W reaches Stendahl our lives will improve beyond anything we can imagine."

Adam laughed. "You should go to work as a spokesperson for the Baltimore & Western Railroad."

"Well, it's a new era, Adam, and we are very fortunate to be taking part in it."

"As long as you are part of this new era, I want very much to be a part of it."

"You're sweet," Sarah said as she reached up and kissed him on the cheek.

-o-

Meanwhile the Jepson brothers were growing more and more brazen and reckless. Even Jehu and Emma Jepson were afraid of them. When Luke ran their car off the street and took out over thirty feet of picket fence in front of Mrs. Manning's home on Main Street everyone assumed they would, at last, be brought to task. But they were not. They continued to drink, to carouse at the Bloody Bucket, to sell tax-free liquor all over the county and generally to do as they pleased without regard to the law or simple good taste.

CHAPTER 16

On Thursday, October 19, 1905, at fifteen minutes after two, Adam boarded the stage to Whitney at the stage stop in front of the Havel Mercantile Emporium. All his life he had heard horror stories of stage travel, stories which had been reinforced by Sarah as she related her experience traveling from the railroad in Whitney to Stendahl by stagecoach. Nonetheless he was excited, almost to the point of becoming physically ill, at the adventure that lay before him, although he maintained an outward calm which he thought was expected of him as a "solid citizen of Stendahl." The fact was that Adam had never been at a greater distance from Stendahl than the Jepson farm, a distance of seven miles. He knew that Ma had been no farther and suspected that Pap, too, had not ventured more than at least ten miles from Stendahl. Now he, Adam Richter, was going to take a two-day stage ride to Whitney and board the train to Baltimore. While the stagecoach trip may well be the awful experience Sarah had described, for Adam it was a brand new adventure that he was eagerly anticipating.

The stage was a light six-passenger Concord coach drawn by four horses. The coach sported multi-coat paint and varnished sheen, but it was badly scraped and peeling in places. The delicate scroll work that decorated its side panels hinted at its earlier grandeur while the scenes on the doors, oil paintings of mythological allegories, were badly faded. The rocker-bottomed body of the coach was hung on wide, multi-ply leather straps called thoroughbraces. All six plush silk seats were taken, as was the outside seat beside the driver. Inside leg room was practically nonexistent. It was a crowded, uncomfortable ride and Adam was pleased that, having arrived early, he had secured a seat by a window. The other window seats were taken by the three women passengers.

Promptly at two-thirty the stage left with a jerk as the horses lunged forward and the body of the coach heaved backward and then violently forward. The road they were following swung north out of Stendahl before turning northeast into the valley of Jefferson Creek. It was nearly eighteen miles from Stendahl to Watkins Cove where they would spend the night. The road, which had been carved of out the countryside with no consideration to speed or comfort, twisted and turned around massive rock outcroppings, scrub-infested hillsides and meandering streams. The coach rocked violently each time it hit a bump or chuckhole.

It was five long hours later that, after four stops to water the horses and let the passengers relieve themselves in the woods, and one stop to change horses, they arrived at the sadly mis-named Pleasant Valley Inn in Watkins Cove. Watkins Cove was a shabby, run-down settlement jammed up against the side of a steep and rocky mountain called High Knob locally and Thunder Mountain on state maps. The town consisted of a country store with two large windows, one of which had been broken and boarded up, an unpainted frame grist mill set by the side of Jefferson Creek, a blacksmith shop, two homes, one of them a log house, and the Pleasant Valley Inn. The place was, if anything, worse than Sarah had described it.

The Pleasant Valley Inn was a rambling old two-story stone building with a tin roof that was in need of painting. The stables were to the right rear of the tavern just beyond the corner of the building where a rainspout directed water to a barrel. About fifteen feet from the barrel, a large pump with a heavy wooden handle sat on a pad of large flat stones, obviously covering a well. Thirty-five or forty feet up the road from the well a small, rickety bridge crossed over Jefferson Creek. To the left of the bridge a worn path led down to the creek to a pool where the locals gathered their water, the inn's well water being available only to guests at the establishment.

Inside the tavern, on the main floor, were four large rooms; a barroom, a dining room, and two sitting rooms. Between the sitting rooms was a ten-foot opening with two double doors that could be folded back to throw the two rooms together. Each of the rooms had a fireplace with a flagstone hearth and a wood-burning grate. The kitchen was in the basement. Upstairs was reached by means of an oak staircase with a cherry hand rail, both well-crafted, Adam noticed. Seven small bedrooms sat on either side of a wide center hall. The entire place smelled of tobacco spit, unwashed bodies, grease and decaying food.

In the dining room a long table ran down the center of the room and two smaller ones against the front wall. Supper consisted of fried rabbit, boiled potatoes, gravy, succotash, day-old bread, butter, apple butter, and coffee. For dessert there was apple pie with heavily-larded crust and too few apples. As Adam thought about it he realized his supper differed from the meal Sarah had received at the inn five months earlier only in that the fried meat presented to her was chicken, not rabbit. Everything, including the coffee, was greasy and lukewarm. After supper a variety of cheap, harsh liquors were available from the bar. Adam did not imbibe.

The four men in the coach were assigned to a small room containing a high four-poster bed with a trundle bed beneath it. In one corner beside the window sat a washstand with bowl and pitcher. There was no water or soap, both available only at the pump outside.

At bedtime Adam pulled the trundle bed from under the four-poster and crawled between two dirty sheets beside a heavy-set traveling salesman. The man had talked a great deal that day, trying to impress the other passengers with his great experience as a traveler. Mostly he struck Adam as an insecure old fart who hoped to cover up his insecurity by talking. Adam reasoned that the more the salesman talked, the less conversation the others would expect of him, as the youngest man in the stage.

Fortunately, the man was a good deal cleaner than either of the other two men in the stage, one of whom was covered with head lice. While Adam was not pleased to be sharing the tiny trundle bed with anyone else – he had not shared a bed with anyone since Pap had died – he reluctantly got into the bed. The other travelers seemed to fall asleep right away. All of them snored. The fat man lying on his back beside him would get very quiet occasionally, as if he had stopped breathing. Then he would jerk and snort and catch his breath in a great commotion.

Exhausted as he was, Adam had trouble falling asleep. His mind kept flitting here and there, conjuring up little pictures of the past: Adam as a boy, cleaning outhouses; Adam sleeping uneasily in the loft at the Jepsons; Adam caring for Ma as she lay dying; Adam laughing with his classmate, Belle, and feeling the pain when she recoiled in horror at the sight of his toothless gums; Adam as the co-owner of Brubaker's Furniture Mill; Adam calling on the beautiful Sarah Gifford. It was as if he were somewhere else, off in a distance, watching someone else named Adam Richter. And this someone else was trying to grow up all at once, to become a respected man in a world where he had always been considered a worthless boy.

Finally, he fell asleep, but he slept lightly, out of a combination of fear and excitement. In the morning, after washing up at the pump and a breakfast of tough beefsteak, greasy eggs, potatoes, and stale bread, they were off toward Whitney at seven o'clock.

Shortly after noon they rolled up to the little wooden shed that served as the railroad station in Whitney. All alighted and four of the passengers, including one woman, purchased tickets on the railroad. Adam's ticket to Baltimore cost $.85. Considering that he would travel in reasonable comfort and arrive in Baltimore after only three or so hours on the train, Adam considered the ticket a bargain. His stage ticket from Stendahl to Whitney had cost $.45 and involved a bone-jarring trip of an afternoon and the following morning during which they had covered only slightly less than a quarter of the distance he would cover on the three-hour trip by train later this afternoon.

Adam's legs were stiff and cramped from the stagecoach ride so he walked around downtown Whitney for a while to loosen up. He judged the town to be roughly twice the size of Stendahl, the difference no doubt being because of the railroad. The most impressive building he saw was the town school, a two story brick building with a belfry and what appeared to be eight rooms. *Eight rooms! Why, that school would have a separate room for each class!*

The main street was paved with cobblestones which gave it a sense of cleanliness that Adam admired and even the side streets he noticed had wooden sidewalks. Whitney was an 'up-and-coming' town and this had to be because of the railroad. As Sarah would probably put it, "Modern life had come to Whitney."

About 1:30 p.m. he took dinner in a dimly-lit place called "Gaddy's Eating House," where he had tough, stringy roast beef with potatoes and turnips, accompanied by bread rolls that were soft and tasty. For dessert he had hot, black coffee and a dish called "Brown Betty," a delightful pudding of apples and bread crumbs. For all this he paid fifteen cents. Then he returned to the station to await the train.

On the train platform he walked to a nearby water pump, removed his teeth and washed them. As he placed them back in his mouth he pondered over how well he had chewed his dinner of tough roast beef. He was accustomed to the teeth now, pleased with how well they worked and with the dramatic change they had made in his appearance. As he thought about it he was quite relieved that Sarah had never seen him without his front teeth. He thought of Sarah and how much he wished she could be sharing this adventure with him. If she were here perhaps he wouldn't have to fight the increasing excitement that was creeping over him as the time for the train's arrival approached. It was unbelievable. He, Adam Richter, was going to take his first train ride, all the way to Baltimore! *Wouldn't Ma be proud!*

The B&O's Capital Limited chugged into the station, amid a hiss of steam and a shower of cinders. Adam boarded and was astounded by the grandeur of the car. The inside was highly-polished, thickly-tasseled, and deeply-carpeted with seats that were upholstered in deep carmine and golden-olive velvet plush. Huge blown-glass globes with electric bulbs – the first he had ever seen – were set into the ceiling over the aisle. He wished it was dark, so that he could see the electric lights glowing in the night, but the scene outside was bathed in the light of early afternoon.

He took his seat, placing his small leather valise beneath his legs and stared out the window. Within an hour the train track was running parallel to the Potomac River and, along-side the river, set apart from the stream by a small levee or bulwark, were the calm, clear waters of the C&O Canal. Occasionally Adam would spot a canal boat being slowly hauled upstream, its small wake created by the steady pull of the mules on the canal path. The harsh contrast of the canal boats moving along propelled by mules and the powerful steam engine roaring past impressed him. It was a graphic example of the rush of progress that Stendahl must soon face.

The train sped on down the Potomac, past Harpers Ferry, and across the rich farmlands of central Maryland. Around six o'clock Baltimore came into view. The city, which was unlike anything Adam had ever seen, bristled with spires, towers, and columns. Bathed in the light of the setting sun, the city was beautiful beyond anything Adam could have even imagined.

He left the train at Camden Station, a three-story brick building dominated by three square towers, the center one he later learned, being one hundred eighty-five feet tall. The city had suffered a devastating fire in February 1904 but the area around the railroad station had not been touched. On the curb outside stood a line of strange horse-drawn vehicles, small two-wheeled carriages where the driver sat on a high outside seat at the rear of the vehicle.

A small black boy rushed up to him, "Cab to your hotel, sir?" Adam replied with as much self-assurance as he could muster, "I will be needing an inexpensive hotel." "Yessir," the boy said, "you'll be wantin' the Eutaw House." He grabbed at Adam's valise, which Adam was reluctant to give up. The boy said, "That's all right sir. I'm jist goin' to lead you to your cab." Adam reluctantly released his grip on the bag and followed the boy, prepared to leap after him if he should try to take off with the valise. The boy led the way to a line of vehicles, chattering as he walked. "Them's hansom cabs, that's what they're called. They're light and they only need one horse. That makes 'em cheaper. Now, the Eutaw House be the oldest hotel in the city. Folks say it was quite a sight when it were built, but that's some time ago. Now it jist be a poor ole hotel, tryin' to keep up with the fancier ones."

The boy opened the door of one of the cabs, placed Adam's bag on the floor, helped him up the step into the passenger compartment, and said, "Eutaw House," to the driver. Then he turned to Adam. "That'll be a nickel, sir." Adam dug into his pocket and pulled out a nickel and handed it to the boy, who stepped back, saluted, and said, "Thank you, sir."

Adam leaned back in the cab and marveled at how far he had come in his life. For the rest of his life this ride to the Eutaw House would be a blur, a ride through scenery as foreign as if he had been on the moon. He was tired, far more exhausted than he had imagined. He wanted now only to get to a room and rest. Even the prospect of supper meant little. He needed to rest, to take in all that had happened to him in the last thirty-six hours.

The cab turned north up Howard Street and after eight short blocks veered left at the northwest corner of Baltimore and Eutaw streets where the Eutaw House, a plain five-story structure stood. An awning extended out over the sidewalk at the corner of the building and ended abruptly about fifteen feet from the front of the hotel. Adam alighted beside a massive gas streetlight. The lobby was small, with a low ceiling, lit with dim electric lamps. Adam took a room on the top floor, the cheapest floor, for twenty-five cents a night, European Plan which, he was told, meant no meals included. He gave the clerk a quarter, picked up his valise, and climbed the five flights of stairs to his room. There he opened the door, turned the knob of the electric switch just inside the door, and stepped inside. Entranced by the convenience, simplicity, and safety of electric lights, he stared at the bulb in the ceiling. Then he turned the light on and off several times. "What a miracle," he thought. It is an instant, non-smelly light that couldn't be knocked over to start a fire like the kerosene lamps in Stendahl.

He set his valise on a double bed that sagged somewhat in the center, and looked around. A small washstand holding a bowl and pitcher sat by the window. On the sides of the washstand were towel racks on which hung a single thin towel and an equally thin wash cloth. Unlike the Pleasant Valley Inn of the night before, the pitcher was full of water and a cake of soap lay inside the bowl. The soap, Adam noticed, was not homemade lye soap like he had used at the pump in Watkins Cove.

Beside the washstand was a plain chair, which Adam appraised with a critical eye. It had obviously been manufactured at a facility where speed was valued over quality. It was sturdy but the saw marks on the back slats and the rough-hewn edges of the seat bespoke of cheapness. He poured himself a glass of water and sat down on the bed. He opened his valise, took out a piece of summer sausage wrapped in paper and bit off a chunk. This would be supper. He was just too tired to go downstairs and eat. As he chewed he looked around the room again. It would be fine.

Then he laughed out loud. It would be *FINE?* For over seven years he had lived in a furniture mill, lit by a kerosene lamp and sleeping on bags of wood shavings. This hotel room with its electric lights would be more than "just fine." Tomorrow, after breakfast, he would begin exploring the city. For now, after a quick clean-up at the washstand, he was going to bed.

Before going to bed, however, he visited the toilet down the hall, the first indoor facility of this sort he had ever seen. He turned on the electric light and looked around. In front of him was a commode. Behind the commode a metal pipe ran up the wall to a porcelain tank. A long chain with a wooden knob at the end hung down from the tank. Adam pulled on the chain. Water rushed into the commode with a roar, and Adam backed away suddenly, crashing into the door. Then he laughed. He had just flushed the commode. He used the facility, allowing the porcelain tank to re-fill, and then flushed it again. He did this twice more, marveling each time at the genius of the whole apparatus.

Considerably rejuvenated by his experience with the flush commode, Adam returned to his room and went to bed. He was no longer as tired as he had been before his trip to the toilet. He was, he now realized, on the brink of a grand, new adventure. The flush toilet and the electric lights were just the beginning.

CHAPTER 17

He breakfasted at 6:30 and spent the rest of the morning wandering around the city, marveling at the paved streets, the crowds, and the majestic buildings. Just outside the hotel he saw a shiny black automobile, moving smoothly and swiftly, if a bit noisily, under its own power. Before the morning had passed, he had seen at least a dozen more. The automobile was, Adam thought, a thing of life and beauty. It gave off only the slightest bit of exhaust, a vast improvement over the horse droppings that littered the city. When – and if – the automobile ever replaces the horse, Adam thought, we will not have to worry about the quality of the air in this country.

The most magnificent building in all Baltimore was City Hall, a huge structure sitting just north of the area devastated by the fire. The building had corniced windows and a mansard roof, topped by a dome which could be seen for blocks. Adam counted the windows on one side of the building – forty-two windows, fifty-one counting the small round ones under the eaves of the mansard roof. He did a quick mental count. There were probably not fifty-one windows on all of Main Street in Stendahl, certainly none as grand as these.

He strolled down to the harbor, passing through the area that had been burned in the fire of the previous February and which was now bustling with activity as the city was being re-built with brick and steel. Light Street was brick-paved and was cluttered with wagons loaded with barrels and jammed with sacks of seed and flour and feed. The street's wharves were lined with offices of the steamboat companies and the harbor teemed with every sort of craft from Baltimore clippers to the gaily painted fishing boats which spread their sails and skimmed over the water.

Baltimore Street, the city's main thoroughfare, was lined with overhead trolley wires, making the street appear to be festooned with cobwebs. Here and there a trolley bobbed along, its wheels grinding on the rails and the sharp, metallic clang of the conductor's bell warning pedestrians to stay off the track.

Having spent his first night in a hotel, albeit a humble one, Adam paid particular attention to other hotels. The Altamont Hotel at Eutaw Place and Lanvale Street, was an imposing, turreted structure of brick and stone. A sign outside announced that rooms could be had at a rate of $2.50 to $4.00, American plan. Adam was pleased that he now knew this meant "meals included." He smiled when he considered that he was becoming, on a very small scale, a man of the world – or at least a man of the world in Stendahl terms.

The most famous hotel in the city, Barnum's City Hotel, which fronted on Calvert, St. Paul, and Fayette Streets at Monument Square, was a six-story structure with cast iron balconies opening onto the streets. It had a flat roof with deeply projecting bracketed eaves and a central tower. Someday, Adam told himself, I am going to stay in a fine hotel like that.

He took dinner at a dimly-lit restaurant on Paca Street where he had two delightful fried crab cakes, the first time he had ever eaten crab. On Franklin Street, between North and Calvert Streets, he came upon a bookstore. He looked at the books displayed in the window and then entered and purchased two books which were recommended by the clerk, a tall, somewhat pompous young man with pince-nez eyeglasses perched on his nose: *The Crossing*, by Winston Churchill, and *The Virginian*, by Owen Wister. If he was truly going to be a "man of the world," Adam thought, he had to read the latest books. And, of course, these books will be complemented by the Sherlock Holmes novels Sarah will be recommending.

Then he asked the clerk if he could recommend a book suitable for a young lady. "She's a schoolteacher and I would like to give her a book that she would enjoy, something fairly new that she is not likely to have read."

The clerk smiled, raised his eyebrows and gestured with his right index finger. "I have just the book for your lady friend, *Beverly of Graustark,* by George Bar McCutcheon." He walked over to a display rack and brought back a book with a gray-blue cover, featuring a stunning young woman.

"This book has just been published and is causing quite a stir. It's a tale of a rich beautiful southern American girl who follows a friend, who happens to be a princess, home to the country of Graustock, which is somewhere in Eastern Europe, not far from Vienna or St. Petersburg. The book has war, bandits, court intrigue, a handsome mysterious stranger, and of course, a dastardly villain. Your friend will love it."

Immensely pleased, Adam added the book to his other purchases and left the bookstore smiling. The beautiful girl on the cover of *Beverly of Graustark* was not one bit more stunning than Sarah Gifford. *I'm going to tell her that when I give her this book,* he thought smiling.

Next he stopped at a brick building on North Eutaw Street, "Gomprecht & Benesch," that advertised "furniture, carpets, and everything for the home." Posing as a man looking to furnish a new home, he was given a tour of the building and left with a printed sheet on which were listed prices for the furniture for sale. He was disappointed, but not surprised, at the low prices. After all, the factory equipment in Baltimore was bound to be powered by electricity and the lathes, saws, drills, and other machines were not only bigger, they would also certainly be faster than the wood-mounted, water-powered machines in the shop at Stendahl.

After studying the prices from Gomprecht & Benesch he stopped at the B & O Fast Freight Transfer Company office at Camden Station and inquired about the cost to ship furniture on the B &W to Maxton, the current end of the line of the Baltimore & Western Railroad. Already knowing the distance from Baltimore to Maxton, he quickly calculated the cost per mile. Then he added the additional miles the road would need to reach Stendahl and had a fairly good idea of the cost of moving freight from Baltimore to Stendahl once the railroad had reached there.

Charles Warren of the B&W had been right when he spoke that night in the Presbyterian Church in Stendahl. Furniture could be built in Baltimore, shipped to Stendahl, and sold at a price considerably below what Brubaker's Furniture Mill would need to charge for a piece made locally. And this would include the cost of shipping on the B&W,

Profoundly disappointed, Adam returned to his hotel and stretched out on his bed. His head was throbbing. He wet the washcloth and laid it across his forehead. He had to think of some way to prevent the loss of his business. He had to think of Will and the others who worked at the mill. What would become of them if it closed? What, for that matter, would become of him? Finally, he fell into a restless sleep. He awoke over an hour later. His headache was gone, but not his profound depression.

Charles Warren had laid it out precisely: small operations such as Brubaker's Furniture Mill were doomed when the railroad reached Stendahl. Perhaps the town would grow by a hundred souls, but they would be getting their furniture from Baltimore.

Still . . . wait a minute, what had Charles Warren said? *The town would grow by a hundred souls, perhaps even three hundred.* That had, at least, been the experience of other towns along the B&W. They would get their furniture from Baltimore. But where, Adam pondered, would they get their houses? Not by way of the B & W. Even the railroad couldn't ship a house to Stendahl. A door was closing – furniture manufacturing in Stendahl was a dying business. But another door was opening – someone would have to build the homes of the new residents who would be attracted to Stendahl. Adam rose from the bed and went downstairs to get supper. He would go to one of the oyster houses on the harbor. There perhaps he could find a place at a table apart from others and eat in solitude. He had a great deal to think about.

-o-

Adam spent the next day, Sunday, wandering the city, taking in all the monuments and other sites. He sat for a while on a bench at the edge of the harbor, reveling in the harbor breeze, and watching the gulls swoop and dive and pirouette. He took breakfast at the Eutaw House, dinner at the Adams Brothers Saloon on East Pratt Street where he bought, but did not drink, a beer for five cents, which entitled him to feast at his leisure on a variety of salty meats, cheeses and pretzels. For supper he was back at the Eutaw House and in bed by eight o'clock. At 6:15 a.m. he boarded the train for Whitney where he would catch the stage to Stendahl.

As he waited for the stage he walked out onto the last street on the eastern edge of Whitney. Three new houses were being built there and at least four others appeared to have been recently constructed. He walked among the houses and noticed that none of them had privies situated out back. Obviously, these homes had indoor flush toilets. As he walked back to get on the stage he pondered over these things. Ideas were forming in the back of his head.

He was back in Stendahl around three o'clock on Tuesday, after another uncomfortable night at the Pleasant Valley Inn in Watkins Cove and a kidney-punishing stagecoach ride into town.

On the train he had began reading *The Virginian,* which he discovered was not about Virginia at all but was a story of the American West. The main character, who was from Virginia, was a silent stranger who rode into the uncivilized West and tried to help establish a sense of law and justice on the frontier. As he read about the ranchers' struggles with horse thieves and cattle rustlers, Adam pictured them as Luke and Paulie Jepson. When the Virginian had to participate in the lynching of an admitted cattle thief, who had been his close friend, the poignancy of the story was somewhat muted for Adam who kept picturing the lynched thief as Luke Jepson.

On his arrival in Stendahl Adam took his luggage home and met with Will to see how things had gone since he had left. Will showed him some furniture they had worked on and went over the books showing what they had purchased in lumber and taken in from furniture sales.

Then, after going over all the records and closing the mill, Adam walked to the Klein home, arriving there shortly after six thirty. Sarah answered the door, smiling. "Adam, what a delight to see you! I was worried that you might not be able to return today. How was your trip?"

Adam described his visit to the city, the hustle and bustle, the automobiles and the various meals he had taken. Then, laughing, he told her of his experience with the flushing toilet.

They both laughed and then Adam handed her the book which had been gift-wrapped by the bookstore clerk. As Sarah opened the package her eyes brightened. "Oh, what a delightful gift! I've heard of this book and have wanted to read it. You're a dear!" She leaned forward and kissed him on the cheek.

Adam pointed at the girl's picture on the book cover. "When I bought this book I was struck by how pretty that girl is. Then I realized that, as pretty as she is, she is not nearly as pretty as you. That's when I *knew* you should have this book."

Sarah smiled broadly, hugged Adam and kissed him on the cheek again.

Wow, Adam thought, *if I had realized she would react this way I would have brought her a whole library!*

They sat and chatted until Adam explained that he really should get back to the mill. Sarah interrupted him. "You can't leave until the clock chimes eight. That's a rule. Didn't you know?"

Adam laughed and sat back down. "I just didn't want to wear out my welcome."

Sarah looked at him intently. "I don't think you could *ever* wear out your welcome here with me."

"Well," Adam replied, "I didn't really want to leave you anyway. I was just trying to be polite."

"True politeness in this instance, Adam Richter, is for you to stay until at least eight o'clock." So they continued to chat and laugh until the clock struck eight.

When Adam was leaving, Sarah leaned forward and kissed him on the cheek again. "Thank you so very much for your visit and for the lovely book. You're a dear."

As he walked home Adam was, he knew, falling in love with Sarah Gifford. It was, for him, a new feeling. But he reveled in it.

CHAPTER 18

Adam was walking on air as he made his way back to the mill. He went to the Perse home and, finding they had finished supper, turned to Will. "Come with me, Will. Let's walk along the mill race. I have a plan to discuss with you."

As they walked it began to rain, a soft drizzle that both men ignored. Adam explained to Will what he had learned in Baltimore. He explained his concern over the low prices furniture shops in Baltimore were charging for their wares. "But," he said, his voice increasing in pitch, "it came to me that we have a wonderful opportunity. We can still sell some quality furniture, but our future lies in building houses. We can make the doors and windows and moldings in the mill and take them straight to the houses we're building and set them right in place. I can oversee the mill, you can oversee a team of carpenters – maybe even two or three teams of carpenters, working on two or three houses at the same time – and we can make a right smart amount of money."

Will nodded in agreement, but Adam couldn't tell if he was really agreeing or just appearing to do so. He went on, "I've been chewing this over all the way home. Old Henry Channing owned that thirty-five acres just west of town. It slopes down to the river, but it's relatively flat and not boggy or anything of the sort. It would be a perfect place to build houses. We could buy that farm from Henry's widow – she's just renting it out for pasture now – put in streets, and build houses for the folks who move into Stendahl when the B & W gets here. What do you think?"

Will stopped, looked at Adam, and then ran his hand over the day-old stubble on his chin. "If we did it right, we could put in streets, line up lots beside the street, and run an alley down the middle of each block so folks could put their privies back there and run wagons up and down the alleys to clean the privies, tend their gardens and the like. How many houses do you suppose we could put in there?"

Will *was* in agreement with the idea. "Don't know without doing some measuring. We'll have to hire Bronson Eddy to survey it for us. Mr. Brubaker left some cash in his safe when he died, probably just about enough to buy the property, if we can get it for the right price. And I doubt Bronson would charge us too much. I think we can do it. And, Will, let's think about not putting in privies but putting in flush commodes and bathtubs in the houses. Make it real modern."

Will looked at Adam, puzzled. "Flush commodes? Bathtubs? Are you serious?"

"Absolutely. I used a flush commode in Baltimore. There was a bathtub beside the toilet, too, a big cast iron tub covered with pure white porcelain. It doesn't seem to me that it would be very difficult to install these things if we put in the water and sewer lines when we develop the property. We'll have to set a water tank at the top of the property. We can fill the tank with water from the river . . . pump it up there with a pump driven by a gasoline engine. I tell you, Will, this property of ours could be the place everyone in town will want to live!"

"As for expansion of the mill, we can teach Tally to do more than just tally board feet. He's already doing all sorts of tasks and we can train him to run some of the machines. Davy can do that. Davy knows how to run every machine in the mill and he can show Tally how. Besides," he shook his head as if he was agreeing with himself, "it will do Davy good to help Tally. He'll feel more important. And he needs to feel more important."

Will smiled. "Davy will love being asked to teach Tally to run the machinery. And he will no doubt surprise both of us at what a good teacher he becomes."

-o-

It soon became apparent that Adam and Sarah were "seeing each other." Adam called on her every Tuesday and, within a few weeks, every Thursday evening. They sat together at church services, walked about town on pleasant Sunday afternoons and, thanks to Cora and Will Perse and Helen and Charles Klein, alternated their Sunday dinners with the Perse and Klein families.

They were in love and anyone who paid the slightest attention to the pair could see it. Adam, whose life had been one struggle after another, was clearly more lighthearted and happy than he had ever been. Life was looking up for him. *Wouldn't Ma be Proud,* he thought often, just to see her son with such a beautiful, lovely young woman. And Pap, maybe even he would have sobered up had he witnessed his son being so successful in his business and personal life.

-o-

Just before Christmas in 1905 Adam and Will visited with Stella Channing. Adam got straight down to business. "Mrs. Channing, I would like to purchase the thirty-five acre tract you own just west of town, the tract I understand you are renting to Grover Needham as pasture. I am willing to pay you top dollar for the land on the condition that you keep our transaction strictly between us."

"What price do you have in mind?"

"I am told the going rate for good land in this area is fifteen dollars an acre. I am prepared to pay you twenty dollars an acre. I believe you have about thirty-five acres there and that would come to seven hundred dollars."

Mrs. Channing pursed her lips and squinted at Adam. "Why are you willing to offer me a premium for this property? Do you have reason to believe it is underlain with oil?"

"No ma'am. I am willing to pay a premium because of where it lies. There is no other land around here that interests me as much as this piece of land. It is perfectly situated for the erection of houses, which I intend to do. I recognize that by telling you this I am giving you every reason to insist on an even higher price. In bargaining with another, I am told, one should never let on how much he wants the property he is asking to buy. But I believe there is much merit in speaking plainly and truthfully with you."

Mrs. Channing nodded. "I appreciate your candor, young man."

Adam continued. "If you do not wish to sell, I will seek property elsewhere, and may well find property equally satisfactory to me. But I would prefer at this time to purchase your thirty-five acres."

Mrs. Channing thought about it for a moment. Obviously, she was doing some calculations. "I am now renting the property for fifty cents an acre. That brings me an income of seventeen dollars and fifty cents a year. If I sell you this land for seven hundred dollars and put this seven hundred at three percent interest with Randall Armentrout that will bring me, let's see . . . twenty-one dollars a year, a profit of three dollars and fifty cents. That is hardly worth my trouble. I like owning land. It means more to me than cash money."

Adam studied the matter for a moment. "How about this, Mrs. Channing. I will purchase the land from you for seven hundred dollars. I will not pay you the money immediately, but will give you a note for the seven hundred dollars with interest at four percent. That will be twenty-eight dollars a year in interest. And, since I do not expect to begin developing the land for a year or two, I will let you continue to rent it out to Grover Needham for fifty cents an acre. So you will have, for the first couple of years at least, an income of seventeen fifty from Grover plus twenty-eight from me . . . for a total of forty-five dollars a year. I will pay you the interest due you at the time of sale and every year thereafter on the anniversary of the sale. When I pay off the note, you can then secure whatever interest you can obtain from Randall Armentrout." He paused for a moment and then added, "Or you may be able to secure a better rate of interest from a private party who is a good risk and needs a loan of money for a short time."

Mrs. Channing smiled. "You paint an attractive picture, young man. I will not haggle with you. Let me dwell on it for a few days and I will be back with you."

"Fine," Adam replied. "I only ask that you say nothing to anyone about our conversation."

Mrs. Channing nodded in agreement.

Two days later she sent a note to the mill saying that she would be willing to sell the property to Adam under the terms he had outlined. Valentine Burner drew up the contract of sale and the deed which Adam did not record but kept in the safe at the mill. Mrs. Channing continued to lease the property to Grover Needham and no one except Mrs. Channing, Valentine Burner, and Will and Adam knew the property had been sold.

Meanwhile, Adam and Will began sketching plans for houses to be built in the new development. "We'll call it 'Brubaker Acres,'" Adam said, "in honor of the old man who has made this possible. I think he would be proud of us, don't you?"

"Yes," Will replied. "And I am certain he would be pleased he left the mill to us."

Adam did not respond.

CHAPTER 19

Every fall, after the harvest season was over and life in Stendahl had slowed down a bit, the Methodist Episcopal church of Stendahl held a week-long revival. Adam enjoyed services. He was absolutely mesmerized by Reverend Rhine's spellbinding oratory, his harsh visions of hell and the punishment that awaited those who had not come to Jesus by the time they died.

He was sitting in his usual seat beside Sarah, about half way up the aisle on the left, listening to Reverend Rhine tell again of the burning fires of hell, when he felt a tap on his shoulder. It was Oliver Finch. He leaned over and whispered into Adam's ear. "Adam, you had better come outside with me."

Adam rose and followed him outside. Oliver was, he could tell, quite distraught. "Adam, the mill is on fire. Don't know how it started, but we're fighting it as best we can."

"Oh my, God," Adam exclaimed. "Let's get up there." Adam slipped back up the aisle, explained to Sarah what was happening, excused himself, and left. On his way out he asked Gerald Hoffman, the church usher, to see that Sarah and her sister got home safely.

Then he raced down Main Street and turned up Mill Street by the Ascher Boarding House. He could see flames leaping out of a first floor window of the mill. He took off running. By the time he reached the mill the first floor was partly engulfed. The bottom floor, which was partially open and stacked with drying lumber, was fully engulfed. Clearly, the first floor was going to go unless they could put enough water on it to keep the fire from going on up through the second floor and onto the roof.

Twenty men and boys were lined up in a bucket brigade, dipping buckets into the mill race and passing them, hand over hand, until they reached Will, Davy, and Tally, who were at the head of the line. The three men were soaking wet from the water slopping out of the buckets as they emptied them onto the flames. Adam ran up and joined them, dumping buckets himself.

An hour or so later the flames began to subside. It was clear they had managed to save the mill, but the building had been seriously damaged. They worked for another hour. Then Adam thanked everyone and sent them home. He met with Will, Davy, and Tally and they decided to stay up all night and make sure the fire didn't rekindle itself. Adam changed clothing and began to survey the damage while the boys were pouring buckets of water here and there when the coals showed signs of getting redder.

By the time daylight came Adam was able to make an assessment of the damage. Most of the lumber on the bottom floor had been ruined. Half of the first floor was burned out. Only the fact that the building exterior was brick standing on a foundation of stone had kept the fire from completely destroying the building. The band saw, the treadle saw, and the lathe had dropped onto the bottom floor and burned. The water wheel shaft was still intact, but it had been pretty deeply charred on the south side of the building, where the damage was worst. It would probably have to be replaced ultimately but, for the immediate future, it would do its job. Half the office floor was gone, the stand-up desk was ruined, and the safe had tumbled onto the bottom floor. Of the twenty windows on the first floor, eight were either gone or too badly damaged to be saved.

He was still trying to understand how it had happened when Will approached. "Two things you need to know, Adam. Neither one of them is very pretty." He pointed out into the lumber yard. "Out there by the end of the curing shed, that's a cross. It hasn't been lit or anything, but it's a cross nonetheless. I wonder if the Klan was involved. The other thing is that old man Reeves who runs the shoe shop told me that, as he was runnin' up here to help fight the fire, he saw Luke and Paulie Jepson hot footin' it down Mill Street, like they was runnin' away from something. He didn't say but it was pretty clear to me he suspicions they set the fire."

Adam pursed his lips. "Wouldn't put it past them. Those no-account thievin' rascals are capable of anything. See if Cora can come down to my house and fix us some breakfast. We aren't going to be able to do anything today but keep the coals down so the fire doesn't start up again. But we have to eat. There's a ham in the outbuilding and plenty of potatoes on the back porch. If Cora can dredge up some eggs and a couple loaves of bread, we can have some breakfast. I'll start on the coffee now."

By eight o'clock they had eaten their fill, mostly in silence. Sarah had shown up, very distressed, and offered to help anyway she could. Adam, touched by her concern, told her that just having the opportunity to call on her twice a week would be very calming and soothing to him. He gave a forced smile. "Just seeing you from time to time will be enough."

Sarah shook her head and spoke boldly, unconcerned about the men gathered there. "No Adam. You mean too much to me to allow you to bear this burden all by yourself. I'm coming here this evening after work and see what I can do. Surely I can be more than just a shoulder to lean on." Then, oblivious to the men gathered around the table, she reached up, kissed him on the cheek, looked deeply into his eyes for a moment, and left for school.

After she had left no one said anything for a while. Then the men simply got up from the table, walked back to the mill and began discussing with Adam what it would take to get back in operation. By noon Adam had determined he would need seven hundred dollars to do everything that was necessary. "I don't have that kind of money. I guess I'll have to go ask Randall Armentrout for a loan. He's used this mill enough, most of the furniture in his house was built right here so I expect he'll be willing to help us if the interest rate is right."

-o-

Randall Armentrout, the president and major stockholder of the Stendahl State Bank, was sitting with his feet on his desk, smoking a cigar, and reading the *Polk County Guardian*. The door to his office was open and acrid cigar smoke was drifting out the door. Adam knocked on the door frame. Randall ignored the knock for about a minute, clearly establishing he was in charge here and would entertain visitors when he was good and ready. Finally he took his feet off the desk, put the paper down, and looked at Adam.

"What can I do for you, Gummy? I hear you had a little trouble last night."

"More than a little, actually, but nothing we can't handle with a little help."

"What you have in mind?"

"I need to borrow four hundred dollars, Mr. Armentrout. I have around three hundred, but I need another four hundred dollars. You set the interest rate, but I need that money to get the mill back in operation as soon as possible. We've got a good many furniture orders and there's substantial money to be made, but we just have to get back in operation."

Randall Armentrout leaned back in his chair, laid his arms across his fat belly and made a steeple with his hands. "Gummy," he said, in a patronizing tone, as though his time was being wasted, "there's something you have to understand. Old man Brubaker may have left you his mill – for God knows what reason – but that doesn't change things regarding you. You're still Job Richter's boy. A boy – barely a man now – whose pap was a no-good-for-nothing drunk, who drowned in that little piss-ant mill race beside the Bloody Bucket. You don't have any education. You don't know anything about how decent people live. In my opinion I don't think you know any more about running a business than my dog Whitey knows about arithmetic." He shifted in his chair and leaned forward onto his desk. "Gummy, this bank is not a charity. I've got a board of directors to satisfy and if I tell them I loaned four hundred dollars to Gummy Richter to re-build his lumber mill, I'd be out of a job."

"Now if you have any sense at all you'll sell that mill to me – in the condition it's in right now – for seven hundred dollars. One thousand dollars if you throw in the house. Hell, I'll even give you a job there. But, if you want my advice, I'd take the thousand dollars and head out west where no one ever heard of Job Richter and you can start over again. What do you say to that? One thousand dollars. Fifty twenty dollar gold pieces. And a chance at a new life. What do you say, Gummy?"

Adam stared at the floor and then began speaking, slowly. "Randall," he said, and then paused to let the fat little man soak in the realization that this was the first time he had ever addressed the president of the Stendahl State Bank by his first name.

"Randall," he repeated, staring unblinkingly at the bank president, "you said there's something I have to understand. There are some things you have to understand, too. First, the mill is not for sale. Not now. Not at any time in the foreseeable future. I may not come from your level of society, but I do know how to run a furniture mill. The last year has

173

shown that. The mill is going to be re-built and re-opened and it will succeed, either with the assistance of the Stendahl State Bank or without it. But it will succeed."

He paused, staring at the banker, then continued. "Job Richter was my father. Yes, he drank too much and he never amounted to very much. But he was my father and, incredible as you may find it, I loved him. He named me 'Adam,' after *his* father." He paused for a moment, and Randall started to speak. Adam held up his hand, palm toward Randall, who stopped talking. Then Adam continued. "Cruel fate has given me the nickname 'Gummy,' a nickname I detest. But my name is 'Adam.' Life has been cruel to me, Randall, in ways and to a degree that you can only begin to imagine from the comfort of your position in this bank. But it has also taught me to be hard when it is necessary for survival."

"I know that, uh, Adam," Randall said. But Adam held up his hand again and stood up. He had the floor and he would not be interrupted.

"So hear me on this." He jabbed his right index finger at Randall Armentrout. "If you ever again speak ill of my father in my presence or if you ever again call me 'Gummy,' I will give you cause to regret the very day your mother gave birth to you. This is not a threat, Randall. It is," he pointed his finger toward the ceiling, "– with God as my witness – a solemn promise."

With that, he turned and walked out the door. Behind him Randall stood up. "Uh . . . Gum . . . Ad . . . Ad . . . Adam . . . uh . . . uh . . . I mean . . . look , I didn't . . . ."

Adam left Randall Armentrout sputtering behind him. He realized keenly now that, even though he was now the co-owner of Brubaker's Mill and had become a rising young success story in the town, he would never be accepted by the leaders of the town as anything other than the drunken Job Richter's son, "Gummy" Richter. It was one of those moments – there hadn't been many in his life – when everything was shockingly clear. He was nobody in Stendahl, a boy from the bottom level of the town's society, and there was no future for him here, no matter how much he might improve himself or how much his mill might prosper.

He stopped and peered into the distance, focusing on nothing. Perhaps he should take Randall Armentrout up on his offer of one thousand dollars for the mill and his house. He could maybe even bargain with Randall and get, perhaps, two thousand dollars. Take the money. Go somewhere, probably out west, and start over, where no one ever heard of Job or Gummy Richter. Leave the Jepson boys behind.

No, he couldn't do that to Will and Davy and Tally and Oliver. They had been giving their all for the mill and he owed it to them to keep the place afloat. And he couldn't leave Sarah behind. It would be unfair to expect her to leave her family here and go to God knows where. He started walking again. No, by God, he would keep the mill afloat, even if Randall Armentrout wouldn't help him. Together with the boys, he would rebuild and prosper yet.

When he reached the mill, Will Perse sensed his mood. "Looks to me like we didn't get the loan."

"No, but I put Randall Armentrout in his place. By God, we're going to re-build this mill – without the help of the Stendahl State Bank!"

That evening Adam and Will, with a concerned Sarah following them, surveyed the lumber in the storage shed. They walked through the ashes of the mill. They calculated that they had enough timber to rebuild those parts of the mill that had been consumed by the fire. But first they would have to saw the logs into lumber. So the first thing that had to be restored and put to work was the gang saw. For now, the drive wheel from the waterwheel could still be used. It was charred at one end, but it would still turn sufficiently to operate the gang saw.

They might need to purchase blades for the saw and have the metal bits and blades for the drills and molding planes hammered out at by Lester Crowell, the town's blacksmith. On the other hand, perhaps the bits and blades could be dug out of the ashes and would still be usable. The concern would be if they had lost their "temper," which occurs when blades have been heated excessively, in which case the blade may not be able to hold an edge. But if they were lucky the metal blades that had gone through this fire may not have lost their temper. They would simply have to see. In any event, the wooden frames of the planes and other metal tools as well as the wooden stands for all the machines would have to be re-built. It was going to be a monumental undertaking.

After they were finished and Will had returned home Sarah and Adam walked down to his house. In the kitchen Adam put a pot of coffee on the kitchen stove, added some wood to the fire and asked Sarah if he could fix something for supper for the two of them. Sarah smiled. "Yes, I would like that. I would like to see what kind of a cook you are. A girl needs to know this sort of thing about a man she is very interested in." Her emphasis was on the word *very*.

Adam turned to her, wrapped his arms around her and kissed her passionately. She returned the kiss and they embraced for several minutes. After he backed away he looked at Sarah intensely and said: "I love you, Sarah Gifford, with all my heart. I'm not sure I can live without you. Will you marry me, I mean after all this mess with the mill is cleaned up and life gets back to normal?"

"Yes. Yes, I'll marry you. So hurry up and get this mess cleaned up. The sooner we are married, the happier I will be."

They embraced and kissed again. Adam smiled. "You know, this may sound strange but as difficult as the mill fire has been for me, and as far 'down' as I have been since it happened, right now I don't think I have ever been happier. I mean it. Knowing that you are going to be my wife is more important than anything in my life." He smiled. "Now let's not spoil this moment by my preparing a lousy supper. All right? Let's go downtown to Mrs. Roscoe's and have a decent meal."

Together they walked down Mill Street, holding hands publicly for the first time, and took an evening meal of stewed veal with dumplings, mashed potatoes and green beans, served with baked biscuits and topped off with Mrs. Roscoe's famous apple pie.

Adam would remember this evening for the rest of his life.

-o-

The next morning Adam gathered his men in the kitchen of his house. "I don't have any money to pay you any more than a dollar a day for at least six months. I know that's barely enough to live on, but it's the best I can do. But once we start making money – which I expect to happen by late next spring – I'll pay you all the back wages you will have lost by then and I'll give you all a fifty cent a day raise. As for me, I am not taking anything out of this business until I've evened it up with you. If any of you can't afford to stay here and work for a dollar a day, I'll understand. You can leave and there'll be no hard feelings."

The room was silent for a while. Then Tally Monroe spoke. "Boys, I reckon we oughta get to work. The sooner we do, the sooner we're gonna see that fifty cent pay raise." The others laughed. They left the kitchen and walked up to the mill site.

They immediately began sifting through the ashes of the mill – dirty, grimy, exhausting work. They recovered almost all of the iron tools that had fallen into the fire. The drill bits and plane irons were still usable, as were a few of the saw blades. The heavy wooden machinery would have to be re-built by hand. Yet, it wasn't quite as bad as they had feared.

They set the safe upright and built a temporary wall around it on the first floor of the mill where it had fallen during the fire. The finish on the safe was blistered and peeling but the papers and other items in the safe had weathered the fire. With the heavy-timbered wall around it and a sturdy lock on the door, the safe would be fine there until they could re-build the office floor above it and raise the safe to its usual spot.

As they were deeply involved in clearing up the mess Lonnie Bierkamp, a local carpenter, drove up to the work site in his wagon. Adam crossed the bridge over the mill race and greeted Lonnie. "Got a load of tools here," Lonnie gestured toward the wagon, "thought maybe you could use them, particularly the heavy planes. You can keep them until you get back on your feet. Meantime, if I need one or more of them, I'll just come back and borrow 'em for a while."

Adam choked up and tears welled to his eyes. "I don't know what to say, Lonnie. That's very kind of you."

"Don't need to say anything. Figger you'd do the same for me. Where do you want to put these tools?"

Adam called Davy and Tally and the four of them moved the tools into the upper end of the mill where they would be safe.

As Lonnie departed in his wagon Adam said quietly, "Lonnie, I'll not forget this. Someday I'll repay your kindness."

Lonnie just nodded his head and drove away.

-o-

The following Monday, Adam crossed the bridge over the mill race and walked straight to the blacksmith shop of Lester Crowell. Lester was hammering a piece of iron on the anvil with a huge hammer while his apprentice, a boy named "Pud" Lehmann, was working the bellows, exciting the fire to a white heat.

Lester stopped hammering when he saw Adam. "Mornin', Adam. Sorry about your fire." You doin' all right? I been meanin' to come by and check on you but," he looked around the shop at all the broken wheels and disheveled tools, "I jist been so busy."

Adam ignored Lester's comments. "I need to talk with you." He looked toward Pud. "Alone."

Lester turned to Pud. "Go on, get another load of coal. Don't come back 'til I call you."

Adam spoke. "Lester, I am going to come straight out. When my mill burned last week there was a big cross stood up in the mill yard. Did the Klan burn my mill because I got Tally Monroe working for me?"

"Why are you asking me about the Klan? I don't know nothin' about no Klan."

Adam exhaled deeply. "Lester, I don't have time to bandy words with anyone these days. Everyone knows you are a power to be reckoned with in the Klan. Even the members of the little girls Sunday School class know. It's no secret. So don't waste our time here this morning telling me otherwise. Did the Klan burn my mill? Yes or no?"

"Adam, I ain't sayin' I belong to the Klan and I ain't sayin' I don't belong to the Klan. But I'm tellin' you this much: the Klan did not burn down your mill. Tally Monroe workin' for you ain't no concern of the Klan. He's a good colored man who don't trouble anyone. You want to hire him, that's your business. It certainly ain't no reason to burn your mill. No, the Klan didn't have nothin' to do with burnin' your mill."

"I have your word on that?"

"You have my word on. And if'n I was to guess I'd say instead of blamin' the Klan you ought to look at those no-good-for-nothin', god-damned sonsabitchin' Jepson boys. It's all over town that they was seen runnin' from the fire that night."

"I didn't mean to offend you, Lester. You can see how I had to know, given the cross in the lumber yard." He stared into the fire for a moment.

179

"And, yes, I had already thought of Luke and Paulie Jepson."

"I don't take no offense to a man simply askin' questions. I see your point, with the cross and all. But if'n I was you I'd be a-goin' after them Jepsons. It's time someone stood up to them mean bastards. I'm a-tellin' you, them boys is no account. They got half this county scared shitless of 'em and somebody needs to come down real hard on them. That's all they understand. Whup their asses real good a few times and they just might be apt to back off a mite. "

Adam turned to leave. "Thank you, Lester. I appreciate your frankness. As for the Jepson's, you know Wilbur Botts will protect them. The sheriff and the prosecuting attorney owe their jobs to Wilbur. They won't lift a finger against those two worthless pieces of trash."

"Wilbur Botts or not, somebody is going to have to do something about them boys."

"I know, I know," Adam said over his shoulder. "You are absolutely right."

CHAPTER 20

In mid-December, about three weeks after the fire, Benny Prout, a messenger boy for the Stendahl State Bank, showed up at the mill. He took Adam aside and handed him an envelope. Adam opened the envelope and read the message:

> *Adam: I'm sorry if I offended you the day we met in my office. After carefully considering the matter, I find I am able to lend you the $400 you require to rebuild your mill. I will, of course, require you to pledge your mill as security for the loan.*
>
> *Randall Armentrout*

Adam handed the note to Oliver Finch, who was working at the desk in the office. He turned to Benny, who said, "Mr. Armentrout said you can write your answer on the note and give it back to me and I will take it back to the bank. I won't read it."

"I know you won't, Benny. I know you won't. But I don't have anything to write to Mr. Armentrout. Tell him I am too busy right now to talk with him but that perhaps, in a week or so, I will be able to find time to drop by the bank and meet with him."

Benny nodded. "Yessir!" and turned to leave.

"Wait a minute," Adam said. He reached into his pocket and dug out a dime which he handed to Benny.

Benny smiled broadly. "Thank you, Mr. Richter," he said, and took off at a brisk walk toward the bank.

Oliver Finch handed the note back to Adam. "You enjoyed that, didn't you, Adam?"

Adam looked at the note again and then placed it in his coat pocket. "More than you will ever know, Mr. Finch, more than you will ever know."

Later that night, after everyone had left, Adam returned to the mill and placed Randall Armentrout's note in the locked strongbox he kept in the bottom of the safe. It's odd, he thought, how things just seem to fall in your lap sometimes.

-o-

A few days later, as he was lifting a charred board on the bottom floor of the mill Adam raked his left hand across the head of a nail imbedded in a post. It tore an ugly gash. He had to stop work, wash his hand in the mill stream, and wrap it with a clean cloth. By the following day the wound had grown red and swollen. At Will's insistence, and remembering how Mr. Brubaker had died of an infection of the blood, Adam went to see Dr. Solomon Glanzer.

"Looks like you're getting blood poisoning, Adam. That's serious. We're going to have to try to reverse it." He picked up a jug that was labeled "alcohol" and poured it liberally onto a cotton rag. "This is going to hurt."

He took the alcohol-soaked cloth and rubbed it vigorously across the wound. It burned like the surface of the sun. Adam closed his eyes and bit his lip. Doc Glanzer probed and pushed at the tear on Adam's hand, massaging blood out of it and pushing the reddened portions of his hand toward the open wound. Then he poured alcohol onto a second cloth and repeated the process. He did this six times, then wrapped Adam's hand in a clean cloth.

He poured about a pint of alcohol into a Mason jar and handed it to Adam. "Take this and do just what I did three times a day for a week. Always use a clean rag. In fact you should boil a batch of rags tonight, just to be certain they're clean. If it doesn't get better in two or three days, come back to see me. This is serious business, Adam. If this doesn't get better, you could lose that hand . . . or worse."

Adam thanked the doctor, paid him fifty cents, and started for the door. He stopped. "Doc, when I was in Baltimore last fall there was an article in the *Sun* that said not everyone's blood is the same. Do you know anything about that?"

Doc Glanzer leaned back against his desk and folded his arms over his pin-striped vest. "Oh, yes. It's called blood grouping. It's been in all the medical journals. There are four types of blood, A, B, AB, and O. The thing is, not all blood types are compatible with each other. So you can't just give a person blood from another person without making sure the type blood you're giving him is compatible with the person's own blood. Would you like to know what type blood you have?"

"I never gave it any thought. Is it difficult?"

"No, not at all. Here, let me take a bit of blood from your arm."

Adam rolled up his sleeve and Doc Glanzer swabbed the inside of his elbow with alcohol. He inserted a needle into the vein on the inside of the elbow and collected blood into a tube. He took two small bottles from a cabinet and poured a sample of fluid from each into two small dishes, then poured a small portion of Adam's blood into each dish and studied the samples carefully. He poured the remainder of the blood sample into a thin tube and placed the tube in a drum-like contraption with a handle like a barrel churn and turned the handle vigorously for about three minutes. He drew off the top portion of the blood into another three dishes. Taking two more bottles from a cabinet Doc poured a small sample from each bottle into each dish. After he studied the dishes for a few minutes and consulted a book which sat on the back of his desk, he turned to Adam. "Well, young man, it looks like you have Type AB blood. That's a rather rare type. Not more than one in fifty, one in a hundred, at best, will have that type."

Adam furrowed his brow. "Is that a problem, Doc?"

"Oh, no. it just means you inherited that type of blood from your parents, that's all. Actually, Type AB blood is a good type to have because you can accept a blood transfusion from anyone. All the other blood types can only receive blood from someone with their type. Type AB blood is fairly rare. I am glad I typed your blood for you. It's good practice for when I have to do it in an emergency." He smiled, looking very pleased with himself. "Say, how are you getting along with Fannie Brubaker?"

"Not getting along at all. She ignores me. I still cut her wood and stack it on her porch, but she never lets on I'm there."

"Fannie has always been an old biddy. No one likes her. Anybody who is around her for five minutes will go sour on her. I certainly understand why Isaac Brubaker left Will and you the mill. Fannie would only have sold it to Randall Armentrout for a song. At least now she has a guaranteed income from you and Will. But you can't please her. No one ever could. She came to me once with a very sore boil. I lanced it and when she came back for a follow-up she refused to pay me. Said God made the boil better, not me. I asked her why she hadn't asked God to lance the boil in the first place. She just snorted and walked out. Never did pay me. But you mark my words, late some night someone will come pounding on my door telling me Fannie Brubaker is sick and needs me. And I'll have to go up the mill race and help her."

"Why don't you just ignore her if she sends for you?"

"Couldn't do that, Adam. Violates the oath I took when I became a doctor. I'll have to go help her, but I don't have to like it. We do lots of things in life because we have to, but we don't always have to like them."

Adam nodded. "You're right about that, Doc." He left the office, holding his left hand close against his body and clutching the jar of alcohol in his right hand. His wound was throbbing.

-o-

Sarah and Adam made their engagement public and Adam ordered a small brilliant cut diamond ring for Sarah from the Sears, Roebuck & Company catalog, after carefully measuring her ring size on the gauge provided in the catalog. The ring cost over eleven dollars.

With hard work and plain good luck, they had the mill back in limited operation about five weeks after the fire. Not all the machinery had been re-built, but the gang saw was turning logs into timbers which made it possible to restore the burned-out section of the main floor and to enclose the bottom floor. Davy had nearly completed constructing the body of lathe, and the heavy-duty crown molding plane apparatus was also coming along. Adam had ordered glass from Baltimore to replace the burned-out windows, which were now boarded up. Without the light from those windows, the mill was darker than they liked, but they were clearly on their way to restoring the mill to its pre-fire condition.

Meanwhile, at Adam's request, Sheriff Emil Lutz had called on the Jepson brothers and informed them that if the mill suffered another fire or any other calamity, they would be under very serious suspicion. "You know you cain't do nothing to us, sheriff," Luke sneered. "So jist go on your way. We didn't have nothin' to do with Gummy's fire, so leave us alone. You don't want Wilbur Botts visitin' you, do you?"

Sheriff Lutz stared at Luke. "Someday, you smart-ass son of a bitch, Wilbur Botts ain't goin' to be able to pull your feet out of the fire. I hope I'm around when that happens."

Luke just looked at the sheriff and then turned to his brother. "Come on, Paulie. We don't have nothin' to discuss with the sheriff."

-o-

By early April of 1906, four months after the fire, the mill was fully back in operation. They had expanded the covered outdoor log storage building and enlarged the bridge over the mill race. The safe had been pulled back up to the office and a new floor laid under it. The lot in front of the mill, which had always been a sea of mud in wet weather, was covered with sawdust and shavings. After every rain Davy and Tally spread another layer of wood chips around the lot. To the selection of furniture on display on the main floor of the mill Adam added a slant-top desk, a small lamp table with a checkerboard inlaid in ebony and maple, and a magnificent walnut four-poster bed. Twice a day Davy went over the furniture with a feather duster.

With the mill finally back in full operation, Adam and Sarah began making arrangements to be married. They met with Pastor Walter Rhine and the wedding was set for Sunday afternoon, May 27. It was to be a small, private affair. Will Perse would be Adam's best man and Helen Klein would serve as Sarah's matron of honor. The workers at the mill and their families were to be invited and Cora and Will Perse asked if they could provide a small reception at their home following the wedding.

CHAPTER 21

Over the past eight months the Jepson brothers had intensified their automotive reign of terror on Stendahl. In the past few weeks alone they had run over six possums, two groundhogs, three cats, and one lamb. Dog lovers themselves, they had thus far been able to avoid killing any dogs. But their reckless behavior had not lessened at all.

On Tuesday, April 10, the boys left the Bloody Bucket thoroughly soused. They fired up the *American Gas* and took off up Main Street, wobbling back and forth from one side of the street to another. As they were making the sharp turn off Main Street onto Jefferson Avenue, Paulie, who was driving, lost control of the steering wheel. The car jumped onto the wooden sidewalk in front of Captain J. C. Ferguson's law office just as Sarah Gifford was coming out the door. The runaway vehicle struck Sarah, threw her backward and her head smacked against Ferguson's brick office building. The nerve fibers inside her brain stem snapped and Sarah was already dead when she finally slid down onto the sidewalk.

Paulie backed the car off the sidewalk and he and Luke rushed over to Sarah. "Well," Luke announced loudly, "she's dead." He looked around the crowd of bystanders who had gathered. "That's too bad, but y'all can all see that this was a accident. I'm sorry, but you can't always control these damned vehicles."

Will was the first to tell Adam who nearly collapsed in shock. He rushed to the accident site and then on to Doc Glazer's office where Sarah's body had been taken. The doctor met him at the door. "I'm sorry Adam, very sorry, but you shouldn't see Sarah's body. Just remember her as you knew her in life."

Adam pushed Doc aside and insisted on seeing Sarah. Then he broke down and cried piteously. Will, who had followed him, took Adam in his arms and tried to console him. After a while Adam stopped crying and insisted on seeing the Jepson brothers. The boys, however, had left town in a hurry and gone back to The Bleaks.

Adam and Will borrowed horses from Jacob Winslow who ran the town stable on Sycamore Avenue and rode to the Jepson place in The Bleaks. There, angry now beyond reason, Adam confronted the brothers.

"You lousy, vicious, mean spirited sons-of-bitches killed the love of my life! Have you no heart at all?"

Luke spoke up loudly. "Listen, Gummy, everyone who saw the wreck can tell you it was a accident. We didn't mean to kill nobody. It just happened. Besides," he shrugged his shoulders, "with all the money you're making at the mill you can have any unmarried woman you want in Stendahl. So calm down."

Adam leaped on Luke, screaming and pushing him to the ground. "Calm down, you say, you son-of-a-bitch. I'll show you how calm I am!" Crying and swearing violently he began pummeling Luke in the face. Then he grabbed him by the hair with both hands and began pounding his head on the ground. "Don't you have ANY feelings for anyone else?"

Paulie and Will pulled at Adam, trying to get him to stop. But, as small as he was, Adam couldn't be stopped. Then, with Luke nearly comatose, Adam stood up and launched into Paulie, pummeling him mercilessly until, sobbing and moaning, he was pulled off Paulie by Will and Jehu Jepson who had come out of the house at the sound of the ruckus.

Both boys were stunned and bleeding profusely as Adam and Will mounted their horses and headed back to town. Little was said but

Will kept telling Adam how sorry he was and assured him he would do anything to ease the pain. Adam said nothing.

The following morning when Adam came into the mill he looked ten years older. His eyes were bloodshot and he was totally disheveled. As Davy and Tally and Oliver expressed their condolences he nodded and quietly said, "Thank you." Those were the only words he had uttered all morning when Sheriff Lutz arrived and insisted that Adam accompany him into the mill's office where he closed the door.

"Adam, I'm awful sorry about Sarah. But you can't go about beating up on folks for what was clearly an accident. Wilbur Botts was in to see me this morning and it was all I could do to stop him from preferring charges against you. Now, we can't have this kind of behavior, do you understand?"

Adam stared coldly at the sheriff, his body quivering with rage. "Oh, I understand. I understand perfectly. We protect Luke and Paulie once again and threaten me for reacting angrily because Sarah Gifford, the love of my life, was killed by their drunken wild-ass behavior. Well, let me tell you something Sheriff, you haven't heard the last of this yet. Now you get the hell out of here and don't you come back. And spread the word – none of you friends of Luke and Paulie who are so terrified of Wilbur Botts are welcome in this mill. EVER! Now get out of here before I beat the shit out of you like I did Luke and Paulie!"

Out on the main floor of the mill Will and Tally and Davy could hear every word that Adam was shouting at the Sheriff.

The sheriff did not reply to Adam but quietly opened the door and walked out of the mill without saying another word.

-o-

Adam was in despair, more deeply than he had ever been in his life. Even the horrendous experience of having his teeth pulled could not

189

begin to compare. Pastor Walter Rhine called on him and tried to console him, but Adam listened blankly to the pastor's words, as if nothing were getting through to him. At work he left Oliver Finch alone in the office and wandered about the mill at random.

In Adam's absence Will, Davy and Tally designed and built Sarah's casket while Oliver sought out silk for the casket's dressing. At Will's insistence the casket was lined with tin which was then overlain with the silk Oliver had secured.

The casket was laid out for viewing in the parlor of the Klein home where Adam had called on Sarah all those Tuesday and Thursday evenings. In what was no doubt a genuine reflection of how the community felt about Sarah, and about Adam as well, it seemed as if the entire town came by to show their respects.

Armistead Watson was there with his wife and his daughter, Ida, who expressed her deep sorrow to Adam but who received a polite, but wooden, response in return. Randall Armentrout showed up and, for once, made no attempt to be funny but was rigidly solicitous to Adam and the Kleins. J. Fletcher Cobb the dentist dropped by as did Doc Glanzer. The entire Stendahl legal community was there, from Judge J. Wellington Truehart, to the prosecuting attorney, Valentine Burner to old Captain J. C. Ferguson to Charlie Luikhart, whose law practice left much to be desired. Even Samuel Oldaker, President of the Polk County Court who had sent Adam to live with the Jepsons, came by to express his condolences. Through it all Adam remained polite but distant as if he were somehow viewing the whole scene from afar.

At the graveside service following the funeral the next day, as Sarah's casket was being lowered into the grave, Adam fainted. Standing between Will and Cora, the two grabbed him before he could slide to the ground. Davy and Tally, who were standing right behind them, quickly reached forward and helped keep Adam from going down.

In the days that followed he was polite but distant with Will and Cora, clearly not wanting to talk. He refused to come to dinner on Sunday and turned down the same invitation from Helen and Charles Klein, who were devastated as well. Twice he walked out the trail to Lover's Leap and stood there seriously contemplating making the leap to his death. But, he knew, his death would do nothing to solve the persistent threat to life in Stendahl presented by the out-of-control behavior of the Jepson brothers.

His retreat from the world continued for over a week and then one day he walked into the mill, called Will into the office and said he needed to talk with him and Oliver. "As you know, I've been through hell recently and it's only now beginning to reach the point where I can think somewhat rationally – about anything other than Sarah. I'm sure you must understand that." Both men nodded silently. "Well, I'm finally getting some limited control of myself and I need to start paying attention to business again. It might even help take my mind off Sarah, at least to a small degree. Anyway, we need to know what we should be planning and thinking about if we're really going to go into the home building business. Before we know it the railroad will be here and we need to protect ourselves from the low-cost furniture that could flood this town then. Our only hope, I believe, is to be ready to start building homes for the folks who are certain to move here with the railroad. We need to be ready to figure out how best to mass-produce the doors and windows and stair rails and the like that we're going to need to make this idea work. So . . . I'm thinking of going to go back to Baltimore and see what I can learn that will help us do this thing right. What do you think?"

Both men agreed that was a good idea and the three of them then discussed briefly some of the things they thought Adam should inquire into.

In the days that followed Adam seemed to be coming out of his deep despair. He dressed with more care, interfaced with others much more pleasantly than he had for the past couple of weeks and, to the delight of those around him, appeared to recovering somewhat from his terrible ordeal.

Then on Thursday, April 26, 1906, Adam once again boarded the stage for Whitney on the way to Baltimore.

CHAPTER 22

He wasn't nearly as excited about this trip to Baltimore as he had been on his first trip. It wasn't merely the fact that he had already been there, that he was a "seasoned" stage coach and railroad passenger and had stayed in a hotel in a major American city. This was a *serious* business trip and what he had to do in Baltimore was infinitely more important than the experience of getting or even being there. He took with him a larger valise than before, one he had discovered under the bed in Mr. Brubaker's spare bedroom. The valise was practically empty but, as he had hoped, no one paid the slightest notice. He endured the long stage ride to Whitney and the dismal night at the Pleasant Valley Inn in Watkins Cove. Even the train ride from Whitney to Baltimore was just to be tolerated.

He arrived on Friday night, spent the night at the Eutaw House where he had a supper of fried pork chops, hash, gravy, green beans, and custard pie. For a dining room in a hotel as modest as the Eutaw House, this supper was a fine meal and Adam went to bed thoroughly satisfied, at least with respect to hunger.

The following morning he went out West Baltimore Street, between Eutaw and Howard Streets, to the establishment of Louis Ash & Son, Clothiers. There he was fitted for two black worsted wool suits. He also purchased a cape Mackintosh rain coat, two pairs of men's shell cordovan shoes, six white muslin shirts, a dozen linen collars, six black silk bow ties, three full suits of gray Merino wool underwear, a dozen pairs of extra-heavy all-wool socks, and a stiff black derby. In addition he bought a pair of Russett Hunting Boots with half double soles cut from the best oak tan stock leather. Mr. Ash assured him these were perfect hunting boots. "You can walk all day in the woods in these boots and your feet will never get tired or wet. Perfect hunting boots! Perfect hunting boots!" At a cost of five dollars and fifty cents Adam thought, they had better be perfect hunting boots! Finally he purchased a twenty-inch canvas cabin bag, three adjustable shoulder or sling straps and a goat skin club bag.

He paid Mr. Ash eleven dollars and seventy-eight cents, the cost of all but the suits, and left the shop, laden with the remainder of his purchases. He was to return on Monday, Mr. Ash said, for a second fitting on the suits and he would be able to pick them up on Tuesday.

From the Ash establishment he went straight to S. Bernei & Sons, at the southeast corner of Eutaw and Lexington Streets, where the sign advertised "dry goods." He purchased a thirty-inch canvas-covered stateroom trunk with a steel lock and key. He loaded his purchases from Louis Ash & Son in the trunk, went back out onto the street, and hailed a cab to the Eutaw House. After storing his trunk under the bed he walked to the bookstore at Franklin Street between North and Calvert where he had purchased three books on his last visit to Baltimore. The clerk who had waited on him during his earlier visit was busy so a little white-haired man came out from behind the counter and asked if he could help.

"I'm looking to purchase two or three books about Sherlock Holmes," Adam said. "I'm told they are very interesting reading."

The man smiled. "Indeed they are. I would suggest you start with *A Study In Scarlet*. This is the novel where Holmes meets Dr. Watson and introduces you to these two fascinating characters. Then you must read *The Hound of the Baskervilles,* which is undoubtedly Sir Arthur Conan Doyle's best Sherlock Holmes tale. Finally, I would recommend *The Sign of the Four*. You will not be disappointed with any of these."

Adam nodded. "Fine, I'll take all three." He left the bookstore hoping that following the literature suggestions of Sarah Gifford might bring him a small sense of peace.

From the bookstore he went to the James R. M. Adams Hardware at Eutaw and Franklin Streets, where he bought a Smith & Wesson .38 caliber hammerless revolver with a 3½-inch barrel and a package of one hundred cartridges. He also bought a corduroy cap with ear flaps, a two-blade jack knife with a rosewood handle, a woodsman's compass, and a rubber horse blanket with gum seams. After thinking about it for a moment he purchased a heavy wool lap robe, measuring sixty-four by seventy-four inches. Then, exhaling deeply, he paid fifteen dollars and forty-five cents for a 17-jeweled Elgin pocket watch with a coin silver case. For an extra dollar and seventy cents he purchased a sterling silver vest chain for the watch.

He carried all these purchases back to the Eutaw House where he placed them, along with the boots he had purchased from Mr. Ash, and the canvas cabin bag and shoulder straps in the valise he had carried, nearly empty, from Stendahl. He put the goat skin club bag in the stateroom trunk with the dress clothing. Then he added up the total expenditures he had made from Louis Ash & Son, Bernei & Sons, and the hardware store. The total came to ninety-six dollars and eighty-two cents. He, Adam Richter, had just purchased goods in the amount of ninety-six dollars and eighty-two cents. *Wouldn't Ma be proud!* More likely, as he thought about it, she would be shocked. But, then, she had never had to do what he was planning. Still, the idea of having spent so much money in one day unnerved him. But he comforted himself knowing that he had the money, that the expenditures were necessary, and that he was going to come out of it all with a great deal more money. Nonetheless, he was so uptight at having spent so much money that he went to bed without any supper. Somehow, in the dark recesses of his mind, he felt that denying himself supper would help make up for his extravagance.

It rained all day Sunday and he spent most of the day in his room. He purchased a copy of the *Baltimore Sun* and read it from cover to cover. The paper was full of stories of the terrible earthquake that had devastated San Francisco nearly two weeks earlier, of the horrific fires that raged out of control, and the breakdown of public order. Adam read and re-read the stories of the terrible damage. Knowing how he had felt when the mill had been set afire, he wondered how the people of that great city could possibly deal with their loss. And if they, like he, had suffered the loss of a loved one, he knew it would only be worse.

In late afternoon he went down to the lobby and watched folks come and go for a while. Then he returned to his room. Aside from the three meals he took in the hotel dining room, and his one brief visit to the hotel lobby, he spent the day thinking about what he was planning.

On Monday he returned to Louis Ash's establishment for a second fitting for his suits. Then he visited the offices of the redundantly-named Baltimore Life Insurance Company of Baltimore City, at the corner of Clay and Liberty Streets, and applied for a term life insurance policy in the amount of two thousand five hundred dollars. He was examined by the company doctor and declared physically fit for the policy. He named Will and Cora Perse beneficiaries of the policy, paid the one-year premium of six dollars and fifty cents, and left the office with a copy of the policy. Then he wandered around town taking in the sights and trying to think if there was anything else he needed to purchase. He wanted to get back to Stendahl to carry out his plans. But he had to wait on the stagecoach schedule and the need to accommodate the fitting of his suits. It made for a long day, especially for a young man who was unaccustomed to loitering.

The following morning he was back at Louis Ash's where he picked up his suits, paid Mr. Ash the twenty dollars due him, and returned to the Eutaw House. He packed the suits into the stateroom trunk with the other "dressy" purchases he had made at Louis Ash & Son and wrestled the trunk down to the lobby and out to the street. He hailed a cab and told the driver to take him to the Adams Express Company on Light Street. There he made arrangements to store the trunk until he should call for it in person. Giving his name as Samuel Griffith, he paid the clerk one dollar and seventy-five cents to cover the first six months storage. Pocketing his claim ticket, he left the express company and walked back to his hotel, comforted by the knowledge that he was avoiding cab fare.

At 6:15 the following morning, carrying his valise which was now full, he boarded the train for Whitney in a driving rain. It was still raining when he arrived there at 11:00 a.m. He took dinner at Gaddy's Eating House and at 1:30 p.m. boarded the stage for Stendahl, arriving there twenty-four hours later, the rain having finally abated. He went home, unloaded the valise, then walked to the Stendahl State Bank carrying the empty valise and went straight into Randall Armentrout's office. "Randall, may I close the door?"

Randall stood up. "Yes, of course, of course. Good to see you again, Adam. Have a seat." he gestured toward a chair seated beside the desk.

Adam sat down. Randall had called him "Adam." That was a good sign. Now he would make Randall feel a bit uncomfortable. He remained silent for thirty seconds or so, looking straight at Randall. Randall stared back, breaking into a half smile with his lips, but not with his eyes. Finally, much to Randall Armentrout's relief, he spoke. "Randall, what I am about to tell you is very confidential. Very, very confidential."

Randall raised both his hands in front of him, palms toward Adam. "Adam, you needn't worry about my leaking any confidential information. A banker is privy to many, many secrets and we have to be extremely careful not to reveal any confidences."

Adam shook his head, as if he agreed with Randall. "Well, this is just about the biggest secret that ever rolled into Stendahl. And it will have a greater impact on the future development of this town than anything that has ever happened – or ever will happen – including the coming of the railroad."

Randall settled back in his chair, his hands clasped across his fat chest, waiting to learn the great secret.

"In fact, Randall, I can't tell you very much in the way of details. But I can tell you this. I need to borrow five thousand dollars from this bank. I am willing to pay you ten percent interest per annum. What's the going rate now, four percent?"

"About that," Randall replied. Adam knew the going rate was three percent.

"Well, I'll pay ten percent, because I am going to make so much money from this deal that ten percent will be a mere drop in the bucket for me. And since your bank will make this deal possible, I think you ought to share in the wealth, too. So ten percent seems fair to me."

Randall scratched his head. "Now see here, Adam, I can't lend you money unless I know exactly what it's for. I'm sorry, but it just won't work that way."

"What it's for, Randall, is the purchase of over fifty thousand acres of wooded land west of here. Fifty thousand acres! And after I strip the timber I'll still own over fifty thousand acres of land which cost less than five cents an acre. Now I can't tell you where it is and I can't tell you who I am buying it from, but I can tell you this: when the railroad gets here and this town starts to double in size, I am going to have all the lumber we need to build fifty, maybe even a hundred homes, and your bank is going to be in the position to lend money to all those new homeowners."

"Will Perse doesn't know about this deal. He's been so good to me since I came to the mill as an apprentice that I want to repay him somewhat. So I'm going to give the lumber to the mill to build the houses we have planned. I'll not make any money by selling the lumber to the mill. My big gain will come from selling the fifty thousand acres of land involved. Of course Will and I will also make money by building all those houses with the timber I'll provide. But the loan I'm asking for is for me alone and I will pledge this land and my half of the mill and my house as security for the loan."

Randall rubbed his hands together and smiled broadly.

Adam went on. "There's no risk, Randall. Every home you lend money on will be pledged to your bank as security. You can require the homeowners to have fire insurance in case a house should burn down. All you have to do is sit here and collect the interest on all those loans. And that's after you have collected ten percent interest from me. I figure it will take me two, maybe three, years to pay you back. That means you'll make as much as fifteen hundred dollars in interest from me alone. And if you lend, say, a thousand dollars each to one hundred home builders, at four percent you'll be making another four thousand dollars a year from them."

Adam could see that Randall was already calculating the money his bank would earn off this deal. The risks, the uncertainties, the vagueness of it all had been pushed into the recesses of Randall's mind. All he could see was thousands of dollars in interest money coming into the bank, at virtually no risk. "But I'll need the money today. And I'll need it in gold coins – twenty dollar coins. As I said, I'll pledge the land and the mill as security, so there's no risk to your bank. But no one, not another soul, can know about this until I have completed the purchase of the timber. And that should happen within the next three weeks . . . four at the most."

"And, one other thing: don't discuss this with Will until the deal is closed. I want to surprise him myself with the news."

"Of course," Randall said as he stood up, rubbing his hands together greedily. "It's a deal. I'll get the loan forms and we can fill them out in here. I'll take the money from the vault myself, so no one else will know."

He left the office briefly and returned with a couple sheets of paper which he handed to Adam. "You fill out two of those, one for me and one for you, and I'll go get your money."

Adam very slowly and carefully completed the forms. When Randall returned, Adam handed them to him. "Here, I've pledged my interest in the mill and the fifty thousand acres of land as security for the loan. Now I'll sign the forms and you can witness my signature." Then he very slowly and carefully signed both forms and handed them to Randall who signed as a witness.

Randall then handed him a heavy sack containing the gold coins. "You'll want to count these, of course."

"No, Randall, I trust you. If you say there are two hundred fifty twenty dollar gold coins in there, I believe you. If we're going to be doing business together for a long, long time, we need to start trusting one another completely."

Randall jumped up and grasped Adam's right hand in both of his. He was suddenly very emotional. "Thank you, Adam, thank you. That's one of the nicest compliments I've ever received." Adam said nothing but thought that was likely not merely one of the nicest complements Randall Armentrout had received but one of the *very few* compliments he had ever received.

After cautioning Randall one more time that the transaction had to remain confidential, Adam left the bank with the sack of coins stashed in his valise. His heart was racing. Five thousand dollars! It had been easier than running a log through a gang saw.

-o-

That night Adam wrote his will, back-dating it to April 4, and placed it in the safe in the mill along with the life insurance policy he had purchased in Baltimore. His will left three hundred dollars each to Davy, Tally, and Oliver, and fifty dollars to Lonnie Bierkamp, the local carpenter who had loaned him his tools after the fire. The rest of his estate he left to Will and Cora, with a provision that Will continue paying Fanny Brubaker fifteen dollars a month until her death. If something happened to him now, Will would own the mill and both houses. With the twenty-five hundred dollars from the life insurance policy, he could pay off the loan to Mrs. Channing. Free of debt, he could develop the thirty-five acre tract and make a fortune building new homes on it. The odds were that Will and Cora were going to be very wealthy some day.

CHAPTER 23

The following day, Saturday, May 5, Adam went to town during the dinner hour, certain he would see the Jepson boys around the Bloody Bucket, getting thoroughly drunk for the weekend. Sure enough, shortly before one o'clock, he caught sight of Paulie leaning against the tumble-down building. He motioned him to come across the street. Paulie staggered over. "What you want, Gummy? You ain't gonna beat me up again are you?"

"No, Paulie, I'm sorry I beat you and Luke up so badly. But, you know, I was very upset that day over Sarah's death and I just went crazy, couldn't control myself. Now I want you and Luke to know I have put the past behind me and I want the three of us to be friends. Do you think Luke would agree?"

"I know he would, Gummy, I know he would."

"That's great Paulie. Now to show you that I want to let bygones be bygones I want to hire you and Luke to help me with something. You have to come alone because I am not paying anyone but you two. But I have a small job that I need two men to carry out and I believe you and Luke are the two men I need."

"What you want us to do and what you payin'?" Paulie asked.

"I'll show you what I want you to do when you show up. I'll pay you a dollar apiece if you come by my house around 7:30 Wednesday night. Can you do that? Or are you too drunk to remember that?"

"We'll be there, Gummy. We ain't turnin' down a easy dollar apiece."

"All right, but come alone. Understand? If you bring anyone else, I'll not use you."

Paulie wrinkled up his big flat nose. "All right. All right. We'll be there. Wednesday night. 7:30. I'll go tell Luke now . . . and we'll come alone. Don'tcha worry, Gummy. We'll be there."

Wednesday night was clear and cold. Adam ate a quick supper of soup beans over a thick slab of bread, washed down with heavily-creamed coffee. Then he went up to his bedroom to the chest of drawers beside the door. He removed the drawers of the chest, placed a thin rug under the legs of the chest and slid it back into the spare bedroom from which Davy and Talley had carried it that very morning. He removed the rug, replaced the drawers, and went back downstairs.

He walked up to the mill and rummaged around in a pile of scrap lumber until he found a piece of oak, about six feet long and two inches square. He cut about a foot-and-a-half off the stick, placed it in a vise, and rounded the stick off with a draw knife. When the stick was fairly well rounded, he drilled a small hole in the bottom and drove a ten-penny nail in to a depth of about one inch, deep enough that the nail would stay put but not deep enough to split the stick. Then he ground off the head of the nail and filed the nail down to a point. At the other end of the stick he drilled a hole through about six inches from the top. He took a piece of leather and cut a strip about three-eighths of an inch wide and sixteen inches long. He threaded the leather thong through the hole in the stick and tied the ends together. He removed the stick from the vise, gripped it tightly, and pounded it on the floor. It was a perfect walking stick. Then, with a rasp, he roughed up the toes of his shoes. He laid the rasp on the workbench, took a long look around the room, and walked out the door.

With a deep sigh he carefully locked the mill, went back to the house and out onto the front porch, where he leaned the walking stick against the wall. Then he returned to the parlor, picked up the Bible which lay on the stand beside the oil lamp and carefully tugged on the five dollar bill which, as he had explained to Will, he used as a bookmark. He made certain at least one-half of the bill stuck out of the Bible. Satisfied it could not be missed by anyone who came into the room, he placed the Bible by the oil lamp.

The evening sun was pouring in through the windows but he lit the lamp and sat down on the cut velvet settee, certain now that, accentuated by the burning lamp, the five dollar bill in the Bible could not be missed by anyone who came into the parlor.

He was very nervous. What if they didn't come? What if they brought someone else? What if one of their drinking buddies was waiting up by the mill for them to finish their chore and go drinking?

Presently he heard them coming though the mill yard. One of them pounded on the door. Adam waited a minute or so, during which time they pounded again. Then he answered the door.

They were half lit already, reeking of alcohol, and as cocky as ever. "Whatcha want us to do, Gummy?" Luke asked. He was grinning, like he had the world by the tail on a downhill drag.

"Got a piece of furniture I need to have moved. Come in here and wait in the parlor. I need to go upstairs a minute. I'll be right back."

Upstairs, he thrashed around in his bedroom and then came back down. In the parlor he made a quick, surreptitious glance at the Bible. The bill was gone. The boys had sprung the trap! Adam exhaled softly.

"All right, boys, come with me." They followed him upstairs where Adam had them move the chest of drawers from the spare bedroom into Adam's bedroom. "Careful, boys," he said. "That's a valuable piece of furniture."

"Oh, shit, Gummy," Luke said. "You think everthin' you got is valuable."

They went back down stairs and Adam gave each of them a dollar, thanked them, and started to send them on their way. As they were leaving the kitchen, he said, "Wait a minute," and went to the back porch where he picked up a rabbit he had caught that morning in a dead fall by the front gate. He cut into the rabbit's mid-section and jabbed about until blood began to appear. Walking back into the kitchen he swung the rabbit toward Luke, spraying blood across his shirt. "Thought you boys might like to have a nice rabbit to fix for your supper tomorrow."

"Jesus Christ, Gummy," Luke cried as he jumped away. "You got blood on my shirt. Hell no, we don't want no rabbit." The boys turned, giggling like schoolboys and tromped across the porch, each carrying their dollar. Luke yelled, "Easiest money I ever made, Gummy. Anytime you need some easy work like that done, just let us know."

"Thank you, boys, I will."

Adam waited, listening carefully, until he was certain the boys were heading back to town to continue drinking. He looked at his watch which registered 7:48 p.m. He walked into the kitchen, picked up his tin kerosene can and carried it into the parlor. There he emptied the kerosene from the parlor lamp into the can, smashed the empty lamp onto the parlor floor and poured a small amount of kerosene onto the floor around the broken lamp. He upset the settee and the rocker and sat down on the leg of the rocker, putting all his weight on it until it splintered. Then he reached up and grabbed one of the curtains in the parlor window and ripped it off the rod, pulling the right end of the rod away from the wall.

From the kitchen he got a wide-mouth Mason jar and very carefully broke it on the parlor floor. He got his straight razor from under the sink, took it into the parlor, and made a quarter-inch slit in the vein of his left arm. Blood poured out of the vein and Adam allowed it to gather in the bottom of the jar until nearly a half inch had pooled there. Then he placed the jar bottom upright in the middle of the parlor floor. He poured some of the alcohol Doc Glanzer had given him onto a clean rag and laid it across the cut and tied another clean rag around his arm to stop the bleeding. Next he went to the root cellar and retrieved the jar of blood he had collected from three rabbits he had trapped earlier in the week. He took a dipper of rabbit blood and flung it across the parlor floor in the direction of the front door. He took another dipper full and spewed it around in the middle of the parlor floor. He then took the jar and spewed the remainder of the rabbit blood across the front porch, taking care that some of it splashed against the front door. Next he then rinsed out the jar and washed the blood off the dipper. He placed the broken jar containing his blood in the middle of a drying pool of rabbit blood on the parlor floor.

He removed the shoes he had scarred earlier, put on the hunting boots he had purchased in Baltimore, went out onto the back porch and grabbed the sack of rocks he had placed there earlier that evening. He stuffed the rabbit he had offered to Luke and Paulie under some rocks in the sack and tossed in his scarred shoes. Then he went through the parlor and opened the front door. Leaving the door open he dragged the sack across the front yard, tore open the gate to the yard, and dragged the sack across the field toward the river. When he had gone twenty yards or so he stopped, took out Pap's watch, and looked at the time. 8:15. He carefully re-set the watch to 7:40 and then smashed it hard against a rock. He heard the crystal smash and brought the watch to his ear. Nothing. The watch had stopped. It would forever set the time of its destruction as 7:40. He dropped the watch onto the ground, dragged the sack another yard or so, and threw the chain to Pap's watch onto the ground in the path he had just created. Next he took one shoe with its deeply scarred toe out of the sack and carefully laid it along the path. A few yards later he dropped the other shoe beside the path. Then he went another fifty yards or so until he came to the river. There he dumped all but a few of the rocks into the river and flung the sack with the remainder of the rocks and the dead rabbit out into the current. He then returned to the house, being careful not to disturb the path he had created

Inside the house he donned the cap with ear flaps he had bought in Baltimore and grabbed the canvas cabin bag he had packed the night before containing the two hundred fifty twenty-dollar gold pieces, the Smith & Wesson pistol and cartridges, jack knife, compass, rubber horse blanket, wool lap robe, Elgin pocket watch and chain, two candles, a box of large matches, a pound and a half of cheese, a summer sausage, a loaf of bread, some hard candy, and an extra pair of shoes and stockings, pants and a shirt.

The two hundred fifty twenty-dollar gold pieces themselves weighed nearly twenty pounds so Adam had sewn over a dozen small bags, filled each with coins and scattered the bags throughout the cabin bag to prevent the mass of coins from settling in one spot and aggravating his back. He had also altered the bag by wiring two shoulder or sling straps to the bag in such a fashion that he could slip his arms through the straps and carry the bag on his back. Finally, he had wired a third strap around the bottom of the bag so that he could tighten it around his waist and keep the bag from flopping on his back as he walked.

Now he threw the bag over his shoulder, snugged it onto his back, tightened the strap around his waist and, leaving the front door open, picked up his walking stick from the porch and, without looking back at the house, walked out to the river. There he took off his boots and stockings, rolled up his trousers and waded into the stream until the water was halfway to his knees. He turned downstream and waded very laboriously for the first quarter mile so as to leave no footprints. Then he very carefully stepped from stone to stone on the riverside until, after a hard mile or so, he came to the iron framework of the uncompleted railroad bridge over the Oremander River. He sat down on a cast iron beam and pulled on his wool stockings and hunting boots. Then he carefully picked his way over the river on the beam and started walking eastward down the unfinished railroad bed. Last night there had been a full moon and, as he had reasoned when planning this trip, tonight's moon gave off plenty light to walk by.

For over nine hours he walked, until the sky began to show the first hint of dawn. There was a steep hillside on his right so he climbed up about a hundred feet above the railroad grade and burrowed into a laurel thicket. He wrapped himself in his rubber horse blanket and wool lap robe, ate some cheese, bread, and summer sausage, and then fell asleep. He woke twice during the day, once to relieve himself and once when he thought he heard someone coming through the woods. It turned out to be a deer, which stared at him for some time and then strolled away.

CHAPTER 24

Tally Monroe was the first to discover that something was amiss at Adam's house. He had arrived at the mill shortly before six o'clock. When six came and Adam didn't appear Tally became concerned, given Adam's long-time practice of punctuality. He walked from the mill to the house and was puzzled to find the house dark. He knocked on the kitchen door. When Adam didn't answer, he opened the kitchen door carefully and stepped inside. He lit a match and looked about. At first he neither saw nor heard anything. Then he spied the disheveled mess on the parlor floor. Seeing the shattered kerosene lamp on the floor and the blood streaking across the floor, he turned and ran out of the house. He didn't stop running until he was at Will Perse's door, pounding and shouting. "Somethin' bad wrong at Adam's. They's been a fight in the parlor and they's blood everwhere."

Will ran to Adam's house and after a quick glance around the parlor, raced upstairs to Adam's bedroom. He lit a kerosene lamp beside the bed. "The bed's not been slept in," he shouted. "Something's terribly wrong here. You run downtown and get Sheriff Lutz." Tally left, running at full speed.

Will rushed back into the parlor. His heart sank. He followed the trail of blood out onto the porch. Something had been dragged across the lawn and through the gate. He heard footsteps, and was joined by Sheriff Emil Lutz with Tally in tow.

"Great God," Sheriff Lutz exclaimed when he entered the parlor, "there's been a hell of a struggle in here. Look over there." He gestured toward the window. "Someone has tore down the curtain and they've broke that rocker. Why, my God, they must have been fightin' like hell in here. And look at all that blood. I reckon that's Adam's blood, seein' as how he's missin' and all."

Will explained that something appeared to have been dragged off the porch, across the lawn, and out into the field toward the river. He and the sheriff rushed out onto the porch. The sheriff looked up at the sky. "It'll be another twenty minutes to a half hour before real good daylight. Then we'll follow that trail." He turned to Tally. "Go get Doc Glanzer. We might find Adam out there somewhere in need of help. Maybe he crawled out there. Who knows? Anyway we need to have the doc here ready to help us. Now go, Tally. Don't just stand there lookin' like you're ready to piss your pants. Go get the doc." Tally took off at a run.

Will saw the Bible on the floor beside the broken kerosene lamp. He picked it up and riffled the pages. "Someone has taken the five dollar bill out of this Bible," he told Sheriff Lutz. "Adam showed me a week or so ago that he used a five dollar bill as bookmark in the Bible. Said it was God's money and it made him feel good to know that the money was being used to mark his place in the Good Book. I think this was part Adam's effort to deal with Sarah's death. Whoever did all this," he swept his arm around the room, "took the five dollar bill, too."

Fifteen minutes later Tally and Doc Glanzer arrived. Will and Sheriff Lutz were just starting to search the field outside the gate when Will found Adam's watch. He picked it up and looked at it carefully. "7:40. Well, I guess we know about when the fight took place. The watch was broken at 7:40. So that tells us something."

Will looked at the watch. Tears came to his eyes. "That was his pap's watch. Adam sure loved that watch. I've heard him say many times that he wouldn't take a farm in Texas for that watch."

The sheriff stooped and picked up something shiny. "This looks like a watch chain." He turned to Will. "Would you recognize his watch chain?"

Will nodded. "Yes, that's his watch chain."

By the time they had reached the river they had found both of his shoes. The sheriff exclaimed, "It's pretty plain to me what happened here. Someone killed Adam and then dragged his body out here to the river." He pointed to the riverside. "Look there, you can see where they dragged him right into the river. We're going to have to search downstream to see if we can find his body." The sheriff held up Adam's shoes. "Look at these shoes. The toes are all scuffed up in the toes, like Adam was being dragged by somebody. Yessir, somebody dragged Adam out here and throwed him in the river. Son of a bitch! Whoever done this sure made a complete job of it."

They rushed back to the house where Doc Glanzer was holding the broken jar with the blood pooled in the bottom. "Sheriff, is it all right if I take this blood back to my office? If it's Adam's blood I will be able to tell you with a reasonable degree of certainty."

"How you gonna do that, Doc?"

"I'll explain later. But if it is his blood, I'll be able to tell you, like I said, with some degree of certainty."

"Take it then. We need to know."

By ten o'clock the sheriff had rounded up around twenty men, including all the men from the mill. He sent them off down the river to look for Adam's body. They searched the river banks as far downstream as Berne, in Wiles County, just to the east of Polk County. All they found were two dead hogs and a deer carcass.

-o-

Thursday night, after it was dark and he had eaten, Adam repacked his canvas bag, threw it over his shoulder and took off once more. He followed the unfinished railroad bed for five hours until it crossed a road. He lit a candle, studied the map he had purchased in the Baltimore

213

bookstore, and consulted his compass. Then he turned north on the road, which was a simple lane cut through banks of pine and small hardwoods. He followed the road for the next two hours, pausing twice to light a candle and check his compass bearing. About midnight he came to a small village. There were lights on in two or three of the homes. He left the road and skirted the town through the woods to the east. Back on the road he trudged on until, at 4:30 a.m., the road crossed over a stream through a covered bridge. He consulted his map once more. When he had determined exactly where he was, he crawled under the bridge, satisfied that he could not be seen from the approaching road in either direction, and prepared his camp for the coming day. He ate some cheese and bread and bathed in the cold water of the stream. Then he wrapped himself in the horse blanket and lap robe and went to sleep.

-o-

When Sheriff Lutz returned home at 8:30 p.m. after a day of searching the river bank, his wife handed him a small piece of folded paper that looked as if it had been torn from a paper sack. Exhausted from climbing over boulders and driftwood alongside the Oremander River, he dropped into a kitchen chair, and unfolded the paper. It was a note, written in crabbed hand.

> *Sherif Lutz – I need to see you imediately on a matter of*
> *grate importance. Pleas come as soon as you can.*
>
> *Maxwell Penderson, Prop.*
>
> *Bluebell Tavern*

Sheriff Lutz sighed deeply. He looked at his wife who was filling a plate from the wood stove. "Just as well put that food back for a while, Edith. I have to go down to the Bloody Bucket." With that he stood up wearily, hitched up his pants, and left for town.

When he walked into the Bloody Bucket, everything grew silent. There were eight or nine men there, all with a glass in front of them. Maxwell Penderson motioned with his head for the sheriff to approach him. "Kin we talk outside? Where no one kin hear us?" He nodded toward a door behind the counter. Sheriff Lutz followed Maxwell out onto a small landing atop a set of stairs that led down to the millrace.

Maxwell took a deep breath and started talking, very rapidly. "Sheriff, about eight last night, Luke and Paulie Jepson come in here laughin' and carryin' on. They was wavin' around a five dollar bill. Paulie said somethin' about 'Gummy Richter had come through agin.' I didn't know what they was talkin' about, but they was flush with money all right. And Luke had what looked to be blood on the front of his shirt. They both love to pull a cork and I thought maybe they had been drinkin' and got in a fight, what with the blood and all. Then, this mornin' about ten o'clock, I heered about Adam Richter disappearin'. I figgered you oughta know about the Jepson boys carryin' on so last night wavin' all that money around and such, 'specially since Paulie went on about Gummy Richter bein' the source of the money."

The sheriff put his hand on Penderson's shoulder. "Maxwell, you done the right thing sending for me. In fact, I think you just solved the case." He followed Maxwell Penderson back into the Bloody Bucket. All but three of the patrons had fled. He confronted the three men who were standing at the bar nursing mugs of beer. "You boys sober?"

One of them said, "Yessir," and the others nodded in agreement.

"I'm deputizing all of you. Raise your right hands. Do you swear to serve as special deputies to the best of your ability until you are discharged? If so, say 'yes, so help me God.'" The men were stunned. None of them said anything.

The sheriff bellowed at them, "Well, do you?"

They all managed to say some version of "yes, so help me God." The sheriff nodded. "All right, now you're special deputies. A posse, if you will. Let's go to the courthouse and I'll get guns for you. We may be in for trouble. You up for that?"

They all shook their heads, "yes," but none too enthusiastically. "Maxwell, you'll have to shut this place down for a while and go get Will Perse. Tell him to meet me at the courthouse. Sorry about having to shut you down for a while, Maxwell."

"That's all right, Sheriff. I'll go get him right now." Maxwell Penderson was happy to oblige the sheriff. When you ran the Bloody Bucket you never knew when you might need the sheriff on your side. All five men left the Bloody Bucket together.

The sheriff was handing out pistols to his three special deputies when Will Perse walked into the courthouse. "What's going on here, Sheriff?"

The sheriff told Will what Maxwell Penderson had told him about the Jepson brothers' behavior in the Bloody Bucket the night before. "The brothers were in the bar around 8:00. You remember the watch was broke at 7:40." Will nodded. "And Paulie was wavin' a five dollar bill around and saying that Gummy Richter had 'come through again.' You remember what you told me about Adam using a five dollar bill as a bookmark in his Bible, and how you noticed the money was gone? Well, I don't think there's any question where Paulie got that five dollar bill and what him and Luke did to get it. Them two sonsabitches has terrorized this county long enough." He looked up at the ceiling and, speaking to no one in particular, added, "Murder. That's a hanging offense." He looked at Will, and then at his three deputies. "I'm gonna see that them mean-ass bastards hang for this. Wilbur Botts ain't gonna pertect them boys this time. This is murder. Even Wilbur can't stop the law this time." He deputized Will and gave him a pistol. Then he led the group outside where he put Will and the three deputies in a wagon, telling Will to drive. With his posse in order he mounted his horse and led the little posse up Main Street toward The Bleaks and the Jepson farm.

It was nearly midnight when they topped the rise in the road and saw the Jepson farm about a quarter of a mile ahead. There were no lights and the boys' car was parked under a tree at the front of the house, a clear indication they were home. The sheriff reined in his horse and motioned for Will to hold up the wagon. "We're going to leave the horses and the wagon here and go on by foot. No need to let them hear us comin'." Down the road they marched, single file, with the sheriff in the lead, followed by Will, with the three deputies coming a reluctant last.

At the gate to the yard Sheriff Lutz whispered his instructions. "Will, here is the only pair of handcuffs I have. I want you to put them on Luke. I think he's the meanest and most dangerous of the two. Make him put his hands behind his back when you handcuff him. That away he can't do us no harm." He looked at the other three. "Daniel," he motioned to the biggest of the three, "you take this piece of rope and tie Paulie's hands behind his back. Any questions?"

There were none.

The sheriff lit the lantern he had been carrying and walked up to the door of the shack. He pounded loudly on the door, shouting at the same time: "Open up in the name of the law! Luke . . . Paulie . . . get your asses out here. You're under arrest."

There was a stirring inside the house. One of the boys, probably Luke, said: "What the hell?"

The sheriff pounded again and repeated his warning. Finally the door opened about four inches. The sheriff lunged at the door, smashing it in Luke's face. Luke staggered back, grabbing his face. The sheriff jammed his pistol under Luke's chin. "Don't move, you son-of-a-bitch, or I'll blow your head off. I mean it. I'm just a-lookin' for a reason to kill your murderin' ass, so you better do what I say. You're under arrest!"

"What the hell for?"

"The murder of Adam Richter?"

"The what?"

"You heard me. Now get your hands behind your back!"

Luke moved his hands toward the sheriff's pistol. The sheriff jammed it viciously under his chin, causing Luke to topple backward onto the kitchen floor. The sheriff kicked him violently in the ribs and shouted, "Roll over, you son-of-a-bitch, roll over! -

Luke did as he was told and Will quickly grabbed Luke's arms, pulled them behind his back and snapped the handcuffs on him. Meanwhile, Paulie was standing in the back of the room with his mouth wide open. With Luke down, the sheriff turned his attention to Paulie. "Turn around, Paulie. Don't give us no trouble and you won't get hurt."

Paulie did as he was told. The sheriff set the lantern down, grabbed Paulie's hands, pulled them back, and motioned for Daniel to tie them. When Paulie was secured, the sheriff pulled Luke up from the floor, picked up his lantern, and led the group out to the road.

"What the hell is this all about, Sheriff?" Luke said. "We never killed nobody. Not Gummy, not nobody."

"Save it for the jury, Luke. Just shut up and walk."

When they reached the horses and wagon, the brothers were rolled onto the floor of the wagon. When the others were on board the sheriff mounted his horse and they started for town.

Occasionally Luke would whine about never having killed anyone and ask what all the commotion was about. Paulie, on the other hand, said nothing. The sheriff's response to Luke's questions was always the same. "Shut up. Save it for the jury."

By two-thirty they were back at the courthouse. The sheriff led the group down into the basement where a room with a stone floor and walls served as the jail. He opened the massive oak door with a large key and shoved Luke and Paulie into the room. "Now, be quiet, you sons-of-bitches. Someone will be here to feed you in the morning."

"Goddammit, sheriff, take these cuffs off, and untie Paulie. We can't even take a piss with our hands behind our backs."

The sheriff slammed the massive door with a thud. "You can piss in your pants as far as I'm concerned. Now shut up!"

The sheriff led his little posse back upstairs where he collected their pistols, thanked them, and told them they could go home.

Will Perse walked home, past the furniture mill, overcome with a profound sense of sadness. In less than twenty-four hours his life had been turned upside down. A man he had come to regard as a son was gone, probably murdered. And his tormentors, who were most likely also his murderers, were in jail. At least he had helped arrest them, he thought. That was the very least he could do for his friend.

CHAPTER 25

The next day, Friday, Adam woke every time someone crossed the covered bridge, clattering on the boards above him. But he was reasonably comfortable there and felt secure from discovery. It had rained all day and the bridge had kept him dry. He decided to try to find another bridge for the next night.

When it was dark he crawled out from under the bridge and headed north on the narrow country lane. The rain had stopped and the sky was clear again. He followed the road at a steady pace for three hours until it came to a fork where the road turned west but a fork to the right led off toward the northeast. He lit a candle and, after consulting his map, took the road to the right, which turned out to be little more than a deer path, with brush that arched over and closed in on him, slapping and stinging him. It was rough going, stumbling along the narrow path through the woods, across creeks, and up and down hillsides. But he had to make time. So he plodded on.

Later, the road merged with another road, wider and better maintained and the going became a bit easier. He followed that road for another three hours, until it topped a long hill and then drifted down into a small town. It was about three o'clock, the middle of the night by any count. He saw no lights in any of the houses and decided it would probably be safe to go straight through the town rather than skirting it through the woods on either side. So he plunged ahead, into the town. Two dogs barked, one of them frantically, but otherwise he passed through without an incident. So far as he could tell no one had seen him.

But shortly after leaving the town he became aware that someone was following him. Despite the bright moon he saw nothing, but he kept looking behind him, knowing someone was there. He could occasionally hear snatches of conversation. That meant there were at least two of them. After he had climbed up and over a small hill and was about a quarter mile down the other side, he looked back and saw two figures – they appeared to be men – outlined against the moonlit sky as they topped the hill. He hurried on until the road turned onto a long straight stretch, taking him out of sight of the two men. Then he began running. He ran until he had calculated the men were about to make the turn onto the straight stretch and then slowed to a walk. Glancing back he saw the men again and noticed they picked up their pace when they had discovered he had widened the distance from them. There was no question now. They were after him!

He had a moment of sheer panic, followed by deep dread. It was the law! They had figured out what he had done and were after him. The game was up. Then he realized that, if it were the law, they would likely be on horseback. There would be more than two of them. No, these men were not lawmen. But they were following him.

A few hundred yards later the road turned again to the left, enough to take him out of sight of the men following him. He broke into a run for about fifty yards. Then he crawled up the bank to his right where he burrowed under a low pine tree. He slipped off his back pack, took out the pistol and box of shells, loaded the pistol, and lay down, facing the road, pistol at the ready. A few minutes later the two men came down the road at a dogtrot. They were slightly winded. Adam heard one of them say, "Where in tarnation did he go to? Sumbitch must have somethin' on him he don't want us to git." The other one said, "I don't know where he could have went, but this runnin' is steamin' up my glasses." The pair slowed to a walk. One of the men removed his glasses and wiped them off. They walked slowly down the heavily-rutted road.

Adam lay quietly under the pine tree for over a half hour – time he could not afford to lose if he was to be within walking distance of Whitney by Sunday morning. It was now 4:15 a.m., or at least that was his guess. He did not dare to strike a match and check the time in case the two men were waiting for him out there in the dark. He had to move on. Slowly he crawled from under the pine tree, hoisted the pack onto his back, and started down the road again, quickly scanning both sides of the road as he went. His right hand was in his coat pocket, tightly gripping the loaded pistol.

A half mile or so down the road he glimpsed something to the left of the road, a brief reflection that he realized could only be the moon reflected off something shiny, something like the lens of a pair of glasses. He stopped suddenly. There was a shuffling behind a bush on the left side of the road. Adam immediately dashed up the side of the hill to his right, digging in with his walking stick for support. The two men scampered out of their hiding place and followed him. Although he was carrying a thirty-five pound backpack, he was in better condition than the two men following him. The uphill climb, although it was not easy for him was more difficult for the two men. They were huffing and puffing. One of them shouted, "Hey there! Why you runnin'? We jist want to talk to you."

Adam did not reply but kept clambering uphill at a fast pace. Finally he reached the top. He dropped over to the other side for about ten yards and then turned and ran along the hillside, keeping to the northeast. When he heard the two men top the hill he stopped abruptly beneath a tall tree. He was panting heavily. The men were standing at the top of the hill, panting, gagging, and listening for any sounds that might tell them where he was. Adam picked up a rock about the size of a baseball and tossed it into the valley below, where it rolled and clattered. One of the men yelled, "He's down there, I just heered him. Let's go." They took off down the hillside.

Adam rushed, as quietly as he could, along the side of the hill. After a while he topped the hill again and clambered back down toward the road. Then he began running down the road at a slow lope. He was free. Or at least it seemed that way.

But perhaps a half an hour later he heard the two men behind him on the road again. It was no use trying to outrun them. He had to confront them, had to get them off his trail. The problem was there were two of them. Despite his small size he knew he could take either one of them, one on one. But the two of them could overpower him. Ahead of him the road dipped a bit and crossed a small stream. He raced down the road, looking from side to side for a place to hide. When he saw a large rhododendron bush on the hillside he leaped off the road and crouched down behind the bush. He took off his backpack and gripped his walking stick tightly in his hands. A few minutes later the two men came trudging down the road. Just as they passed him, Adam stepped out into the road and swung the stick at the man closest to him. The stick collided with the right side of his head just behind the ear, and the man collapsed with a dull "oof." His partner, who was at least six feet tall and sturdily built, turned and faced Adam.

"You little son-of-a-bitch. I'm gonna teach you a lesson."

"Come right ahead," Adam sneered. One thing about being small is that no one is afraid of you. In Stendahl the boys had all learned that, small as he was, Adam would make even the biggest of them sorry they had taken him on. But this man was a stranger and to him Adam appeared to be only a small boy, easy prey. That was good. Adam had learned long ago that being underestimated is an enormous advantage.

Adam gripped his walking stick tightly. Suddenly, before he could swing the stick, the man rushed him and the two of them fell to the road, with Adam on the bottom. Adam dropped the stick, jabbed his thumbs into the man's eyes, and clawed at the eyes with his thumbnails. The man screamed and rolled off Adam, grabbing at his eyes. Adam jumped up and kicked the man viciously in the side, just beneath the ribs. He kicked him again, this time on the side of his head. Then he kicked him in the side again. The man moaned sharply, fought for his breath, and lowered his hands to his side. At that moment Adam dropped astride the man, using his knees to pin the man's arms to the ground, and began pummeling him in the face. Blood spurted from the man's nose and he started coughing violently. Finally he croaked, "Enough.! I've had enough! Please! Stop! I'll not give you no trouble."

Adam stopped hitting the man, glanced back to see that the other man was still lying beside the road motionless, and asked, "Why are you two following me?"

The man said nothing. Adam slapped him hard aside the head.

"Ow! We was drinkin' and seen you come through Nixes Mill. Thought, since you was travelin' all quiet like at night, maybe you might have somethin' valuable on you. Why are you out sneakin' around at night anyway?"

"I'm in a hurry to get somewhere, that's all. I walk all day and half the night. Only sleep a few hours every night. I've been doing that for over two weeks now. Could have come through – what did you call that town?"

"Nixes Mill."

"I could have come through Nixes Mill in the daylight as well as after dark. Just happened that when I got to Nixes Mill it was dark. Now, what am I gonna do with you two?"

The man Adam had hit with the club began to stir, moaning deeply. Adam reached into his coat pocket and took out his pistol. He pointed it at the man he was holding down. "You see this?"

"Jesus! Yes I see it! You ain't gonna shoot us are you?"

"I can't have you following me ready to jump on me all the time. I'll never get where I've got to get at that rate. Either I shoot you or you take off back up this road as fast as you can and leave me alone. I don't have anything valuable on me, just a little food and some spare clothes. But I have to get where I'm going."

"Where's that? Where you come from? And where you goin'?"

"You ask a lot of questions for a man who is liable to get shot in the head."

"All right. All right. We'll leave you alone. Don't know about racin' back up the road right away though. Jake there, he don't seem to be in much condition to do any runnin' anywheres. And I know I ain't."

Adam stood up slowly, keeping the pistol pointed at the man's head. Then he backed away. The man sat up, wiped at the blood on his face with his hand. "Jesus! You done me a lot of trouble. Me *and* Jake there." He ran his tongue around inside his mouth. "I think you even loosened a tooth."

"If it's loose, it'll tighten up on its own. Just leave it alone. Now I'm going to start down this road again. I'm going to have this pistol in my hand until daylight. If I see you fellers behind me again, I swear to God I'll shoot you both."

"We ain't givin' you no more trouble, sonny. That's the truth."

Adam picked up his bag and slowly put it on. The man sat in the road and watched him. His partner was still moaning and moving around a bit. Hoping they would trouble him no more, Adam started down the road with his pistol in his hand. Every few yards he looked back. The man had not moved. After about a quarter mile the road turned to the left. Adam made the turn and then stopped. He waited two or three minutes and then walked back around the curve, looking toward the two men.

The man he had beaten was on his knees beside his companion. His back was to Adam and he did not appear to be interested in following him. With a heavy sigh Adam started back down the road. Still, every few yards, he checked behind. He saw nothing.

After another half hour the road branched, the main road going off to the left, heading northwest, and a smaller, obviously less-traveled road, heading to the right. That would be northeast. He knew without consulting his compass that he had to take the road to the right, so he plunged ahead. This was, he decided, a lucky break. If the men were determined to follow him, he figured they would more likely take the main road when they came to this junction.

An hour later, bone-weary and hungry, and still nervous over the prospect of being jumped by the two men at any moment, he noticed it was starting to grow lighter in the east. It was time to find a place to spend the day. The road was now making its way along a hillside, with a steep incline on his left and a sharp drop to the right. In the growing dawn he began looking for a hiding place on the hillside above him, on the uncertain theory that travelers on the pathetic road would be more likely to spot someone sleeping in the woods below the road than someone on a hillside above it. After a while he could hear a stream gurgling ahead of him. He trudged on to the stream, drank his fill of water, filled his canteen, and then splashed up the stream bed for fifty yards or so before moving out onto the hillside in search of a place to spend the day. Having walked in the stream bed, he knew he had left no footprints to announce his departure from the road. If the two men were still following him and were looking for signs of his departure from the road, they would find none.

He walked along the hillside until he came upon a copse of pine. He crawled into the middle of the trees and removed his pack. His back hurt and his feet were swollen. It was nearly daylight now. He raked up a thick pile of pine straw with his hands and made a mattress. He opened his bag, pulled out his horse blanket and spread it on the straw. Then he took out the sack containing the remnants of his food. The bread was all gone, but there was some summer sausage left along with a small piece of cheese. He cut both in half, put one half back in the bag and ate the remainder. When he had finished he took a long draw of water from his canteen, wrapped himself in the blanket and lap robe, and lay down. He stayed awake for some time, anxious for any sound of traffic along the road. Finally, hearing nothing, he fell asleep.

CHAPTER 26

On Friday morning Wilbur Botts rode up to the courthouse in his buggy. He tied the horse's reins to the hitching rail, dismounted wearily, and followed the boardwalk around the courthouse. A small, weatherbeaten wooden sign bearing the single word, "Sheriff," hung out perpendicular to the wall. Wilbur opened the door and saw Sheriff Emil Lutz sitting behind a massive oak desk. On the wall behind the sheriff was a gun rack containing three rifles and a bulky billy club. The sheriff looked as if he had been expecting Wilbur.

Wilbur offered no greetings but immediately launched into the reason for his visit. "I hear you got the Jepson boys locked up down there." He gestured toward the basement of the courthouse.

"Yep," the sheriff replied. His face was set. He did not offer a chair to Wilbur, did not smile, did not utter another word.

"Surely you don't think those boys murdered Gummy Richter, do you? I mean, they've been a bit frisky and caused some trouble from time to time. But they ain't murderers."

"That," Sheriff Lutz said, "is for the jury to decide. But, if you ask me, it sure looks like they're guilty." He leaned forward, elbows on his desk. "Look, Wilbur, I've turned my head time after time when them boys has got into trouble. You know that. I've always accommodated you when it come to them boys. But, Wilbur, this is murder. I cain't let them boys go free. The people in this town is up in arms about Adam Richter's disappearance. If I let them boys go, *I'll* get strung up. I cain't help you here, Wilbur. I just cain't."

Wilbur looked at the sheriff for a moment. Then he slowly shook his head from side to side, turned, and walked out of the office without saying a word.

Emil Lutz went over to the tiny burner that stood under the window, picked up the coffee pot, and poured himself a cup of coffee. From the window he watched Wilbur Botts ride up the street in his buggy. The sheriff pursed his lips and nodded his head. *After all these years,* he thought, *I finally feel like I really* **am** *the sheriff of Polk County.*

-o-

Ten minutes later Wilbur Botts walked into the office of Valentine Burner.

"What can I do for you?" Valentine asked.

"You're surely not thinking of seeking an indictment for murder against the Jepson boys, are you Valentine? You know there's an election in two years. And you know you need my help to get reelected."

"Have a seat, Wilbur," Valentine said, motioning toward a split-bottomed chair. He licked his lips for a moment and then began, staring intently at Wilbur, who had settled into the chair. "I know I owe my position as prosecuting attorney to you. And I know you can have me defeated in the next election. But, until that election, I am the prosecuting attorney of Polk County. In that capacity, I fully intend to seek an indictment against Luke and Paul Jepson for murder in the first degree. If I get that indictment – and I am certain I will – I intend to seek conviction of those no-good bastards for murder and see them hang for what they did to Adam Richter. If I don't get reelected, I guess Nancy and I will just have to make do on my income as a private practitioner of the law. But I am not going to violate the oath I took when I became prosecuting attorney by taking it easy on those boys. The folks in this community – and I include myself in that description – have turned a blind eye to those boys and their crimes for far too long. But this is one crime that cannot be ignored."

Wilbur stood up. "I'm disappointed in you, Valentine. You're going to regret this, I promise you."

"No, Wilbur, I'll not regret doing my duty in this case. You can take this office and shove it up your arse as far as I am concerned. But I'm trying those boys for first degree murder. And if you threaten me again or give me any reason to believe you are trying to improperly influence me in the performance of my duties, so help me God, I'll seek to have you indicted for obstruction of justice. Now, get the hell out of here and don't let me ever see you in this office again."

As Wilbur left the prosecutor's office, his face was blood red and he was grinding his teeth. He mounted his buggy, cracked the whip violently over his horse's head, and took off up Main Street like a chastised dog that had just been kicked.

-o-

Three days after Adam's disappearance Randall Armentrout appeared at the mill office where Will was talking with Oliver Finch. He barged right in, interrupting the two and waving a paper at them. "Will, you need to know about this," he announced with no introduction. He shoved the paper at Will and took a long drag on his cigar, wreathing his head in blue-gray smoke.

Will looked it over carefully and then looked up at Randall, with his eyebrows raised. "What," Will said, "are you trying to do with this, Randall?"

If Randall noticed this was the first time Will had called him anything but "Mr. Armentrout," he didn't let on. He rolled the cigar around in his mouth. "Why it's a note Adam signed when he borrowed five thousand dollars from the bank. You can see right there where he pledged his half of the mill as security for the loan. That and the fifty thousand acres of timber he was buying."

Will studied the paper for a moment, then looked up at Randall. "Uh-huh," he said, accenting the second syllable. "You're saying that this paper is proof that Adam Richter owes the Stendahl State Bank five thousand dollars. Is that what you are saying?"

"That's exactly what I'm saying," Randall said, as his double chin wobbled. "Just read the goddamned instrument. You *can* read, can't you? Or are you a half-wit like your brother?"

Will glared at Randall. "Randall," he said, "I don't know what's going on here, but that isn't Adam's signature on that document. And that writing, where it says he pledges the mill as security, that's not Adam's writing either. And what's this about fifty thousand acres of timber?"

Randall tore the cigar from his mouth with his left hand and grabbed the paper from Will with his right. He looked at the paper and then up at Will. "Will, I sat right there at my desk in the bank and watched him sign that paper and write that bit about pledging the mill and the timber land as security. Saw him write that with my own eyes. The timber was why he needed the loan . . . he was buying fifty thousand acres of timber land to build houses when the railroad comes to town. Said he was going to surprise you by giving this timber to the mill at no charge. Hadn't he told you about that?" He put the cigar back in his mouth and puffed on it violently.

"No, this is the first I've ever heard about any timber purchase. And he shared just about everything with me concerning the business here. Let me have that paper again." Will studied the paper very carefully. Then he shook his head from side to side. "That's not Adam's signature and that's not his writing. Look at this signature. Look at the A in 'Adam.' Adam never made his A's all fat and round that way. He always made his A's with a point at the top. He told me one time he deliberately made his A's like that so they would look like the A that Abraham Lincoln made in his signature, with a curve at the bottom and rising to a sharp point at the top. And the R in 'Richter.' He never made his R's like that. His were tall and thin, not short and round like this one." He studied the document for a moment. "Matter of fact, Randall, the A in 'Adam' and the R in 'Richter' look just like the A and R in your signature, where you signed as a witness. And the 'd' and the 'e's' in the word pledge there, they look just like the 'd' and 'e' in your name. What are you trying to do here, Randall?"

Randall grabbed the paper again and looked at it carefully, the blood draining from his face. His brow was deeply furrowed. He was chewing furiously on the cigar. "Will, I sat right there in my office and witnessed Adam sign this document. And he wrote that paragraph about pledging his half of the mill and the timber land. I didn't write it. I was in the vault getting him the five thousand dollars." He looked at Oliver Finch. "Oliver, you remember how I used to go into the vault and get money for folks who were taking out a loan. You remember that, don't you?"

The expression on Oliver Finch's face never changed. "I wouldn't know a thing about that, Randall. I was always busy in the teller's cage or limping around the bank like I was drunk."

Randall cast Oliver Finch a look of pure disgust. Then he turned to Will and sneered, "Will, I swear to God, that's his writing. I don't care what it looks like."

Will stood up straight and looked Randall right in the eyes. "That is not Adam Richter's writing. I don't understand what is going on here, but that is not his writing. You can ask anyone who is familiar with his handwriting. Adam Richter did not write this. And that is not his signature. Tally Monroe can't read and write, but I'll wager even he would tell you that's not Adam Richter's handwriting."

Randall looked as if he had been slapped in the face with a wet fish. He took the cigar out of his mouth again and shook the paper at Will. "I do not appreciate your insinuations – that I forged this document. I am going to get to the bottom of this, just you wait. I am going to get to the bottom of this and when I do, by God, I will own this place." He turned and stomped out of the building, leaving behind a cloud of cigar smoke. But his threat was hollow; his voice lacked conviction. Randall Armentrout, the arrogant, loud-talking, cigar-chomping president of the Stendahl State Bank, had had the wind taken out of his sails. That was something new around Stendahl.

Will looked at Oliver Finch. "What do you suppose that was all about, Mr. Finch?"

Oliver shook his head. "I declare, that cheap son-of-a-bitch will try anything. But this is the first time I ever saw him try to rob the dead.

CHAPTER 27

If there was any traffic on the little road below him that Saturday, Adam was unaware of it. He woke twice to quench his thirst, once to relieve himself, and otherwise slept the entire day. Obviously, he decided, the two men who had been after him stayed on the main road and did not take this less-traveled road as he had. The risk of their being out on this road tonight was slight. At least he hoped that was so. As it grew dark, he packed his knapsack, crawled out of the copse of pines, and headed north, with his hand still tightly gripping the pistol in his coat pocket.

He had been walking about seven hours when the road suddenly widened and dropped precipitously into a narrow valley. At the foot of the hill the road was intersected by a creek, about fifteen feet wide and a foot or two deep. On the far side of the creek was what appeared to be a fairly well-maintained road, which Adam recognized as the stage road into Whitney. The stream, then, had to be Elk Creek, which emptied into the Potomac at Whitney. He waded the creek and walked along the road paralleling the stream for about an hour. At last he could see in the distance the lights of Whitney. Here and there were lights from a house or other building, but most of the lights, he knew, were from the railroad shops at Whitney. He was only about a half hour's walk from the train station.

To his left was a large field which provided no cover. To his right, across Elk Creek, was a steep hillside, about three hundred feet high. He waded the creek and scrambled, hand over foot, up the side of the hill. He reached the top and went down the other side for a distance of twenty-five feet or so, just to keep out of sight. He found a small thicket of rhododendron and burrowed in, wrapped himself in the horse blanket and lap robe, and went to sleep.

He awoke at midday on Sunday, parched. He had forgotten to fill his canteen in Elk Creek. The canteen had only a swallow of water, which was lukewarm and tasted of metal, but he drank the water and lay down again. This time he couldn't go back to sleep. He was thirsty, but didn't dare show himself in daylight to traffic on the road beside Elk Creek by filling his canteen. But more than his thirst, he was nervous about tonight. Would he be recognized as he got on the train to Baltimore . . . by someone from Stendahl who happened to be in Whitney to catch the train that Sunday afternoon, or by the ticket agent who had sold him his ticket on his two previous trips to Baltimore? Would he look suspiciously scruffy after four nights on the run from Stendahl? Would word of his disappearance have reached Whitney? If it had, would anyone care?

He tried to reason out all the potential scenarios and, the more he thought about it, the more nervous it made him. Finally, sleep being impossible, he unwrapped himself from his robes and lay against the side of the little ravine he was hiding in. He consulted his watch. It was one o'clock. Four hours before he could leave. Four long, miserable hours.

Finally, he dozed off. He woke every fifteen minutes or so and checked his watch. Then, around 4:30 p.m., he got up, took out his clean shoes, pants and shirt, and changed clothes. Now at least he wouldn't look as if he had been in the woods for four nights. At five o'clock he walked out of the ravine and to the top of the hill. He looked to his left and right as far as he could see. No one appeared to be coming. He slid down the side of the hill, getting his shoes and pants dirty. He waded the creek, stopping to get a drink of water and wash off both his shoes and the lower parts of his trousers. Then he walked out onto the road beside Elk Creek, unnoticed as far as he could tell, and began walking toward Whitney.

There was no stage coach from Stendahl on Sunday so the chance of someone from his home town being there to recognize him was slight, but still he was much relieved when, on his arrival at the station around 5:40 p.m., he was the only person there. He bought his ticket from the agent who – another lucky break – was not the same agent who had sold him his tickets on the previous two trips. The train was due at 6:10 p.m. By six o'clock five other folks, four men and one woman, were at the station. He recognized none of them and they paid him no attention, even with his ear-flapped cap covering his cheeks. Better to look silly in a cap, he reasoned, than to have someone remember the mole on his face.

The train was late, arriving at 6:25 p.m. Adam entered the car, took a seat in the rear, and stared out the window. The conductor, a different one from his earlier trips, punched his ticket and left him alone. He looked out the window and watched the scenery rush by in the growing dark. The first great hurdle was over!

-o-

The train pulled into Camden Station around 11:00 p.m. Adam hailed a cab for the Howard House, a flop house hotel he had identified on his last trip. He paid the man at the desk fifteen cents for a room on the top floor, registered as Samuel Griffith, climbed the stairs to his room, and went to bed, pleased to be able to get a room by himself.

The following morning, a Monday, after he had shaved, dressed and eaten breakfast, he grabbed his bag and took a cab to the Adams Express Company. He gave the clerk, a nervous little man with red hair and freckles, the ticket he had received when he had stored his trunk there a month earlier. When he had retrieved his trunk, he tipped the clerk a quarter and asked him, "Is there someplace where I can freshen up a bit?"

The clerk smiled broadly at the generous tip. "Yessir, you can use our toilet. It's around the side of the building, the second door. It will be unlocked. You know this place was burned to the ground in the fire of 1904. But we rebuilt right away and when we did we put in a modern toilet for our customers. Like I said, it's around the side of the building," he gestured, "second door."

Adam lugged his trunk and canvas cabin bag to the toilet, locked the door, washed up, and changed into one of his black wool suits, with a white muslin shirt and black silk bow tie. He pulled on a pair of wool stockings and slipped into a pair of shell cordovan shoes. He topped off his outfit with his black derby. He admired himself in the mirror over the sink. The transformation was amazing. A poorly dressed working man had entered the toilet and a successful member of the upper class, dressed grandly, if not downright magnificently, was about to leave the toilet.

Finishing up, he emptied his cabin bag of the gold coins and packed his dirty clothes in the bag which he then stuffed in the trunk, relieved that he would not have to carry it on his back any longer. Into the goat skin club bag which he had taken out of the trunk he placed the bags of gold coins, a spare muslin shirt, black bow tie, a pair of stockings and an extra pair of underwear. With everything repacked he left the toilet carrying the club bag and dragging his trunk. He slowly trudged behind the Express Company and across the alley into the next street, so that the clerk who had given him his trunk would not notice the transformation in his appearance. He traveled about a block, turned right and walked to the next corner. There he hailed a cab.

"Mount Royal Station," he told the cab driver. The driver, obviously impressed with the fare he was picking up, dismounted and loaded Samuel Griffith's trunk into the storage compartment in the rear of the cab. Adam kept his club bag, with the gold coins in it by his side. Then he tipped his hat, mounted the cab and took off.

For many years the railroad coming into Baltimore from Philadelphia and New York to the north ended in the northern section of the city.

There was no physical connection between the main line of the B&O from the west and the lines to the North, which were now also operated by the B&O. This had been a serious bottleneck. For many years, cars were dragged through the city by horses from one train line to another or ferried from one terminal to the other across the neck of Baltimore harbor. In the 1890's the problem was solved by linking the two B&O routes via a tunnel under downtown Baltimore.

Adam, who wanted to get as much distance between himself and Stendahl as possible, did not want to take the train at Camden Station and ride on the tunnel to Mount Royal Station. He feared that he might meet someone at Camden Station who would recognize him. So he had the cab drive him through the city to the station itself where he bought a ticket to Philadelphia for fifty-five cents. The train would not leave for four hours. He checked his trunk with a red cap at the baggage room, tipped the man generously, and took a leisurely dinner in the lunch room of the station, with his club bag, loaded with gold coins, at his feet. Then he went back into the two-story waiting room and purchased a copy of the *Baltimore Sun*. He took a seat on a bench along the wall opposite the train side where he was least likely to come into contact with anyone. Opening the *Sun,* he held it just below eye level, where he could appear to be reading but could watch anyone who might approach him. He sat there nervously for an hour and forty minutes. Then, precisely at 3:43 p.m., the train pulled into the station.

Adam watched as his trunk was loaded into the baggage car and then entered the luxuriously-appointed car. He watched the other passengers for any sign of recognition. There were none. At 4:10 p.m., right on time, the train pulled out of the station, headed for Philadelphia.

He was free at last. Or, at least, he had reason to believe he was free.

CHAPTER 28

Having seen no one he recognized since leaving Stendahl five days earlier, Samuel began to relax and, for a time, dozed on this last leg of the day's journey. The B&O train from Baltimore pulled into the line's massive and ornate Philadelphia Terminal at 24th and Chestnut Streets at 6:12 p.m. Samuel hailed a cab and asked the driver to take him to the best hotel in the city. Ten minutes later the cab stopped at the entrance to the Bellevue Stratford Hotel, at the corner of South Broad and Walnut Streets. "Here she is, sir," the driver said. "The 'Grand Dame of Broad Street,' we call her. She's the most luxurious hotel in the country, over a thousand rooms. A ballroom you won't believe."

As Samuel paid the cab driver and a uniformed bellhop rushed up and unloaded the trunk. "Welcome to the Bellevue Stratford, sir," he said, as he reached out to relieve Samuel of the club bag. Samuel gestured, "no" and the bellhop turned, swung his right arm out and pointed toward the entrance. "Right this way to the registration desk."

Trying not to appear as too much of a hick from the back country, Samuel glanced up at the hotel's facade. It was truly magnificent. Ten, fifteen, maybe even twenty stories tall – it was difficult to tell at a glance – with ornate carvings, cornices and bay windows decorating the marble face of the building. He turned and followed the bellhop up nine marble steps, through gleaming brass revolving doors, into the lobby, a fantasy land of gold and creme and chandeliers, with golden marble columns and a beautiful tiled floor.

Samuel took a deep breath. *This is a long way from Brubaker's Mill in Stendahl.* He took a late supper in perhaps the most elegant room he had ever seen, a massive domed dining room with heavily-draped archways and a huge chandelier hanging from the dome, which Samuel estimated to be at least forty feet from the floor.

He went to bed exhausted. But he could not sleep. He kept replaying the events of this day: his Baltimore transfiguration from a shabby working man to an upper-class businessman, the escape from Baltimore on the B&O; the ride to Philadelphia, and the security he now felt at being only one out of a million and a quarter people in the nation's third largest city.

Of one thing he was certain: Adam Richter was dead and Samuel Griffith had a promising new life ahead. On that happy note he finally fell into a dreamless sleep.

The next morning he took a cab to the Pennsylvania Railroad's Broad Street Station on the northwest corner of 15th and Market Streets, across Penn Square from City Hall. The building was enormous, with a web of gothic spires and arched windows. The structure was, Samuel knew, the world's largest railroad passenger terminal, serving sixteen tracks.

Samuel paid the cab driver and a man wearing a uniform with a red cap approached the cab, took Samuel's trunk and led him to the ticket counter inside the ten-story stone building. There he checked his trunk, and purchased a ticket to Chicago for $4.20. The train was already in the station and Samuel was aboard and bound for Chicago by 7:20 a.m., his club bag snugly by his side.

He took a seat at the back of the car and spent the day watching the countryside pass by, deep in his thoughts, leaving his seat only to take dinner and supper in the dining car. He reveled in the sight of the changing scenery as the train roared across the rolling hills of Pennsylvania, through Harrisburg, Altoona, and Pittsburgh, crossed the Ohio River and glided into the flat lands of Ohio, through Crestline and Lima, and into Fort Wayne, Indiana, in the growing dark. At 10:40 p.m. Central Railroad time, sixteen hours and ten minutes after leaving Philadelphia, the train pulled into Chicago's Union Station.

He spent the night in the Palmer House in Chicago and early the following morning he once again checked his trunk and, with his club bag gripped tightly in his right hand, boarded the Illinois Central bound for Council Bluffs, Iowa. Nine hours later, in Council Bluffs, he purchased a ticket on the Union Pacific Railroad for San Francisco and boarded an open-section sleeping car. The car was made up of pairs of seats, one seat facing forward and the other backward, situated on either side of a center aisle. As night time approached, the seat pairs were converted into the combination of an upper and a lower "berth," each berth consisting of a bed screened from the aisle by a curtain.

Samuel had been on the Union Pacific only three hours, and had just finished dinner in the dining car, when the porter came through his car and made up the beds for the night. He spent a relatively restful night in the upper berth and awoke the following morning as the train stopped at the station in Laramie, Wyoming. After a hearty breakfast of two eggs, pancakes with maple syrup, and coffee he returned to his seat to watch the scenery, leaving only to visit the dining car for dinner and supper, both of which were superb meals.

After a second night in the upper berth, he was awakened by the slowing down of the train as it came into Winnemucca, Nevada. That day he marveled at the spectacular scenery as the train wound its way through the Rocky Mountains on its way to the Pacific coast. Finally, just before 10:00 p.m. on the cool night of May 18, 1906, Samuel Griffith dismounted the train in San Francisco. As the red cap was helping with his luggage he asked, "What would be a nice, reasonably-priced hotel?"

"Well," the man said, "there's not much left standing after the quake. But the St. Francis Hotel has put up a temporary building in the court around the Dewey Monument in Union Square. I would recommend you go there."

"All right," Samuel said, "that sounds fine."

"The St. Francis — the temporary one in Union Square," the man said to the cab driver. His trunk was loaded and Samuel climbed into the cab with his club bag, sat back and watched the city go by. The Red Cap had not been exaggerating. San Francisco was still recovering from the devastating earthquake of the previous April and piles of block, heaps of lumber, charred remains of buildings, and other debris lined the streets. At the hotel he registered under the name "Samuel Griffith," took a room on the second floor, unpacked and went to bed.

After breakfast the next morning he hailed a cab to the main post office. When he arrived at the post office he told the driver to wait while he retrieved his mail. He approached a caged window where a tall, pock-faced postal clerk, whose dark brown hair hung down over his right eye, greeted him with no interest at all. He told the postal clerk, "I'm here to pick up the mail for Samuel Griffith, addressed to 'General Delivery, San Francisco, California.'" The clerk went into a back room and returned a few minutes later, carrying a handful of newspapers, rolled up and tied with a piece of cord. "The only mail for Samuel Griffith was these papers," the clerk said. "But how do I know you are Samuel Griffith?"

"Who else but Samuel Griffith would know to call for Samuel Griffith's mail?" Samuel said as he handed a nickel to the clerk. The clerk took the nickel and handed the pile of *Polk County Guardians* over to Samuel as if he were unloading clothing bearing yellow fever germs. Back in the cab Samuel looked through the collected issues of the *Guardian*. There were two issues, beginning with the issue of May 2, the first one sent out in response to the pre-paid subscription request which Adam had mailed from Baltimore to Stendahl on April 30. The last issue was for May 9, the day he had fled Stendahl. Samuel peered out the window and calculated. It was now June 2. Since Adam Richter's disappearance would have been discovered on the morning of May 10, the *Guardian* of May 16, would be the first to make a note of it. So it would be at least another week before he would read about it.

Well, best to sit back quietly and see what happens. Meanwhile the city of San Francisco would no doubt be in desperate need of a furniture manufacturing plant that could turn out high quality furniture at a reasonable price on a short notice. Somewhere in this city, Samuel thought, such a mill must surely be available for purchase at the right price.

-o-

Samuel soon learned that an issue of the *Polk County Guardian* would arrive at the main post office in San Francisco on the Thursday or Friday of the week following the issue's publication. So he made a regular visit to the post office every Friday afternoon and picked up the previous week's *Guardian*. On May 25, he picked up the May 16 issue. The story of Adam Richter's disappearance – and apparent murder – dominated the paper. Samuel read with great interest the interviews of Sheriff Lutz, Tally Monroe, Will Perse, and Maxwell Penderson. He was particularly fascinated by the interview with Esau Siple, habitue of the Bloody Bucket, who had been deputized to help arrest the Jepsons the night following Adam's disappearance. Siple related how the posse had sneaked up on the Jepson house and captured the boys before they knew what had happened. "Luke Jepson kept insisting he and Paulie had not killed nobody, 'specially not Adam Richter, who Luke kept calling 'Gummy.' But," Siple said, "the sheriff showed Luke no mercy."

Samuel Griffith read and re-read that issue of the *Guardian*. The description of the path made by the apparent dragging of Adam's body to the river, along which the sheriff had found the watch Adam had

245

inherited from his father, the chain for the watch, and Adam's shoes, all fascinated him. Nowhere, Samuel noted with great interest, was there so much as a hint that anything had taken place but a brutal murder and the disposal of the victim's body.

-o-

On Friday, June 22, Samuel Griffith made his weekly trek to the main post office to retrieve his copy of the *Polk County Guardian*. The front page of this issue carried a surprising piece of news, headlined **Local Banker Kills Self!**

> At 3:45 p.m. on Friday, June 8, fifteen minutes before the regular monthly meeting of the board of directors of the Stendahl State Bank was to commence, Randall Armentrout, the president of the bank, locked the door to his office, sat down in the swivel chair behind his desk, opened the top drawer to the desk, and removed a Colt Model 1901 Navy .38 caliber revolver from the drawer. He placed the barrel of the pistol in his mouth, pulled the trigger, and blew off the back of his head. Bank officials refused to speculate on the reason for Mr. Armentrout's suicide but rumors persist that at least $5,000 is missing from the bank's vault. It is rumored that Mr. Armentrout tried to cover up the missing money by means of a document which is

widely perceived to be a forgery. However, none of these rumors have been
confirmed.

Samuel Griffith read the article in the cab as he rode back to his hotel
from the post office. If the article gave rise to any emotional reaction
on the part of Mr. Griffith, it was not evident to the cab driver when
Mr. Griffith paid the fare, to the doorman at the hotel who helped Mr.
Griffith alight from the cab, or to any of the guests or employees of
the hotel.

CHAPTER 29

The grand jury met on June 19, the third Tuesday in June. Valentine Burner laid out the case to indict Lucas and Paul Jepson for murder in the first degree. As was the custom, Luke and Paulie were not present for the presentment to the grand jury, nor was counsel for the two defendants present. In fact, until the indictment, no counsel was appointed to represent them.

Valentine Burner's presentment to the grand jury took about a half hour. He very carefully laid out only the basic facts on which his case would be founded. The grand jury had enough for an indictment, but not anything that would tip the prosecution's hand before the trial. It would be a classic "trial by ambush," with each side trying to surprise the other and sell its case to the jury.

The grand jury voted with no dissent to indict the Jepson brothers for first degree murder, a hanging offense. And, from the looks on the faces of the jurors, there wasn't a man present who wouldn't be willing personally to pull the lever to open the trapdoor to hang both Luke and Paulie.

-o-

Charlie Luikart, who had studied law under Major J. C. Ferguson (so called because he had been a major in the Confederate army during the war), was appointed by Judge C. Wellington Trueheart to represent Luke and Paulie. It was not a particularly fortuitous appointment for Luke and Paulie since Charlie's practice consisted mostly of title work and wills. No one could remember the last time Charlie had appeared in court. Truth to tell, Charlie was at best only a half-assed lawyer. But unless the judge wanted to assign the Jepson boys' defense to old Wilbur

Froebel, who hadn't drawn a sober breath since Jesus was a boy, Charlie was the only lawyer left in Stendahl.

A brash, self-assured man in his forties, Charlie Luikart stood just over five feet ten inches tall, with blond hair and a drooping moustache which he fancied made him look like President Roosevelt. He had married late, only two years earlier, to an older woman, the widow of a substantial merchant whose store was the only serious competition to Havel's Mercantile Emporium. Mrs. Luikart ran the store, with the help of her two teen-aged daughters, and Charlie dabbled in wills and title work and fancied himself a pillar of the Polk County legal establishment.

Charlie was thrilled with the appointment to represent Luke and Paulie Jepson. He went around Stendahl telling how he was going to give those boys "the best damned defense you ever saw." To anyone who would stand still long enough, Charlie would explain that the boys' guilt simply could not be proved. He, Charlie Luikart, was going to teach Valentine Burner a thing or two. Finally, after having told his story to practically anyone in town who would listen, he called on Valentine Burner, who was sitting in his office before the long oak table that served as his desk. The table was stacked high with books and papers, and Valentine was in the process of writing in a yellow legal pad. He looked over his shoulder at Charlie.

Charlie plopped into a chair. "You know you ain't gonna get a conviction in this case, Valentine."

"That so? What makes you so certain?"

"You got no corpus delicti."

"What do you mean, 'no corpus delicti.'"

"Well, where's the body? Ain't no one told me you come up with Adam Richter's body. You gotta have a body, a corpus delicti. You oughta know that."

Valentine swivelled his chair around and faced Charlie. "Charlie, you dumb son-of-a bitch, didn't Major Ferguson teach you *anything*? 'Corpus delicti' doesn't mean 'body of the deceased.' It means 'body of crime.' I don't have to come up with Adam Richter's body. All I have to do is prove he was murdered. That's it. That's the 'corpus delicti,' the 'body of crime.' If you had to have a body to prove a murder, we'd never get a conviction because every murderer would chop up the victim into little pieces and burn them. All I have to prove is that a murder was committed and that the Jepson boys committed it. I am going to do just that, and in ways that will make your head swim. The best thing you can do for Luke and Paulie is to tell them to get right with God because they're going to meet Him at the end of a very short rope before long."

Charlie's mouth dropped. "Don't see how you're gonna to do it, prove a murder, that is. And I don't see how you're gonna tie Luke and Paulie to the murder. Remember, Mr. Hotshot Prosecuting Attorney, you have to prove their guilt 'beyond a reasonable doubt.'"

"Charlie, when I am finished presenting my case the only doubt in that courtroom will be whether you ought to hang with those two boys, just for the crime of defending them." He swiveled his chair around, presenting his back to Charlie, who sat there for a moment and then stood up and left the office.

CHAPTER 30

The trial commenced at 9:00 a.m., on July 9, 1906. The little courtroom was packed with onlookers, counsel, the court reporter, and the twenty-four men who had been summoned for jury duty. It took but two hours to select a jury. Of the first twelve men called, Charlie Luikart struck three, two peremptorily and one for cause. The "for cause" strike was against Jasper Lindholm, and was based on Charlie's assertion that Jasper lived near the Jepsons in The Bleaks and would be prejudiced against them. Valentine Burner argued to the judge that Jasper, being a neighbor, was just as likely to be prejudiced in their favor, but he was willing to leave Jasper on the jury, "out of a sense of fairness," he told the judge. Charlie sneered at Burner and argued to the judge that Jasper was more likely to be prejudiced *against* Luke & Paulie because everyone in the Bleaks knew the brothers would steal anything that wasn't glued, nailed, or held down by gravity. Jasper was excused by the judge.

Valentine Burner struck only one juror, Henry Paige, because Burner knew Paige to be a shiftless, no-good, thieving, liar who would likely identify with the Jepson boys. His strike, being a peremptory one, took Henry off the panel.

With the jury empanelled, Judge C. Wellington Trueheart addressed the assembled body in a deep, stentorian voice. Judge Trueheart was fifty-four years old, over six feet tall, and weighed well above three hundred pounds. He had about him what could clearly be called a "presence." And he knew it. His mother had named him Caleb Wellington Truehart at birth and had always insisted on calling him "Caleb," which had been his maternal grandfather's name. When he started school he had been known by the other children as "Welly." But when he donned the black robes of a judge, he insisted on being called "C. Wellington." Since he was the judge, he got his way in this as in most matters. His manner was pompous, even overbearing, but he was a fair judge and cared deeply about the law. He tolerated no shenanigans in his courtroom and expected counsel to comport themselves as gentlemen, even as they fought over the life or death of the accused in the dock.

After the courtroom had been quieted, C. Wellington cleared his throat and addressed the jury. "Gentlemen of the jury, the case you are about to hear is a capital case, meaning that the accused are facing the possibility of being executed if they are found guilty. Since the lives of two young men rest in your hands, I don't need to tell you how important it is that you carry out your responsibilities to the absolute best of your abilities. I am certain all of you are aware of the crime for which the two accused will stand trial. You have no doubt heard some of the details or read about them in the *Polk County Guardian*. But I ask you to expunge from your memory all you may have heard or read about this crime and listen to the evidence which will be presented to you with a perfectly open mind. It is one of the most ancient and honorable principles of Anglo-American jurisprudence that a man is innocent until he is found guilty. And that guilt must be proved," here he paused and gestured at the jury, "beyond a reasonable doubt. That means that if you have any reasonable doubt that these two boys, or either of them, committed the crime of which they are accused, you *must* acquit them. That is the law. It is part and parcel of what we call 'the law of the land.' It has been the law of this particular land since the founding of the Jamestown Colony in 1607, and it is the law here, today, in this courtroom."

The judge went on to explain how the trial would proceed. Valentine Burner, the Prosecuting Attorney of Polk County, would lay out the evidence in support of the Jepson brothers' conviction and Charles Luikhart, the defense counsel, "appointed by this honorable court," would lay out the evidence suggesting that the brothers were not guilty. Each lawyer, the judge pointed out, would cross-examine the other side's witnesses in an effort to support his side.

"Out of all this," the judge concluded, "the truth should emerge and you will have the necessary evidence on which to base a verdict of guilty or not guilty."

The judge then ordered a fifteen minute recess after which he mounted the bench again and nodded toward Valentine Burner. "Counsel, you may begin."

-o-

Valentine Burner stood and hiked his pants. He adjusted his vest, tugged at his sleeves, and turned to face the jury. He let his eyes roam up and down the two rows of six jurors, pausing briefly to lock eyes with every one of them. All the while he spoke not a word. Then he looked down at his hands, wrung them together and shook his head slightly, as if in deep thought. He sighed deeply and audibly. He was, clearly, raising the tension in the room to a fever pitch. Then he began.

"Gentlemen of the jury, you are facing perhaps the most awesome task you will ever be called upon to perform . . . in your entire lives. I am going to ask you to send two young men to the gallows. I am going to ask you this because our sense of justice, our sense of fairness, our sense of right and wrong, requires it. I am going to lay before you the gruesome, even macabre, details of a horrid crime that screams out for retribution. I am not asking you for vengeance. I am asking you to affirm that this community has standards of decency and justice such that will not permit us to turn our backs on a dastardly crime and see it go unpunished. I am asking you to uphold the law. The law! I am asking you to remove from our midst two criminals – two evil, foul, despicable young men – who have forfeited their right to live among us. When I

255

have presented my case, you will have no alternative but to vote for a conviction of murder in the first degree."

Then he turned his back on the jury and pointed at Luke and Paulie Jepson. "These two miscreants, gentlemen of the jury, placed themselves in the position of God, of determining whether a man should live or die. And they chose that he should die, in the most wretched and dismal fashion." He turned back and faced the jury. "Now, gentlemen of the jury, it is this community's turn to cleanse the cancer that has so long dwelt among us. Listen carefully, you are about to hear the story of a grisly murder. And you will hear evidence that will leave no doubt that these two defendants are guilty of that murder." With that he slowly returned to his chair.

The judge nodded at Charlie Luikart, who rose and started toward the jury box. Charlie was nervous and it showed. He was out of his element and he knew it. He stopped before the rail separating the jury box from the counsel area, looked at the jury, and began in a halting, shaky voice.

"Gentlemen of the jury, the state is about to place an enormous burden on you. You are being asked to send two men to the gallows for no other reason than that a beloved citizen of this community has disappeared." Charlie's voice was clearer now. His confidence was returning. He straightened up a bit, and went on. "That's all. Adam Richter, a beloved citizen of Stendahl – known to everyone in this room – has disappeared and Luke and Paul Jepson have been dragged into this courtroom to pay the ultimate penalty because everyone is upset over Adam's disappearance. In fact, that is all there is to the prosecution's case. Adam Richter has disappeared and someone has to pay. Because Luke and Paul Jepson have an unpleasant past relationship with Adam Richter, they have been chosen to pay for Adam's disappearance. Chosen, I must emphasize, without any evidence whatsoever."

256

"But please take note of what the prosecution will not do in this case. It will not present any evidence regarding the discovery of Adam Richter's body. Simply put, there is no body to bring before you. In fact, Mr. Burner will not offer any evidence that will prove, beyond a reasonable doubt, that Adam Richter is actually dead. There will be no evidence that Luke and Paul Jepson had a struggle with Adam Richter. There will be no evidence that they were even near Adam Richter's home on the night of his disappearance. The prosecution will, no doubt, go on and on about the more unsavory aspects of Luke and Paul Jepson's lives. And I am not here to tell you that they are upstanding citizens of Polk County. But I am here to tell you that nothing," and here he paused and then shouted, "NOTHING, ties these two boys to the disappearance of Adam Richter. They are not on trial for having been troublemakers in this county. They are not on trial for the unsavory things they may have done to Adam Richter and others in this county in the past. They are on trial for murder in the first degree – a hanging offense."

"It is precisely for cases like this that our law provides that you cannot convict someone of a crime if you have ANY reasonable doubt as to their guilt. So I ask you to watch carefully as the prosecution lays out its case. Watch what the prosecution does NOT present. Then think about it: try to find just what actually proves – beyond a reasonable doubt – that Luke and Paul Jepson murdered Adam Richter. I submit to you that, at that time, your minds will be filled with all sorts of reasonable doubts. And you will have no choice but to acquit these boys."

Charlie turned, looked smugly at Valentine Burner, and walked to his seat.

CHAPTER 31

Valentine Burner then called his first witness, Sheriff Lutz.

Mr. Burner: State your name and occupation please.

Sheriff Lutz: Emil Lutz, Sheriff of Polk County.

Mr. Burner: How long have you occupied this office?

Sheriff Lutz: I was elected Sheriff of Polk County in November 1896. I took office the following January 1st and have served in that capacity ever since. Let's see, that would be ten years this coming November.

Mr. Burner: On July 19 of this year . . . that would have been a Thursday, did anything out of the ordinary occur related to your position as sheriff?

Sheriff Lutz: I was at home that mornin' having my breakfast. Tally Monroe, the colored man who works, er, who at that time worked, for Adam Richter, came poundin' on my door and yellin' for me. He said somethin' awful had happened at Adam Richter's house and would I come quick. I strapped on my gun and run all the way down to Adam Richter's home with Tally. When I got there they was a awful mess. A awful mess.

Mr. Burner: What do you mean, "an awful mess?" Would you describe what you found when you got there.

Sheriff Lutz: They was blood everwhere, and signs of a powerful struggle. The curtain had been ripped off the window, and one of the chairs – a rockin' chair – had a busted leg. Furniture was overturned and throwed about. It was a awful sight. Like I said, blood everwhere. Will Perse was there and, of course, Tally

259

Monroe who had come to get me. The front door was open – Tally said it was open when he first come in – so I went out onto the porch. You could see streaks of blood on the porch and out in the yard you could see where somethin' had been dragged out through the gate.

Mr. Burner: What did you do after you went out onto the porch?

Sheriff Lutz: Well, I told Tally Monroe to go get Doc Glanzer, that maybe Adam had been hurt bad and was lyin' out there in that field in need of some help. Then me and Will went back inside and searched the house all over to see if'n we could find anything important. That took about ten minutes. We didn't find nothin'. By then it was good light and me and Will started follerin' the trail of whatever had been drug across the field towards the river. We hadn't gone fifteen feet when we found a silver watch, which Will recognized as belongin' to Adam Richter. Will said it had been Adam's daddy's watch. A little further on we found the chain to that watch. By the time we had followed that trail to the river we also had found two shoes which Will said belonged to Adam. It looked to us like someone had killed Adam Richter and dragged his body out to the river and dumped it in.

Mr. Luikart: Objection, your honor, the sheriff is just speculating about what he saw.

Judge Truehart: Sheriff, please confine your testimony to what you saw. The jury doesn't need to hear what you think happened. Just tell the jury what you saw.

Sheriff Lutz: Sorry, your honor.

Mr. Burner: Did you examine the watch you found?

Sheriff Lutz: Yes I did. I noticed it was stopped, apparently broken. The time it had stopped showed twenty minutes to eight.

Mr. Burner: And what time was it when you found the watch and looked at the time it registered?

Sheriff Lutz: It was about ten to six.

Mr. Burner: That was ten 'til six in the morning. So if the watch was stopped at twenty 'til eight – 7:40 – that would have been the night before? Is that right?

Sheriff Lutz: Yes sir. That would have to be the case 'cause it wasn't 7:40 in the mornin' yet when we found the watch.

Mr. Burner: What, if anything, did you conclude from this, Sheriff?

Sheriff Lutz: Well, it seemed pretty clear to me that whatever struggle had caused the watch to be broke had took place at twenty to eight – 7:40 – the night before.

Mr. Burner: You mentioned there was blood all over the place when you got to Adam Richter's house. Can you tell the jury anything else about that?

Sheriff Lutz: Like I said, they was blood everwhere. They was a broken jar – a Mason jar – on the floor of the parlor. It had about a half inch of blood in it, like someone had been cut bad on the broken glass and blood had collected in the jar. I said I wondered if that was Adam Richter's blood. Doc Glanzer was there by that time and he said if we would let him take the blood back to his office he could tell pretty certain whether it was Adam Richter's blood.

Mr. Luikart: Objection, your honor. This is ridiculous. Blood is blood and there's no way anyone could say that was Adam Richter's blood, or President Theodore Roosevelt's blood. I want to strike this testimony and any testimony Dr. Glanzer may attempt to offer regarding the identification of the blood in that jar.

Judge Truehart: Mr. Luikart, like you, I don't know where the testimony about the blood in the jar is taking us but I'm going to allow Mr. Burner to introduce whatever testimony or other evidence he may have. If it turns out to be, as you say, 'ridiculous,' we'll deal with that issue at that time. Proceed, Mr. Burner.

Mr. Burner: What happened next, Sheriff?

Sheriff Lutz: Well, I told Doc Glanzer to take the jar of blood with him. I didn't know what he could do with it to identify it as Adam Richter's blood. But it wasn't doing us any good sittin' there in the middle of the parlor floor drying up along with the rest of the blood in the room. So he took it. I haven't heard nothing about that blood since that mornin'. I mean, whether Doc Glanzer identified it as Adam Richter's blood or what.

Valentine Burner then led Sheriff Lutz through the story of the message from Maxwell Penderson, the proprietor of the Bluebell Tavern, the sheriff's visit to the tavern, what Maxwell Penderson told him that led him to decide to arrest Luke and Paulie, the swearing in of a posse, and the arrest and incarceration of the Jepson brothers.

Charlie Luikhart's cross-examination of Sheriff Lutz was brief and consisted for the most part of having the sheriff repeat the number of times Luke Jepson insisted that he and Paulie had killed no one. His final series of questions were an attempt to lend some credibility to Luke Jepson's pleas.

Mr. Luikart: Sheriff Lutz, did Luke Jepson ever admit to you that he and Paulie had pulled Adam Richter's teeth when he was living at the Jepson farm?

Sheriff Lutz: Yes sir. Several times when we was haulin' him and Paulie to jail that night he said, "I admit me and Paulie pulled Gummy Richter's teeth."

Mr. Luikart: And did he ever confess that he and Paulie had set fire to Adam Richter's furniture mill?

Sheriff Lutz: Yes sir, he also mentioned several times that same night that he and Paulie had set fire to the mill.

Mr. Luikart: So he admitted that he and Paulie had pulled Adam Richter's teeth and that they had set fire to his mill. Did he ever admit to killing Adam Richter?

Sheriff Lutz: Oh no, sir. He kept insistin' that he and Paulie hadn't killed no one, certainly not Adam Richter. He admitted that Sarah Gifford had died after the brothers car had struck her. But that was an accident, he said. Other than that accident Luke Jepson insisted he and Paulie had killed no one. And he said that to me ever time I saw him in the jail after that. In fact, ever time I have seen him since I arrested him, he has insisted him and Paulie didn't kill Adam Richter. Of course, I don't believe him. No one does.

Mr. Luikart: Your honor . . . .

Judge Truehart: Gentlemen of the jury, I'm going to ask that you disregard the sheriff's statement about not believing Luke Jepson's protestations of innocence. What the sheriff believes or doesn't believe about Mr. Jepson's guilt or innocence, is not a matter for you to consider. You alone are to decide the question of guilt or innocence.

But the damage had been done. Not that it was really necessary. The sheriff's actions had made it plain he believed the Jepson brothers had killed Adam. His saying so was only icing on the cake, so to speak. And the jury would not be able to disregard what the sheriff had said no matter how much the judge instructed them to do so. Sheriff Lutz had made himself the thirteenth member of the jury. And he had cast his vote for conviction. Not one member of the jury would be able to forget that.

Valentine Burner then called Doctor Solomon Glanzer to the stand. After establishing that Dr. Glanzer had treated Adam for a cut he had incurred on his hand during the cleanup of the mill after the fire, and after going through the details of that treatment, Valentine led straight into the most damaging piece of evidence he had against the Jepson brothers.

> Mr. Burner: Did anything else of note occur during Adam Richter's visit to your office to treat his hand?
>
> Charlie Luikart rose slowly. Judge Truehart looked down at him.
>
> Mr. Luikart: Your honor, what does all this have to do with the case at hand? Why are we wasting the jury's time, and your time and my time, hearing about the treatment of Adam Richter's hand by Doc Glanzer?
>
> Judge Truehart: Mr. Luikart, like you, I don't know where Mr. Valentine is taking us, but he is permitted to develop his case as he sees fit. If it turns out that this line of testimony is of no significance to this case, we will deal with it at that time. You may answer the question, Dr. Glanzer.
>
> Dr. Glanzer: As Adam was leaving my office he mentioned having read in the newspaper when he was in Baltimore that it had been discovered that human beings have

different types of blood. He asked if I knew what that was all about.

Mr. Burner: What did you tell him?

Dr. Glanzer: I told him, yes, that the medical journals were full of information about the discovery that there are four different blood types, or blood groups, to be more precise. The blood groups are designated A, B, AB, and O. He seemed quite interested in this. You know, Adam Richter, despite his impoverished beginnings, was a very intelligent young man who was interested in a great many things. I think his interest in blood groups was a reflection of his inquisitive nature.

Mr. Burner: Doctor, would you explain, in language that we non-physicians can understand, just what this blood grouping or blood typing is all about.

Dr. Glanzer: Very simply stated, experiments with blood transfusions, the transfer of blood from one person into another person's blood stream, have been carried out for hundreds of years. But over the years many patients have died when receiving blood transfusions, while others were healed by the transfusions. It was not until quite recently, in 1901 to be precise, when the Austrian Karl Landsteiner discovered that human blood is divided into four groups that blood transfusions became safer. You see, as I explained to Adam Richter, all human blood may look alike, but not all blood groups are compatible with each other, which explains why sometimes blood transfusions work very well in healing someone who has lost a great deal of blood, while at other times the person receiving a blood transfusion will go into shock. Mixing blood from two individuals can lead to blood clumping or agglutination if the blood from the two individuals is not compatible.

Mr. Burner: What do you mean, 'if the blood from two individuals is not compatible?'"

Dr. Glanzer: Well, it is a little bit confusing. A person with Type O blood can only receive a transfusion from another person with Type O blood. On the other hand, a person with Type O blood can donate blood to any other person. For that reason a person with Type O blood is called a 'universal donor.' A person with Type AB blood can receive blood from a person with any of the four blood groups, but this person can only donate blood to another person with Type AB blood. For this reason a person with Type AB blood is called a 'universal recipient.' Generally speaking, a person with Type A blood can only donate to and receive blood from another person with Type A blood and a person with Type B blood can only donate to and receive blood from another person with Type B blood.

Mr. Burner: All right. So, to simplify your testimony further, you are saying, are you not, that not everyone can safely give blood to everyone else? Nor can everyone safely receive blood from everyone else. Is that correct?

Dr. Glanzer: Yes, that is correct.

Mr. Burner: Doctor, what determines our blood type?

Dr. Glanzer: Blood types are inherited and represent contributions from both parents.

Mr. Burner: I see. Now, doctor, do you have any information as to the distribution of blood types within the population? By that I mean, what percentage of the population is likely to have one type of blood as opposed to another type?

Dr. Glanzer: According to data I have seen, perhaps only four or five persons out of a hundred will have Type AB blood. That means that, out of the 350 people living here in Stendahl, for example, only about eighteen people are likely to have Type AB blood. On the other hand, nearly one hundred sixty of our citizens are likely to have Type O blood, one hundred forty will have Type A, and forty folks will have Type B.

Mr. Burner: Do you happen to know what type blood Adam Richter had?

Dr. Glanzer: Yes I do.

Mr. Burner: How is it that you happen to know his blood type?

Dr. Glanzer: Well, as we were having this conversation about blood groups, I asked him if he would be interested in knowing his blood type. After I assured him it would not be difficult or painful to ascertain his type, he agreed. So I drew a bit of blood from his arm and performed the test that determines blood grouping.

Mr. Burner: What did you discover?

Dr. Glanzer: His blood type turned out to be Type AB, which as I explained, is the rarest of the blood groups

Mr. Burner: Once again, doctor, how many folks in Stendahl are likely to have Type AB blood?

Dr. Glanzer: Most likely, around eighteen.

Mr. Burner: That would be eighteen out of the entire population of Stendahl?

Dr. Glanzer: Yes, men, women, and children. Eighteen out of the entire population of three hundred and fifty. That's right.

Mr. Burner: But the other blood types would be much more prevalent?

Dr. Glanzer: Yes, as I explained a moment ago, out of the three hundred fifty residents of Stendahl, nearly one hundred sixty are likely to have Type O blood, one hundred forty will have Type A, and forty folks will have Type B.

Mr. Burner: But only eighteen are likely to have Type AB blood.

Dr. Glanzer: That is correct.

Mr. Burner: Now, doctor, you took a broken Mason jar with about a half inch of blood pooled on the bottom back to your office on the night Adam Richter disappeared. The jar was discovered sitting on the floor of Mr. Richter's parlor, surrounded by blood on the floor. Is this correct?

Dr. Glanzer: Yes sir.

Mr. Burner: What did you do with the blood in that jar?

Dr. Glanzer: I ran the rather simple tests required to identify the blood group to which this sample of blood belonged.

Mr. Burner: You typed the blood from the Mason jar taken from the floor of Adam Richter's parlor on the night he disappeared?

Dr. Glanzer: Yes sir.

Mr. Burner: What did you discover?

Dr. Glanzer: The blood in the bottom of that jar was Type AB.

Mr. Burner: The same type as Adam Richter's blood? The same type that is likely to be possessed by only eighteen folks in all of Stendahl?

Dr. Glanzer: Yes sir, that is correct.

Mr. Burner: Now, Dr. Glanzer, is there any doubt in your mind about the results of this test? That is to say, are you absolutely certain that the blood in the bottom of that jar is Type AB?

Dr. Glanzer: Absolutely, sir. The test is quite simple and I am certain beyond doubt that my identification of the blood as Type AB is correct.

Valentine Burner thanked the doctor and returned to his seat. The jurors followed Valentine back to the prosecution table and then looked at one another, as if to say, "Well, what about that testimony!" Charlie Luikart sat at the defense table, between Luke and Paulie Jepson, looking like he had just been shot at and missed and shit at and hit. He was scribbling something on a paper on the table in front of him, but it was clear that this testimony was a huge surprise to him. Judge Truehart, aware of the shock Doc Glanzer's testimony had been to the defense, ordered a fifteen minute recess.

CHAPTER 32

By the time Charlie began his cross-examination, he had recovered his composure – after a fashion. At least he made a attempt to show the jury that Doc Glanzer's testimony was no big deal to him and that he was about to put it in the proper perspective.

Mr. Luikart: Doctor Glanzer, you don't know for certain that the blood in the jar you took from Adam Richter's parlor floor was Adam Richter's blood, do you?

Dr. Glanzer: Well, I know it was either his or blood from one of seventeen other people in this town who are likely to have the same blood type. Since it was in a jar on the floor of Adam Richter's parlor, I think the odds would favor it being Adam Richter's blood.

Mr. Luikart: But you don't know that for sure do you? You are just making an assumption.

Dr. Glanzer: An assumption based on some pretty sound facts.

Mr. Luikart: Now, when you say that only around eighteen people in Stendahl are likely to have blood Type AB, that is an estimate, based on what?

Dr. Glanzer: That estimate is based on figures found in the medical literature that state out of one hundred persons; five are likely to have Type AB blood. Since there are three hundred fifty folks living in Stendahl, I multiplied five by three-and-a-half and came up with the figure eighteen. It's actually seventeen-and-a-half.

Mr. Luikart: That figure is an estimate, is it not? So that actually more than eighteen folks in Stendahl could have Type AB blood. Isn't that correct?

Dr. Glanzer: Yes, that is correct. But it is also possible that fewer than eighteen folks in Stendahl could have Type AB blood. In either case, however, the variation from eighteen would most likely be slight, probably fewer than ten in either direction.

Charlie Luikart should have stopped his cross-examination at this point. But, like many lawyers, he asked one question too many.

Mr. Luikart: So you are saying that not just eighteen, but perhaps as many as twenty-eight folks in Stendahl, could have Type AB blood. And that, too, is just a guess. You really don't know how many folks in Stendahl have Type AB blood, do you?

Dr. Glanzer: No, I don't know to a certainty. The figures I have given here today are just an estimate. But even if you assume these numbers – which, I remind you, have been provided by medical experts – are off by one hundred percent, that would still mean that no more than thirty-six residents of Stendahl are likely to have Type AB blood. That's still a very small number. And the blood that was of the same type as Adam Richter's was found in a jar on the floor of Adam Richter's parlor, a room that was disheveled and covered with blood. I think it's a pretty far reach to assume it was anyone but Adam Richter's blood.

Mr. Luikart: Your honor, I move to strike that last answer and to ask you to instruct the jury to disregard Dr. Glanzer's outrageous assumptions.

Judge Truehart: Mr. Luikart I'm going to let Dr. Glanzer's answer stand and the jurors can consider for themselves whether his assumptions were, as you suggest, outrageous.

Having fairly well established that the blood in the jar – and by inference, the blood strewn about Adam's parlor – was of the same rare Type AB as Adam's, Valentine Burner called Will Perse to the stand to bolster Sheriff Lutz's testimony about finding Adam's watch, watch chain, and two shoes, along the trail which Will described as "looking like something had been dragged out to the river." Will also testified about Adam having told him he used a five dollar bill to mark his place in the Bible he kept on a table in the parlor. He testified that Adam had told him, "I figure it's God's money anyway, and I like to see it put to God's use, marking my place in His word." Will testified that one of the first things he noticed when he looked around the parlor at all the mess that morning was that the five dollar bill was missing from the Bible. "I picked up the Bible," Will said, "and flipped through the pages. The five dollar bill was gone. Someone had taken it."

Tally Monroe then testified about going to the house for breakfast on the morning of May 24 and finding the place all torn up. He described the mess in the parlor, the blood on the floor and in the broken Mason jar, and the front door to the house being open to the porch. He also testified that the day before he and Davy Perse had moved a chest into Adam's bedroom from a spare bedroom upstairs.

Then Valentine called Maxwell Penderson, the proprietor of the Bluebell Tavern, to testify about what had transpired at the Bloody Bucket the night Adam disappeared.

Mr. Burner: Please state your name and occupation.

Mr. Penderson: Maxwell Penderson. I am the proprietor of the Bluebell Tavern in Stendahl. Most folks calls it the "Bloody Bucket," but its real name is the Bluebell Tavern.

Mr. Burner: What, if anything, unusual occurred in your tavern on the night of May 9 of this year?

Mr. Penderson: It was just a usual sort of night, a handful of boys was sittin' around drinkin' quiet like, mindin' their own business. And then, about eight o'clock, maybe a quarter 'til eight, Luke and Paulie Jepson come into the place. They was all excited, laughin' and jumpin' around. Luke had what looked like blood on the front of his shirt and he was wavin' a five dollar bill around and sayin' something about how Gummy Richter had come through agin. Then he took a dollar bill out of his pocket, slapped it down on the bar, and ordered a whiskey. Paulie done the same thing.

Mr. Burner: Did either Luke or Paulie buy drinks for anyone else in the bar that night?

Mr. Penderson: Oh no. Them boys was so tight they squeaked when they walked. They'd never buy nothin' for nobody else. They was quick to take a free drink from someone else, but they never bought nothin' for nobody else.

Mr. Burner: Did there ever come a time when you went to the sheriff and told him about the Jepson brothers' behavior that night?

Mr. Penderson: Yessir. The next day, after I heard about Mr. Richter's disappearin' and all, and about it looked like they was a robbery at Mr. Richter's house, and there bein' blood all over the place and all, I sent word to the sheriff that I needed to see him. He come by and I told him what had happened the night before. That's when he deputized the boys in the bar and sent me off to find Will Perse and have him come to the courthouse.

Mr. Burner: (Nodding to Mr. Luikart.) Your witness, counsel.

Mr. Luikart: Did either of the Jepson brothers talk about where they got their money?

Mr. Penderson: Luke who said somethin' about Gummy had come through agin. That was all.

Mr. Luikart: It is passing strange, is it not, that if the Jepson brothers had just killed Adam Richter, Luke would have been going on about Gummy Richter having 'come through' again?

Mr. Burner: Objection, your honor. That calls for an opinion on a matter on which the witness is not qualified to testify.

Judge Truehart: I'm going to let the question come in. You may answer, Mr. Penderson.

Mr. Penderson: As far as Luke and Paulie Jepson is concerned, nothin' they could do would ever strike me as strange. Them boys is two of the meanest, low down, plain ornery sons of . . . guns I ever knew. I got nervous ever time they come into the tavern. Nothin' they could do would be strange enough to surprise me.

Once again, Charlie Luikart had asked one question too many. This time he had taken the teeth out of any claim he could have used in his closing argument, that it was unlikely Luke would have bragged about Gummy Richter "coming through again" if he had just killed him. Now, while he would certainly use that argument as he wrapped up his defense of the Jepsons, Maxwell Penderson had laid the argument to rest.

After Maxwell Penderson's testimony, Valentine Burner rested the state's case. Judge Truehart then recessed the trial until nine o'clock the following morning.

The next morning Charlie Luikart called Luke Jepson to the witness stand.

Mr. Luikart: State your name and occupation.

Mr. Jepson: Luke Jepson. I run a farm out in The Bleaks with my brother Paul and my pa, Jehu Jepson.

Mr. Luikart: Please tell the jury what happened on the night of May 9, 1906.

Mr. Jepson: Well, Paulie ran into Gummy Richter on the street the Saturday before and Gummy had asked for me and Paulie to come by his house on Wednesday night. Said he had a job for us, that wouldn't take long and he would pay us well. Said we wasn't to tell anyone about it.

Mr. Luikart: Did he tell Paulie what the job was?

Mr. Jepson: No, Paulie just told me Gummy had said we was to come by his house about 7:30 Wednesday night. Said the job wouldn't take long and we was to say nothin' to nobody.

Mr. Luikart: So did you go by his house on that night?

Mr. Jepson: Yes. We went by around 7:30 and he let us in. Said he needed to go upstairs and check something. He went up the steps. I stepped into the parlor and saw a five dollar bill stickin' out of the Bible. I took the bill and stuck it in my pocket. He come back downstairs and told us to foller him upstairs. There he asked us to move a chest of drawers from a spare bedroom into his bedroom. We moved the chest and then went downstairs where he give us each a dollar. Then as we was leavin' he said "wait a minute" and went out onto the back porch and returned carryin' a dead rabbit. He flung it at me and got blood on my shirt. He asked if we wanted it for supper the next night. I said, "no and look what you done to my

276

shirt." Then we left. That's the last I ever seen of Gummy Richter. And I swear to God me and Paulie never killed him. We never did. I stole the five dollar bill and we set fire to his mill and we even pulled his teeth. But we never killed him. So help me God!

Mr. Luikart: (Nodding to Mr. Burner.) Your witness.

Valentine Burner stood up, stared at Luke Jepson with a look of disgust, like he was looking at a cockroach just before stomping on it, and finally said, "Your Honor, I have no questions of this witness."

Charlie Luikart rested his case. The judge called for a short intermission, and closing arguments began at around 10:00 a.m. Both summations were brief and to the point. Valentine Burner summed up the evidence he had presented, argued that there was no other conclusion than that the Jepson boys had killed Adam Richter and disposed of his body in the river. He scoffed at Luke Jepson's explanation of why he and Paulie were at Adam's house the night he disappeared: that they had been asked to move a piece of furniture into Adam's bedroom that had already been moved there earlier that day by two of Adam's employees. He noted that the defense had put on no evidence except Luke Jepson's denial of any involvement in Adam Richter's death and that, given the weak excuse Luke had given for being at Adam's house that night, wouldn't hold up.

Charlie Luikart attacked the blood grouping evidence presented by Doc Glanzer, arguing that there was no way anyone could know how many folks in Stendahl had Type AB blood short of typing the blood of every citizen in the town. He argued that it was suspicious that Adam Richter had had his blood typed and that it was equally suspicious that no body had been found. Thundering that "Not one respectful piece of evidence has been presented that Adam Richter is actually dead," he reminded the jury that the judge had instructed them they had to believe the Jepson's were guilty "beyond a reasonable doubt."

"This case," Charlie declared, "is full of nothing but reasonable doubt. Do fingers of suspicion point to the Jepson brothers? Of course, they do. But do they point to the brothers 'beyond a reasonable doubt?' No they do not!"

The jury was out for one hour and forty-three minutes, over twenty minutes of which were taken up by jurors' visits to the privy behind the courthouse. One vote was taken. It was twelve to zero in favor of conviction of murder in the first degree.

When the verdict was announced in the courtroom, Luke Jepson jumped to his feet and screamed: "WE DID NOT KILL GUMMY RICHTER!" The judge gaveled him into silence. Then he asked for the Jepson brothers to stand and announced the sentence. "Luke and Paul Jepson, the jury having found you guilty of murder in the first degree of the late Adam Richter, it is the sentence of this court that you be hanged by the neck until you are dead. You are hereby remanded to the state penitentiary at Little Creek where the warden will see that the sentence is duly carried out."

He rapped the gavel and announced, "This proceeding is closed."

CHAPTER 33

Samuel Griffith read and re-read with great interest the *Polk County Guardian's* reports of the trial, which included verbatim transcripts of the testimony of all the witnesses. Then, on Friday, September 28, 1906, while sitting in the lobby of the temporary St. Francis Hotel, he read in the September 19 issue, an article headlined: **Killers Hanged!**

Shortly before midnight on the night of September 14, in the courtyard of the state penitentiary in Little Creek, Luke and Paul Jepson were hanged for the murder of Adam Richter. Luke Jepson died first. When asked if he had any last words, he said in a quiet voice: "Me and Paulie is being hung for a crime we did not commit. If'n you want to hang us for pullin' Gummy Richter's teeth or for settin' fire to his mill, or for killin' his girlfriend in that accident, so be it. But we didn't kill Gummy Richter. He set us up. I hope, wherever he is, he is proud of what he done." With that, the trap was sprung and Luke Jepson was launched into eternity. His brother Paul, who had no last words, followed him to the gallows. Thus ends the tragic story of the mistreatment and murder of one of Stendahl's finest citizens, Adam Richter. Citizens of this community who were willing to express an opinion of the hanging of the Jepson brothers generally felt that justice was done. Will Perse, who worked with Adam Richter and to whom Adam Richter's share of the Brubaker Mill was left in Richter's will, said, "I feel nothing but sadness. Luke and Paulie Jepson deserved to die, but hanging them cannot begin to repay this community – and my family in particular – for the loss of Adam Richter. He was a rare human being. I will always miss him."

Samuel Griffith was alone in the lobby of the St. Francis that morning. But anyone else who might have chanced to be sitting there would have been surprised to see him toss the newspaper he had been reading into the trash can and stare off into the distance for a long time. Then he reached into his mouth and removed his false teeth – both uppers and lowers – and turned them over and over, examining them carefully. He then placed them back in his mouth, wriggled his jaws a bit to settle the teeth in place, stood up, and walked out the door of the hotel. The doorman distinctly heard him say as he exited the hotel, "Time to go buy a furniture mill!"

Epilogue

In the summer of 1936, in celebration of their fiftieth wedding anniversary, Will and Cora Perse took a train trip to the West Coast. They visited San Diego, Los Angeles, and San Francisco, toured the movie studios in Hollywood, took a bus through the giant redwoods north of San Francisco, and tasted the wine in the early wineries of the Napa Valley. On their third day in San Francisco they rode the Powell Street cable car, over the hill from Fisherman's Wharf, to Market Street. After getting off the cable car at the foot of Powell Street, Cora went into a drug store to purchase a package of chewing gum. Will waited outside the drug store, idly watching the traffic pass by on Market Street.

Suddenly, as a streetcar rumbled by, he saw, in the third window back from the front entrance to the car, a slight little man who bore a startling resemblance to Adam Richter. The man had a beard but he also had a large black mole on his right cheek above his beard. Despite the beard, Will felt he was looking at Adam Richter. He was so startled he raised his arm, pointed at the man, and shouted, "Adam!"

The man looked up and his eyes locked with Will's. He smiled slightly, nodded his head, and raised his right index finger to the brim of his hat in a sort of salute. Then he turned and faced forward. Will never saw him again.

Will never mentioned this incident to Cora or to anyone else. But until his death in 1943, at the age of eighty-seven, Will Perse remained certain that the man he had seen in the streetcar in San Francisco that August day in 1936 was Adam Richter.

-o-

The June 30, 1948, issue of the *San Francisco Chronicle* carried the following obituary:

Samuel Griffith, the shy, reclusive multimillionaire owner of three furniture manufacturing mills in the San Francisco Bay area, passed away yesterday at the age of sixty-six. A generous donor to charitable causes, Mr. Griffith was best known for his practice of hiring first-rate men to manage his manufacturing plants and then letting them run the operations with little or no interference from him. Mr. Griffith reportedly met weekly with each mill manager at his home just north of the city where he went over the details of the previous week's work at the plants and made minimal suggestions for the coming week. Employees at Mr. Griffith's mills were routinely paid higher wages than other employees in the area and jobs at his establishments were much sought after. Mr. Griffith was a person of small stature and a very private man with a particular aversion to being photographed. He seldom ventured from his home and, on the rare occasions when he did, he was almost never recognized as the wealthy furniture manufacturer who paid his employees premium wages. At Mr. Griffith's request there will be no memorial service. His body is to be cremated and his ashes strewn in San Francisco Bay.

Orphaned as a child, Mr. Griffith had no surviving relatives. According to a spokesman for Mr. Griffith, his estate, rumored to be in excess of six million dollars, is to be placed in trust with the income from the trust to provide for dental care and formal education for the orphans of the San Francisco Bay area. Mr. Griffith was reported to be especially interested in seeing that orphans receive training and education in grammar, deportment, and mathematics, in order that they might rise to the highest levels in their communities.

The End

36204145R00157